Heartbreak Symphony

Heartbreak Symphony

LAEKAN ZEA KEMP

LITTLE, BROWN AND COMPANY
NEW YORK   BOSTON

Little, Brown and Company
Hachette Book Group
1290 Avenue of the Americas, New York, NY 10104
Visit us at LBYR.com

First Edition: April 2022

Little, Brown and Company is a division of Hachette Book Group, Inc. The Little, Brown name and logo are trademarks of Hachette Book Group, Inc.

The publisher is not responsible for websites (or their content) that are not owned by the publisher.

Library of Congress Cataloging-in-Publication Data
Names: Kemp, Laekan Zea, author.
Title: Heartbreak symphony / Laekan Zea Kemp.
Description: First edition. | New York : Little, Brown and Company, 2022. | Audience: Ages 14 & up. | Summary: Set in the Monte Vista neighborhood of San Antonio and told in alternating voices, teenaged musicians Aarón and Mia grow close as they share and struggle to overcome the emotional pain of their troubled home lives.
Identifiers: LCCN 2021016141 | ISBN 9780316460385 (hardcover) | ISBN 9780316460330 (ebook)
Subjects: CYAC: Emotional problems—Fiction. | Family problems—Fiction. | Musicians—Fiction. | Mexican Americans—Fiction. | San Antonio (Tex.)—Fiction.
Classification: LCC PZ7.1.K463 He 2022 | DDC [Fic]—dc23
LC record available at https://lccn.loc.gov/2021016141

ISBNs: 978-0-316-46038-5 (hardcover),
978-0-316-46033-0 (ebook)

Printed in the United States of America

LSC-C

Printing 1, 2022

For JD, they're alive in us

Aarón

MAKING MUSIC IS LIKE SUMMONING A GHOST. PLAY the right melody, strike the right chords, and people remember the past with their whole bodies. What it felt like to fall in love for the first time. What it felt like to have that heart you never knew could be so big, broken.

The right song sinks its teeth in us and makes us feel in places we thought were numb. The right song hangs us high above the clouds and makes us dream.

My mother's favorite song was "The Book of Love" by Peter Gabriel, and when life gets quiet, when life gets loud, I close my eyes and sometimes I can hear the strings washed in synthesizer. I can feel the rise and fall of the notes in my chest. I can feel her unfurling my clenched fists and wrapping her arms around me.

I *feel* things that I can't unlock otherwise.

It's been eight months since she died and the only thing that makes life bearable is being the one to turn the key, to find the song that finally reaches the person who's been hiding in the corner of the dance hall all night, to watch it slide over their body and wrench them onto their feet.

Sometimes it's just a toe tap, a jiggle of the knee. Sometimes a tear falls. Sometimes it's a smile so small you can barely see it. And it's those moments that keep me coming back to these grimy dance halls and smelly gymnasiums, DJing every family reunion and quinceañera that comes my way.

Because it's better than being home on the weekends with my dad and my brother who have stuffed their grief so down deep that it's like we live on two separate planets—one where Mom is a bittersweet memory and the other where she never existed at all. Because when I'm the one controlling what's coming through those speakers, I can change my whole mood with one swipe of the play button. I can remember her when I want. I can forget it all too.

The seven-foot robot standing next to me shrugs. "Or maybe you're the only DJ, and I use that term loosely, ending up in smelly gymnasiums and dimly lit refectories because you're also the only one without a flashy pseudonym and an oversized headpiece with an ironic costume to match." The robot frowns. "You need some style, kid."

At first glance he looks like one of the party decorations or maybe even tonight's second act. What kid doesn't want a giant walking, talking robot leading everyone into La Macarena?

But he's not and the only one glancing in his direction is me because I'm the only one that can actually see him.

I wish I knew *what* he is. All I know is he's been following me around since the funeral. A ghost as invisible as I am when I'm roaming the halls of Monte Vista High School. All my sadness wrapped up in shiny tinfoil and shaped like an oversized child's toy. He keeps playing games with me like one, his latest some deranged version of cat and mouse with my sanity being the mouse.

But just because he's (probably) not real doesn't mean he's wrong. Maybe I wouldn't still be here, half an hour after the party was supposed to have ended, if I had a flashier setup or a larger-than-life persona. Maybe then I wouldn't be so invisible. But being invisible has its perks. For one, none of the drunk partygoers have attempted to make small talk with me. I'd definitely call that a win.

"I'll admit," the robot says, "that is pretty impressive considering some of these people have been drinking for three hours straight. Well, at least all the white people who showed up at four because that's what the invitation said."

Some of them were already buzzed by the time the family finally arrived. But is it even una fiesta real if the birthday boy doesn't arrive late to his own party? He showed up bouncing in a souped-up muscle car with hissing hydraulics. The kid should have been wearing a helmet, but that would have messed up his perfectly gelled hair.

The robot scoffs. "If these people wanted to cumbia the night away, they shouldn't have booked the church during peak funeral season."

"I didn't know funerals had a season."

"*Everything* has a season."

It's not just about the wake, I think. *I've got shit to do too.*

"Mm-hm, sure you do."

Two little girls with bare feet and cake-stained faces elbow each other on the way to my setup.

The taller one asks, "Can you play 'Yo Perreo Sola'?"

The robot lifts a hand to his mouth. "Not sure that's an age-appropriate request…"

The smaller one stamps her feet. "No, Nayeli, you said it was my turn!"

Neither of them can see me rolling my eyes behind my sunglasses—my only attempt at creating a mysterious persona.

"Not to mention the fact that you've played that song twice already." The robot groans. "Seriously, kid, one more and I'm popping every single balloon in this goddamned place."

The girls walk right through him, still shoving each other.

"I want Bad Bunny."

"I want the baby shark song!"

There's hair pulling now. The little one screams.

"Bad Bunny!"

"Baby shark!"

I override them both and load "La Carcacha" into my queue. The girls perk up at the sound of el güiro and drag each other back onto the concrete area that's been marked off as the dance floor, before hiking up their skirts and spinning in circles under the strobe lights.

I scan the other dancers for birthday boy's parents. The priest stands in the doorway, probably looking for them too. They're supposed to be setting up food in here for the wake that's just wrapping up down the hall. Some of the family is already here, all dressed in black and clutching rosaries.

My cell phone buzzes on the table. I check the screen.

ACADIA AUDITION 8PM

Shit. I'm not gonna make it.

The robot shrugs. "Maybe showing up and vomiting your guts out onstage is worse than not showing up at all."

"You don't get it," I growl.

"Enlighten me."

I remember finding the flyer about the auditions on the floor outside stats class, the little stars someone had doodled around the words SCHOLARSHIPS AVAILABLE.

And my first thought was *I need to show Mom.*

A gut-wrenching reflex. The worst kind of muscle memory.

But then the truth caught up to me, grabbing that big veiny muscle and squeezing hard. Until my next thought was *I can't.* Because she's gone.

The alarm on my phone goes off again and there's something otherworldly about it. Like she's calling me from another dimension.

You can do this, Aarón. You can do it for me.

I glance toward the exit. I have exactly ten minutes to run six city blocks, catch the 37 bus, then change out my dirty DJ shirt for a clean button-down, all while engaging in a battle of psychological warfare with myself.

The robot raises a hand. "And don't forget about me."

I glare at him. *How could I?*

But people are still dancing. If I leave, they'll notice.

"So a distraction, perhaps?" The robot beams.

"Don't you dare," I snap.

Suddenly, there's a pop, the music dying out in a static hiss.

"What did you just—?"

The robot raises his hands. "It wasn't me!"

A woman in a black dress is clutching the power cord next to the generator. She's breathing hard, eyes narrowed like she's ready to take that cord and string it around all our necks. But then it slips from her grasp like she's just woken up from a dream. Or maybe she thinks she's in one right now.

My mom's funeral felt like that. Like we were all wading through fog, thinking we'd been swallowed into some kind of parallel universe.

"Party's over," the priest interjects. "Thank you all for coming. If you'll just start making your way toward the exit…"

The woman who pulled the power cord still looks shaken, trying not to make eye contact with the disgruntled dancers.

And I wonder for the first time who's inside that casket. Because the look on her face tells me they were *everything*.

Suddenly, I'm angry all over again. Because someone she loves is dead. Because my mom is too. Because you can't just take the sun away and expect everything else to go on living.

"Is that what you call this?" the robot gestures around the room. *"Living?"*

This time when the alarm sounds it's like an electric shock. A sign that I *could* be. If I was just brave enough to try.

I pack up my stuff and race through the exit doors, my backpack bouncing like a ton of bricks. I pray the laptop doesn't shatter against my keyboard.

Please let Señora Muñez be waiting for the bus. Please let Señora Muñez be waiting for the bus.

Señora Muñez is ninety years old. If she's waiting for the bus, Mr. V will have to put it in park so he can get out and help her up the ramp. She'll hold his arm in a death grip, trying to make small talk while the other passengers look on in annoyance. She'll start calling Mr. V *Enmanuel* because that's her oldest son's name. He'll correct her, a reminder that Enmanuel is dead, and then she'll burst into tears while Mr. V and the other passengers desperately try to console her.

If Señora Muñez is waiting for the bus, I can make the audition.

If Señora Muñez is waiting for the bus, well, it could change everything.

I round the corner, bounding over broken sidewalk and past Speedy's gas station. A horn blares. A pickup truck almost swipes me as I'm crossing the driveway. I wave my hands, more of a prayer than an apology.

Please let Señora Muñez be waiting for the bus.

I see the bus stop on the other side of the school building and cut across the grass, trying not to remember all the times I puked my guts out on the track. My twin brother, Miguel, was always the star athlete, not me.

But I try to channel his speed as I cut through the courtyard and zigzag across the parking lot. When I emerge on the sidewalk directly in front of the bus stop a truck is idled, blocking my view. It pulls away as I cross the street.

And on the other side... Señora Muñez is *not* waiting for the bus.

I look down the road, searching for taillights.

Instead, there are two cats spitting at each other, wrestling over something rotten. I sit on the empty bench and I don't want to feel it. But I do.

I'm relieved.

I'm a coward.

The street is quiet, but my skin can feel what my eyes can't see. Bass jumping a few blocks over at Speedy's. Mutts snapping at the holes in the chain-link fence lining the highway. My father's alarm screaming in his ear to get ready for his night shift.

The relief I was feeling just a few seconds ago is replaced by a pang. Because he's the reason I have to get out of here. Because orbiting a black hole is exhausting.

My phone buzzes again and I silence it.

It was stupid. I'm stupid.

"You're scared." The robot stretches his arms across the back of the park bench. "The difference is slight, but there is one."

"Can you be quiet?"

"I don't know. *Can* you?" He shrugs. "I'm in *your* head, kid. Not mine." The robot that is *just* a figment of my imagination sighs like he's the one being inconvenienced by my constant presence instead of the other way around. "Hey, not just *any* robot. I think you mean, the robot that is the stage persona of a musician who you idolize a little too much and who is also just a figment of your imagination. I'd call it an obsession, really. And I'd be flattered, you know, if the whole thing didn't have this creepy serial killer vibe, which come to think of it, I shouldn't actually be worried about since I'm already dead."

"You're not dead," I say, even though I have no idea.

Xavier López, aka La Maquina, who is a musician that I deeply admire but am in no way obsessed with, has been missing for almost a year, and I may or may not have been collecting clues in an attempt to find him. But just to make sure he's okay.

"Like I said. *Creepy.* Also you forgot to mention the love letters."

"They're not 'love letters,'" I snap.

They're more like updates; neighborhood news to let him know that he still matters. Like when the Little League baseball team he sponsors, the Flying Chanclas, took photos in their new uniforms, robot patches sewn onto their sleeves, or when La Puerta Abierta held their annual Easter egg hunt on the soccer field he paid for, every kid in the neighborhood waddling home with baskets overflowing with candy thanks to a generous donation that I *know* came from him.

"If you know it came from me, then why the hell would I need an update?"

"Because someone should say thank you." I shrug. "Shouldn't they?"

And because this isn't the first time La Maquina has had a mental breakdown and disappeared. Reminding him he matters might be the key to pulling him out of it.

"And if I don't want anyone to pull me out?" the robot asks. "What then?"

My stomach twists. Because I don't know what happens then.

In the quiet, I'm bombarded by the sound of my own heartbeat, still racing. I let it swell in my ears until I'm dizzy with it. And yet, I still don't know it quite as well as the night screams and chattering TV screens. The monotone voice at the crossing lights mixed with the Spanish guitar intro of *Amor Eterno*.

I know the sounds of this neighborhood *better* than my own heartbeat.

They usually make me feel safe. But right now, sitting on this park bench instead of the bus, weighed down by the chains of my own indecision, I wonder what it would feel like to not exist within this symphony. To leave Monte Vista and live in a fancy dorm, the sounds of instruments I've probably never even heard of wafting down the corridors.

But then I remember that Monte Vista is not a symphony. Not to the people in the new high-rise apartments on the edge of our neighborhood. Not to the teachers at Acadia or the judges who would have been listening to my performance tonight.

When they drive through our barrio or see it on the news, they don't hear a song. They hear sirens. Secrets.

If I had gotten up on that stage, if I'd played something for them, maybe that's all they would have heard. A secret language they'd rather make disappear than try to understand. Or maybe they *would* have understood. Maybe if I could have arranged the notes just right, they would have heard something they could understand. Something they could accept.

Forgive.

Around the neighborhood, gas ranges click on, flames gasping for air. It's dinnertime, voices swirling around hot stoves and cramped kitchen tables, families full on big belly laughs and posole. There's static—someone adjusts the radio. "Soy de Rancho" plays as bare feet dance on linoleum floors.

I wait for something inside me to click and catch fire too.

Maybe I need a match.

I tap my cell phone screen, igniting the sound in my headphones that always saves me. Suddenly, Monte Vista is behind glass, drums punching at the barrier, making everything rattle and shake. Sometimes I turn La Maquina's music up so loud that I can feel my skull filling with cracks.

But that's when things slither out. Sometimes those things are choruses and drumbeats. And sometimes they're giant robots that follow me around wherever I go, whispering things, calling me crazy. The one thing my brain hasn't been able to create is a remedy. Maybe I just haven't found the right song yet, something to turn my cracks into puzzle pieces.

"Or maybe there's just no figuring you out." The robot grins, his mouth a neon U.

Suddenly, the whir of an engine pulls my gaze and the brakes squeal as the 37 bus comes to a stop in front of me.

The doors open with a gasp. "Hey, Aarón, sorry I'm running late. I know you have your audition tonight."

I look past Mr. V and see Señora Muñez dabbing at her eyes with a handkerchief. There's a pharmacy bag on her lap.

She was waiting for the bus. She was waiting for the goddamned bus.

"S'okay," I mumble because I can barely open my mouth.

I sit across from Señora Muñez, not sure if I want to kiss her or start crying too. Because now I have no choice. *I have to do this.*

I think I'm going to be sick.

At the next stop, I consider hopping out and saving myself from what is guaranteed to be a total shit show, but then the doors open and the thing that's usually pumping blood through my veins starts to go haywire. Like when you drop an Alka-Seltzer in a soda bottle and the whole thing fizzes and explodes.

Because there is Mia Villanueva, hair in a bun, lips like the pink seam of a peach, holding her trumpet case and scanning the empty seats.

▪ ▪ ▪ ▪ ▪ ▪ ▪ ▪ ▪ ▪ ▪

After God flooded the earth, he fashioned a rainbow as a promise—that no matter how bad a storm seemed, it wouldn't keep raining forever.

In the weeks leading up to my mom's death, the rain didn't stop. It pelted me in her hospice room. Stung me in my sleep.

Until the day she died.

When the nurses told us she was gone, I ran out of the sliding glass doors, down the next street and the next, and when my legs finally slowed, it was her voice that made me look up.

"Does it look brighter to you?"

Mia was standing on the sidewalk outside Speedy's, head hanging back.

"What?" I followed her eyes to the cobalt sky above our heads.

It was electric, pocked with silver clouds. Even the trees looked different, the leaves so vibrant, I could barely look at them without squinting. And I *felt* her. In the colors too saturated to be real. In the sunlight and birdsong and warm gentle breeze.

As if the second my mother slipped away, God took the best pieces of her and scattered them like glitter.

And I almost didn't notice; wouldn't have if it hadn't been for Mia stopping me in my tracks. The rainbow after a yearlong storm that I was so sure would swallow me whole.

"Maybe I'm wrong." Mia furrowed her brow.

"No." I shaded my eyes, taking in the way she sparkled like everything else. "You're not wrong. I see it too."

I wanted to tell her that my mom was dead. I wanted to tell her that sometimes when I walked past the empty band hall and heard her playing her trumpet alone, I thought about stopping and asking her what it felt like. How she survived it when she lost her dad; when we were twelve and the other kids wouldn't stop staring at her, like if they looked in her eyes long enough, they might be able to see how it happened.

But when she smiled and walked away, taking that sparkle with her, I didn't try to stop her.

I didn't tell her that our hearts now carried the same scar.

Just like I never mustered up the courage to ask her out.

Just like I never mustered up the courage to do *anything*.

Now there are just a few weeks until graduation and I'm still choking.

* * * * * * * * * * * *

"Mia, your audition is today, isn't it?" one of the other bus riders, Mrs. Molina, asks.

She nods and I can tell by her blanched knuckles that she's nervous.

"You're going to be amazing," Mr. V promises.

Her tense smile disappears as she heads to the back of the bus. And then Mia Villanueva, the girl that turns my brain to static, comes to stand directly in front of me.

"Hey..."

I glance to my left. The seat is empty. I look to my right at the seven-foot robot sitting next to me. But I know she can't see him.

"Is this seat taken?"

I shake my head, too hard and too fast. Then she sits, her leg brushing mine, and I stop moving. Everything stops moving. The other bus riders. The cars that just a few minutes ago were whizzing past the windows. The people on the sidewalk. The clouds overhead. Everything stands perfectly still, pressing every millisecond of this moment into a memory.

But then Mia's fingers start tapping her bare knee, and everything is set in motion again, my heart pumping at warp speed.

"You okay?" she asks.

Words somehow force their way to my lips. "I don't know." I find her reflection in the window across from us, too afraid of looking at her directly. "You?"

"Same." Then she turns to face me. "Are you auditioning tonight?" She nods to the keyboard sticking out of my backpack.

I swallow. "Yeah..."

"Me too," she says. "I think..."

The tires graze the concrete curb, signaling our arrival at the auditorium.

"Buena suerte, mija." Mrs. Molina reaches over and pats her hand.

Mia heads for the exit but not before looking back at me one last time. She means *Aren't you coming?*

But for some reason I'm not moving.

I. Can't. Move.

Mia's face softens and I can't read what's there. Disappointment? Anger? Betrayal?

"She barely knows you," the robot interjects.

My mouth falls open, but I don't know how to speak to her. I don't know how to tell the truth. That I'm scared.

She knows it anyway and I can tell by her eyes, shifting

from me to the stairs of the auditorium, that she feels it too.

The last of the exiting passengers are almost down the steps.

Say something.

I inhale, but the words are stuck.

"Wish me luck?"

Then she heads for the exit, disappearing into the crowd headed for the concert hall as I bury my phone and all its useless alarms in my bag. Because my songs are not a symphony and nothing I've made will catch the world on fire.

2

Mia

IN MY FAMILY, DOUBT IS AN INHERITANCE. IT CHASED my mother out of her bed in the middle of the night, into our 1998 Chevy pickup truck, and off to God knows where the year I turned twelve. It kept my father in an alcoholic chokehold that squeezed the life out of him six months after she left. It's forced my brother Andrés to breathe his muffled poetry behind the elastic of a luchador mask, and it's taught my other brother, Jazzy, that the only way to avoid a broken heart is to break the other person's heart first.

Some nights it pulls up a chair at the dinner table; others it stares at us from the dark corner behind the television. But we are never allowed to mention it by name. We are never allowed to show how it haunts us.

And the hardest part is that Doubt does not lie. It just doesn't tell the whole truth.

For the past two days, Doubt's half-truths have frozen me to the back row of bus number 37, holding my hand and whispering in my ear. *You can't let them see you. They'll hate it. They'll hate it.* And tonight, it will be the only member of my family watching from the audience as I perform for a spot at the Acadia School of Music.

"Psst." A sharp hiss makes me jump. A girl in a black dress and a tight shiny bun waves a hand at me. "Hey, what number are you?"

I stare down at the number stuck to my chest.

Her eyes widen. "You're right after me." She turns her attention to the stage. "Can you see what number she is?" Adrenaline paints her cheeks a rosy pink. "Eighteen. Three more musicians and then I'm up."

I feel myself pale in reply. Three more musicians before her means four more musicians before me.

"Are you going for one of the scholarships?" she asks.

I swallow, tasting bile.

The school received an anonymous donation along with explicit instructions to hold auditions for students from Monte Vista, Real, Los Feliz, and Grant Avenue. Places these fancy private university people would never actually step foot in, which is why they needed an incentive.

Although, that hasn't stopped some of the rich kids from the west side from showing up anyway. I heard some of their parents had a problem with special auditions being held for mostly Black and brown kids and have been screaming about reverse racism.

I think it's funny since Acadia has been holding auditions

on the west side for years at donors' homes, pretending they were just invitation-only fundraisers. In other words, the white parents loved the pay-to-play policy when they were the only ones who could actually pay to play. But this donation has changed everything.

No one knows who the anonymous donor is, probably some social justice vigilante who will step out of the shadows sooner or later once this whole thing goes viral. But what we do know for certain is that Acadia never would have given us a chance without all that money hanging over their heads.

That's why every kid I've ever known who thinks they can sing, dance, or play an instrument has shown up in their Sunday best. Which is why I'm surprised by the girl's question—am I going for one of the scholarships? Of course I am. Doesn't she see it all over my face? In the sweat staining the sides of my dress? The dress that isn't even mine but that I borrowed from one of the other hair-dressers at the salon where Jazzy works.

"Yeah, I'm going for one of the scholarships," I finally say.

"Me too. Where you from?"

"Monte Vista."

"So, I guess you've heard the rumor then..."

"What rumor?"

Someone in the next row shushes us.

The girl gives them a dirty look before leaning closer. "The rumor that La Maquina might be the anonymous donor. He's from your neighborhood, right?"

I nod. I've heard the rumor.

But no one's seen or heard from Xavier López in months,

and part of me thinks this is just another desperate attempt by people to bring him back from the dead, or Mexico, or wherever the hell he ran off to. He's been missing for almost a year, so the possibilities are endless.

But letting go of your hometown hero is hard, especially for people who love his music so much he's not just their hero but some kind of god. Unless he really is dead, which would definitely negate that whole theory, and which, honestly, is probably closer to the truth. I've known addicts. My father was addicted to alcohol and my mother was addicted to freedom. I know where they ended up.

But maybe as long as people still have La Maquina's music, they'll never be able to think of him as a ghost.

My trumpet teacher, Mr. Barrero, says that's what happens when you're a great storyteller. Once the story has a life of its own, there's no making you disappear.

I turn my attention back to the girl onstage and at first she looks totally in control. But the longer I stare, the more I can see that she's grasping at the notes. Because all that practice hasn't tuned the only instrument that matters.

Her heart.

I can't *hear* it.

Because the girl is not a storyteller.

I try to tell myself that's the difference between me and every tight-lipped musician that's taken the stage. They are experts at telling other people's stories. Beethoven, Chopin, Bach. But I grew up with different fairy tales, ones I told myself, alone in the dark behind my closed bedroom door. Where monsters wore my mother's face and the best heroes knew how to hide.

As applause signals the end of one performance and the beginning of another, that's all I want to do. But I promised myself I wouldn't run again.

That I would try.

That I would *fight*.

The next performer is a violinist. His hair is slicked back, some gel dried white to his forehead. The first few notes of Caprice no. 5 by Paganini leap from the strings like flint stones igniting a spark. He sets everything on fire. The crowd erupts.

My skin is hot. Like I'm dangling over those flames, ready to drop any second.

"Are you okay?" the girl asks.

I wipe my brow with the back of my hand. It's soaked.

"Stage fright?"

I nod even though *stage fright* does little to describe what is actually happening inside my body right now.

I barely hear the girl as she says, "Good luck," before rising to her feet.

Which means I'm next.

She maneuvers under the spotlight, stone-faced. But as she cradles the violin, I can't help but search for signs— that I should bail; that I should do what I do best and hide.

It doesn't take long for me to find what I'm looking for.

The girl's instrument glints beneath the light, catching her smile. She looks shiny and new. But then she shifts, bow tearing across the strings as she angles closer to center stage. She's trying to find her mark.

So are the judges. I watch as their eyes narrow in on the tiny piece of plastic sticking out from the neck of the girl's dress. One of them motions to her collar, pointing it out to the woman sitting next to her. The dress only looks new because it is, with the tags still on it and everything.

The faster the girl plays, the more exposed it becomes. And as the judges take their eyes away from her performance, noses down over their scorecards, I realize that just because this anonymous donation guarantees that two of us will get in, that doesn't mean they're going to treat us any differently once we get there.

"Number twenty-two?" Someone stands over me and I jump.

My forearm instinctively presses to my chest, hiding my number. But she already saw it.

"Come this way, please."

I stand, knees quaking. Because I can't follow her to that stage. I can't even move.

The woman tries to wave me forward.

My trumpet case is sweaty in my hand.

"Miss!" she hisses.

That's when I realize the auditorium has erupted in cheers again. The girl bows, finished.

I take one last look at the judges. They can sense I'm causing some sort of disruption. The spotlight feels like it's already reaching for me.

And suddenly, I am frozen.

I am nine years old standing under an artificial sun. I look down at my brothers as they squirm in the fourth row. My father has Jazzy by the arms, trying to hold him still. My mother snaps at them both and then everyone turns to look. While I hold the old trumpet Mr. Barrero let me borrow because my parents couldn't buy me one. While I silently plead for them to stop.

Stop. Please. Stop.

But my mother's anger is left over from that morning when my father called her a puta and she called him a drunk. He yells the same thing now, Jazzy crying and trying to break out of his hold. No one is looking at me and then everyone is looking at me. Holding my trumpet, cheeks stained with silent tears as a wet shadow appears on the front of my skirt.

Now I'm watching that little girl from the audience. She reaches out her hand, sobbing, begging me to drag her offstage. To replace her with someone strong. To be strong.

Be strong, Mia.

But I can't. Because I'm sobbing too.

Before the woman beckoning me to the stage can see the tears, I bolt, running without thinking.

There are people outside on the steps. I push through them and someone calls after me. "Watch where you're going!"

But I don't know where I'm going. I'm just going. Going until my lungs are screaming, until I'm halfway home.

A car races past, reggaeton bumping loud from the speakers, and I press myself to the wall of Speedy's gas station. Lights buzz above me and I think I'm going to be sick.

Get out your phone. Call Andrés.

Unlike the woman who tried to coax me toward the stage, I know he won't think I'm crazy. At least, not for running. For signing up to audition, sitting through over a dozen other performances and waiting my turn—all that he'll think was nuts. But only because Doubt whispers in his ear as often as it whispers in mine.

What I don't know is whether or not Doubt is the *only* voice or if he hears our father too. Exasperated and talking a mile a minute about dreams and hope and promises. Like he knew one day he was going to disappear. Like he could already feel it happening.

The night of the talent show we were running late. I was alone in the back seat of the car, counting the seconds tick by while I watched my parents through the kitchen window. They were still inside the house, backlit by the six o'clock news, yelling at each other.

I pinched my eyes shut, stomach aching at the thought of missing my turn.

A door slammed. My father slid into the driver's seat and I found his eyes in the rearview mirror.

"We're going to be late," I said.

"No." He turned to face me. "I won't let that happen." He reached back and squeezed my knee, his hands rough.

They should have been scrubbing plates at the Chinese buffet, but he took off work because he said it was important. As we idled in the driveway, I couldn't help but think he was wrong.

"It's okay." I looked down. "It's stupid. We don't have to go."

"Mia."

I met his eyes. They were serious. Maybe even a little sad.

"Do you love playing?"

I shrugged.

"Mia, do you *love* it?"

I nodded, cheeks warm.

"Then it's not stupid." He sighed, facing out the window. But I could still see his reflection, eyes narrowed as his entire body sank into a memory even older than I was. "Before you and your brothers were born, I thought about who you might be. What you'd like." He smiled to himself. "Your passions." Then he frowned. "Your fears." He tapped his pointer finger against the steering wheel. "Maybe one of you would want to be a doctor or an actor or maybe even an astronaut. And for a second it all felt possible. Like all your mother and I had to do was bring you into the world and that would be enough." He exhaled. "But it wasn't enough. Hoping. Praying. Bargaining with God. It wasn't enough. Because the *where* mattered so much more."

He flexed his fingers, staring down at the scars and callouses. "More than whatever I could build for you with my bare hands, more than whatever battles I could fight for you, where you took your first breath..." He shook his head. "It was the only thing that *really* mattered.

"So we left Mexico even though it was dangerous. And with every step, those dreams I dreamed for you and your brothers, they started to feel possible again. They started to pull me toward our new home." He turned to face me. "They carried me, Mia. On days when I didn't know if I could keep going, your dreams carried me. And that's why you have to hold on to them." He took my hands, squeezing them between his palms. "You have to hold on to them *so tight* because someday when you don't know if you can keep going, they will carry you too."

The tears come again. Harder this time. Until the sob is rattling in my teeth. Because what he didn't say is that before the dreams can carry me, I have to be able to carry them first. And they're *so* heavy.

Like if I drop them, if I let them go, I'll be crushed under the weight of all that I could have been. Just like he was.

A car honks and I quickly wipe the tears from my cheeks before I walk beneath the harsh gas station lights, dodging grease stains on my way to Andrés's truck.

"¡Ay, Mamacita! ¿Adónde vas?" One of the Zapatos who's always posted up outside Speedy's hangs out the window of his purple Pontiac Firebird.

I glare at him as I pass. "¿Perdiste algo?"

Andrés steps out of the truck. "¡Sí, como tu cabeza!" He slams the roof of the car. "That's my sister, pendejo."

My catcaller just laughs. "Oh shit, güey. I thought your sister was still, like, twelve. Why's she dressed up all fancy?"

We both ignore him as I get in the car.

Andrés doesn't ask about the audition. Instead, he looks over at me and says, "You hungry?"

I'm not. In fact I still feel like I could puke, but I know he's just trying to make me feel better. When he pulls up to Pen's Pastelería food truck, I'm suddenly hopeful that it just might work. It's parked near Devine Lake, strings of lights running from the truck to a pair of pecan trees and casting a warm glow over some plastic tables and chairs that are almost full.

Chloe, a girl who graduated from Monte Vista High School last year, leans out of the order window. "The usual, Andrés?"

He slides over a ten-dollar bill. "Throw in a few chamucos." He shrugs in my direction. "Someone needs a pick-me-up."

"Be ready in five."

Andrés and I find two empty seats across from a woman who's tearing off pieces of a sopapilla and feeding them to her toddler. The little girl is transfixed, watching a young guy tune his guitar.

"Open up." The woman stuffs another piece of sopapilla into her daughter's mouth.

Andrés's eyes flash with something dark. He looks away, and I know I'm not the only one who can't see someone else's mother without thinking of our own. Andrés had her longer than I did, which means his memories always take longer to shake off. Especially in moments like this when I'm sitting here with puffy eyes and makeup smeared across my face, desperately in need of the kind of comfort and advice that a parent should give.

But we don't have parents anymore. We only have each other. So he does what he always does, places his giant hand on top of my head, squeezing and mussing up my hair, a sad smile on his face that says he knows he'll never be able to fix what's wrong. Not really. Because what's wrong is so much more than blowing a stupid audition. What's wrong is me.

"You look like a raccoon." Andrés wipes some mascara from my cheek. "What were you doing hiding behind

Speedy's anyway? You know kids your age shouldn't be hanging around there after dark."

"*Kids my age?* I'm not a kid anymore, Andrés. I'm seventeen and I graduate in a couple weeks."

"Well, according to Zapato you're still twelve and I'd like to keep it that way."

I groan. "Please don't be a stereotypical big brother right now."

He shakes his head, dropping the argument. Andrés is a closet poet whose primary conviction is shining a light on the ways stereotyping harms the Latinx community. Being a stereotype in real life is out of the question.

Mr. Martín, unofficial president of the Monte Vista retirees club, comes to sit next to us. He slaps his knee along with a mediocre rendition of "La Camisa Negra." "My nephew." He wags a finger at the woman feeding her little girl. "That's my nephew, Joaquín, up there."

Joaquín's right hand plucks the strings while his left jumps from one end of the guitar's neck to the other. He reaches a high note and his voice cracks, but somehow the imperfections make it even more endearing. Okay, *slightly* more endearing. He holds out the next note, much longer than necessary, and all my ears can focus on is the fact that it's flat.

"Kid's good," Mr. Martín says.

He's not *that* good. At least not from a technical standpoint.

My trumpet teacher, Mr. Barrero, says I'm *too* technical sometimes. He's been teaching me the trumpet since I was seven years old and I'm still trying to harness whatever magic he does. Which is hard to do when you're not sure if you believe in magic. But I believe in stories...and the one this guitar player is telling is definitely true.

When our alfajores, chamucos, and coconut flan arrive, I mostly pick at them, my stomach still tied in knots. My dress suddenly feels like a straitjacket and the fake pearls around my neck are hitting my collarbone in just the wrong way. I rip them off, the clasp popping and landing in the gravel.

Andrés licks some caramel off his thumb. "I told you that you didn't have to go back up there again."

The first night of auditions, I actually made it all the way to the stage. I walked beneath the spotlight and then I kept walking, off the opposite side of the stage, through the emergency exit, which set off the alarm, and then all the way home.

The next day I only made it as far as the check-in line. Each time I was struck by a memory, *a feeling*, like something was going to go terribly wrong. I could sense a monster lurking around every corner. But now I know that the monster wasn't lying in wait, ready to jump out and devour me. It already was. From the inside.

"How was your group?" I ask, transferring the shame onto Andrés. He's been going to this poetry group for months and still hasn't been able to read a single thing without wearing his signature luchador mask, which he claims is some kind of commentary on Latinx stereotypes but really it's just a way for him to hide.

"About the same as your audition, I guess." He reaches for one of the uneaten alfajores on my plate and scarfs it down.

I look back at Joaquín, at all his defects on display. But as he plays, he looks like he's holding on for dear life. Like everything he's feeling has pushed him to the edge of a cliff and he has to keep strumming, keep screaming into the void to keep from falling off. He looks like he likes the way it feels.

When I'm alone in my room, playing for no one but me, sometimes I can get *close* to that feeling. But the closer I get, the more Doubt starts to pull me in the other direction. And the current is so strong. I wish I knew how to fight it.

I look right at Andrés and say, "There's something wrong with us, you know."

He nods. "Probably."

I know he isn't satisfied, but he's gotten too good at convincing himself otherwise. Even though I can tell all he wants is to be different. To be able to tell himself a different story. That has to be why he started going to his poetry group in the first place.

What if I want to tell myself a different story too?

I try to say it out loud, to give us both permission. But I can't get the words out. Maybe he wouldn't want me to.

He's too afraid. So are you.

Doubt places a finger over my lips and I let it. Then I turn back to Joaquín who's singing the most off-key rendition of "El Canción del Mariachi" I've ever heard. And I resent him for making me believe it is beautiful. I resent myself even more for believing I could never make such a thing.

3

I GRAZE MY KEYBOARD AND THE LED LIGHTS ABOVE my bed flicker red. I tap the synth in front of me and now I'm underwater, the lights washing everything blue. I bring up the bass until I'm a thousand feet below the surface where no one can reach me, the sound through my headphones submerging me somewhere safe. Somewhere I don't have to think about the audition and the fact that I totally blew it. Again.

Touching the drum pad pocks the ceiling in flecks of gold, twinkle lights turned makeshift stars that my mother and I tacked to the plaster when Miguel and I started sleeping in separate rooms.

"I know you're afraid," she'd said, pulling me into her lap. "But there's no reason to be." She looked up and I followed her eyes, her arms slowly rocking me. "There's an entire universe looking after you while you sleep. Think of that…" She kissed me on the forehead. "People have marveled at the stars for centuries, but out of all of the little boys in the world, they're shining on you."

Miguel poked his head in. But he wasn't looking at the lights. He was looking at me in our mother's lap and suddenly I felt too big to be in her arms, my face turning red as I wriggled free.

"Your room next, Miguito?" She pinched his cheek and he groaned.

"I don't need a night-light. I'm not afraid of everything like Aarón is."

For so long, I thought that was true; that the biggest difference between my brother and me was that I was afraid and he wasn't. But really the biggest difference was that no matter how old I was, I still let myself *need* her, and Miguel refuses to need anyone.

She was wrong, though, about the stars. She thought they would make me feel less lonely, but the truth is, there's nothing lonelier than looking up at the stars; at the distance between them, twinkling even though they're already ghosts.

But they're also a reminder—that the most beautiful things die twice. A star implodes but it isn't gone. When the light finally disappears, that's when a thing really dies.

So the key to cheating death, the key to living forever, is to make enough light that *nothing* and *no one* can ever snuff it out. Which is why every song I write has a bit of my mom in it, her voice stripped from old home videos and laid over violins and guitar solos and synthetic heartbeats that trick me into thinking she's still here.

"Is that what you're doing with me?" The robot lounges on my bed. "Pretending I'm alive like you do your mother?"

There's a difference, I want to tell him, between *pretending* and *hoping*. Hoping requires something tangible. Like an X-ray with no menacing shadows. Blood work that comes back cancer free. A photograph of the person, alive and well on an island off the coast of Belize.

The wall above my computer is covered in them, plus printouts and newspaper clippings—all the evidence I've been collecting since the news broke that La Maquina had disappeared. All of it staring back at me, waiting for me to put it together.

My mother's diagnosis wasn't a mystery. There were no clues to examine or threads to unravel. There was nothing I could do except watch her slip away.

But La Maquina is nothing if not an enigma, his disappearance a problem I might actually be able to solve. Most people think that he's dead, but they're wrong. Because even if he is…there's still the light.

I mute the keyboard and scroll through my music library until I find his first single, "Thirteen Heavens." The sound ratchets up and I lean back, feeling the vibrations in my teeth. Until there's nothing inside my skull but synth and drum machine.

I turn back to the keyboard, tapping out my own beat beneath La Maquina's. Like he's right in front of me, serving the sound like a ball over a net, waiting for me to hit it right back at him. Like he's asking me questions I've never even thought of and I'm conjuring answers in a language I'm still desperately trying to learn.

We talk like this, back and forth, until the lights strung around my room seem to multiply. Red bleeds into every dark corner and suddenly I'm not underwater anymore. I'm sitting in the middle of the left atrium, pumping blood this way and that. Until my own heart is racing.

I paint with the sounds, long strokes that make the hairs on my arms stand on end, and as I do, every note on the scale draws my eyes to a different clue on my wall.

There's something about the clippings when they're awash in different shades. The red emboldens the lines, headlines popping, faces in photographs more ghoulish, suspicious. I turn everything blue, then green, trying to coax out some important detail. A road sign, a piece of jewelry, a distinctive tattoo. So far they've all been dead ends.

My fingers flex over the keys, summoning the sounds of what I know: On February 3, *Complex* magazine runs an article titled: "The Precise Mechanics of a Mental Breakdown: How the Most Anticelebrity Celebrity Is Manufacturing His Own Demise."

It was scathing, comparing his music to the Popsicle stick figures of someone in a mental ward. La Maquina goes on a Twitter tirade, claiming the article is complete bullshit and that every word he said was taken out of context. He claims it harms people with mental illness...

"Which it does," the robot adds.

...and that the media has been trying to destroy his mental health for years. Because he doesn't fit into their box. Because he doesn't apologize for it.

"And I *never* will."

He stops tweeting in English and starts tweeting in Spanish. He stops tweeting in Spanish and starts tweeting in Nahuatl. He stops tweeting in any alphabetic language and starts using dots. But it's not nonsense. It's Morse code, the same almost indiscernible clicks he buries deep in the underbelly of his songs.

Twenty-four hours later all of his social media pages go dark.

The robot puffs a ring of smoke. "Poof!"

Fans are sent an email with a countdown clock. The internet freaks, thinking he's going to release a new album on Thanksgiving Day. The people who hang around his fan forums, the people who follow him on tour, they know better. Thanksgiving Day is the day La Maquina's mother passed away from ovarian cancer. When the countdown clock strikes zero, La Maquina doesn't release any new music. Instead, he removes every song he's ever made from all streaming services.

The robot laughs to himself. "Suckers..."

Then crickets.

The robot makes a chirping sound.

"Are you done with the ridiculous commentary?" I spit.

He shrugs. "Are you done pretending to be sane?"

I ignore him, checking my email sent folder for any sign of a response:

The Mexic-Arte Museum put up a new
installation of photographed street art
inspired by your music.

The Belen Rojas Community Center gave
away a year's worth of Paco's Pizza to the kid
with the best LEGO sculpture of your robot
persona.

Someone tagged the Sage Street water tower
with the chorus from your song "Cleave."

No response. The robot mimics the sound of blowing
tumbleweeds.

I scroll through a few forums next, looking for anything new.

There's reference to a bullshit sighting in Miami.
Another ridiculous conspiracy theory about alien abduc-
tion. My DMs are full of more of the same, as if being the
president of La Maquina's fan club somehow makes me lead
investigator. If any of the other club members knew I was just
a senior in high school, still living at home, with an annoying
roommate no one else can see, they'd probably accuse me
of being the one to make La Maquina disappear in the first
place.

"Those people believe in aliens," the robot scoffs. "I
doubt an imaginary friend would be much of a stretch."
He reaches his arms behind his head. "Although, I do enjoy
the idea of me being stuck on a UFO somewhere with Elvis

and Tupac. Obviously, Tupac and I would become best friends and we'd shove Elvis through a porthole for stealing Black people's music."

I shake my head. "So *that* you're willing to entertain but the idea of you being alive *anywhere* else—"

There's a burst of air as my bedroom door flies open and I shove my voice back down, praying Miguel didn't just hear me talking to myself.

He rips off my headphones. "Dad says stop playing with your Christmas lights and come eat dinner."

I'd rather go to bed hungry than share any breathing room with Miguel, but lately I don't really have a choice. Since Mom died, our father's been in this constant tug of war between wanting us close and wanting us as far away as possible. Our faces carry too many memories and because we're twins, when we're side by side it's double the dose.

Dad's already at the kitchen table. "You keep listening to that music so loud, you're going to bust your eardrums." He eyes the Coke can Miguel just popped open with a hiss. "You think Coach Miller lets his athletes drink that basura? You treat your body like trash and that's exactly how it'll perform."

Miguel got a basketball scholarship to the local community college and it's all Dad talks about. Maybe he thinks it's a safe topic, something to celebrate. As if he doesn't notice Miguel bristle every time he brings it up. Maybe he doesn't want to.

Just like all of the other things we pretend never happened.

Like how Miguel was shooting the winning basket in the championship game while Mom was taking her last breath. Or how she was holding my hand but calling for Miguel just a few minutes before. How the cancer was so cruel, it hid me in his shadow even then. Or how Dad was working a double shift, retaliation from his manager for all the time off he'd been asking for.

"Yeah, well Coach Miller's not here." Miguel takes a big gulp.

"But *I* am," Dad says.

And that's why Miguel can't stand playing anymore; why I overheard him telling the girl he's dating that he doesn't even want to go to school in the fall. Because Dad's got ten years' worth of night games and weekend tournaments and early morning practices he's trying to make up for. Things he missed while he was busy being the model employee, working his ass off to buck every stereotype, to earn a fraction of the respect his white coworkers were born with.

But then Mom got sick and getting time off was like pulling teeth and he learned that no matter how hard of a worker he was, that's *all* he was. A name on a timesheet. Another cog in the machine. Now he manages Miguel with the same ruthlessness his bosses manage him. Not willing to let another thing die. The dreams he has for Miguel. The dreams he wishes Miguel had for himself. They've been Dad's life support for the past eight months—the scholarship, Miguel's shot at being the first person in our family to earn a college degree.

As Miguel crumples his napkin in his fist, I can see that

the weight of it is crushing him. But he doesn't argue. He doesn't say a word. No one does. Because we don't know how to fill the silence the way she did. Because it's not worth tearing our hearts open to try.

In the quiet, I glance between them, trying to guess which memory they might be trapped in. Maybe the one from two summers ago when Mom suddenly decided the house needed a new coat of paint and when a mix-up at the store left us with six cans of sherbet green she refused to return them.

"The Holy Spirit chose these colors," she laughed. "And we don't argue with angels."

Or maybe they're thinking about when Miguel and I turned nine, and she and Dad took us to the drive-thru safari near San Antonio. Miguel was practically hanging out the window while I was hiding on the floorboard, terrified of the long tongues reaching out for food.

Mom crawled into the back seat with me and sat me on her lap. She held my arms down and said, "You're safe, Pepito."

The next thing I knew a giraffe was slobbering all over me while everyone laughed. Once I realized that I was still alive and that the giraffe's tongue actually kind of tickled, I started laughing too.

"Not everything in this world bites, Pepito." She mussed my hair. "Sometimes life just wants to give you a big juicy kiss."

Or maybe they're thinking about our family trip to the beach when Miguel was trying to lure me into the waves while Mom and Dad stood on the sand. Dad was working the sunscreen into his hands before slathering it on Mom's arms.

The wind carried their voices.

"Mayra..."

"What is it, Bruno?"

He moved her hand to the skin under her armpit. "Do you feel that?"

■ ■ ■ ■ ■ ■ ■ ■ ■ ■ ■

"You're doing it again."

"What?"

Miguel points at my plate with his fork.

All of the food has been chopped so finely it's practically dust. That's when I notice the sweat on the back of my neck.

Sometimes when my brain starts rewinding too quickly, the bitter and the sweet memories all jumbled into one, my body goes on autopilot. I fold and refold the laundry too many times. I brush my teeth until they bleed. I cut up my food into the smallest pieces while my father and Miguel look on with dread.

"Sorry," I say.

I feel naked, the thought of eating making my throat clench. I try to focus on the noise around me—the refrigerator humming, the low murmur of the television. I hear the voice of the news anchor say, "A new executive order out of the White House cancels renewals for all work visas, effective immediately."

From the corner of my eye, I watch my father reach for

the remote and click off the TV. Another thing we don't talk about—my father's status.

"Aarón…" My father nudges me. "You need to eat."

I just nod, still trying to breathe. *Breathe. Just breathe.*

"Why does he have to do this weird shit every fucking time?" Miguel throws himself back against his chair. "You make us remember her, you know? You're the reason we can't move on."

"Miguel…" My father's voice is weary.

"What? I'm sick of this. We're about to graduate and Aarón's over here still having fucking panic attacks. All because Mom babied you too goddamned much."

"That's enough."

Miguel keeps his head down, jabbing his fork into the food on his plate. Then he mumbles, "I'm not going to take care of you, Aarón." Then adds a little louder, "When Dad's gone, I'm not going to take care of you."

The fork trembles in my hand as I fight hard not to let the tears well up, to hide from Miguel how much it hurts for him to prod at these wounds, to hide that they still bleed. But he knows. *He knows* and he's had enough.

"It's been eight months, Aarón. Stop being such a girl!"

"Watch your language, Miguel." This time my father stabs at his food like he's trying to murder it. "I don't want to hear anything else about your mother or your brother, or you're going to your room."

Through the living room curtains, lights dance in the dark. Then one by one they go out, car doors slamming shut. I hear boots on the pavement, voices.

We all drop our forks, listening.

When my father moves to the glass, Miguel and I follow.

Across the street, I can see the Salazars through their living room window. Mr. Salazar is sitting in his recliner, bouncing his new baby girl on his lap. His other daughter is perched on her knees in front of the TV while Mrs. Salazar lounges on the couch reading a book. All four of them behind that single pane of glass. The kind of family you'd put on a postcard or maybe in a magazine ad.

It's hard to see the other bodies at first. Four of them moving through the front yard—bulky and hunched over like they're invading enemy territory. But this isn't another country far away. This is here. This is *home*.

What are they doing in our home?

"What's happening?" Miguel hisses.

Their motion sets off the porch light and then all our questions are answered.

The glow of the TV spills through the crack in the door until the men look less like soldiers and more like ghouls. But they don't wait for Mrs. Salazar to ask questions, for her to let them inside. They shove her back and then my father does the same to us, forcing us away from the window.

"Stay back." He shakes.

I hear the rumbling of the SUVs. I hear Mr. Salazar's little girl scream.

"No, you can't take him!" Mrs. Salazar pleads.

Doors slam shut. Engines rev. Tires squeal off into the night.

For a long time, Dad just stands there, clutching the curtains like they're rooting him to the spot. His shoulders heave as he watches the commotion. Something breaks like glass. More sobs.

"Dad...?" Miguel creeps closer.

But he's frozen.

Mr. Salazar isn't the first to be taken, and there's a fist around my gut, clenching hard, because I know he won't be the last.

My father finally turns to us, his black eyes dim, and in that moment, I know he is afraid.

But just like his sadness, he doesn't speak it aloud. Instead, he shoves it down. Swallows it like poison. Swallows it so we don't have to. Another cancer without a cure.

And for a second, I wish I could reach for him, to feel his flesh and bone and *know* that he's still here. To let him know that I'm still here too. Even if we can't fill the silence for each other. Even if we don't need each other the way we needed her.

I'm still here.

Mia

MR. BARRERO IS ALREADY IN HIS GARAGE AS I HEAD up the driveway. He's *always* in the garage. It could be over a hundred degrees and he'd still be out there fiddling with broken things, trying to make them whole again.

The first day I saw him he was cleaning something shiny—brass. No one had taught me not to talk to strangers, so I walked right up to him and asked him what it was.

He said, "A speaker for your soul. The soul goes in through the mouthpiece and comes out the other end as sound."

Then I asked him what a soul was. He looked me up and down, probably surprised that I could grow up in our Catholic neighborhood without knowing what a soul is.

"It's you," he finally said. Then he tapped his chest. "Do you want to listen?"

I'd only ever been to the doctor a few times—once

when I had to get my shots so I could be enrolled in kindergarten and the second time when I got the chicken pox. But I could still remember the cold press of the stethoscope making me jump.

So I wouldn't feel as scared, the doctor let me listen to my own heart. *Pom-pom, pom-pom.* At five years old, I was frozen, listening to the rhythm, *my* rhythm. But not something I had made. Something made by the *something* that had made me.

I clutched the rubber end of the stethoscope when the doctor tried to take it away, desperate to savor the sound like a ticking bomb. I never wanted to forget that there was something inside me that could destroy.

Mr. Barrero held up the speaker for my soul and I pressed my lips over the mouthpiece, expecting to hear the same dull thudding sound.

"Now inhale," he said, and I puffed up my cheeks. "Then blow."

I did as he said and what came out of that old trumpet were the dying breaths of a hoard of geese being set on fire.

But then Mr. Barrero said, "Try again," only this time he placed his fingers over some of the tone holes and the sound became a smooth, solid thing.

My lips leapt off the mouthpiece, startled.

He laughed. "You're a natural."

"What does that mean?"

He wrinkled his nose, amused. He looked from the trumpet to me and said, "'A natural' means you were born to do something."

After that, I started bugging Mr. Barrero every day,

asking him to let me play, to show me how. I didn't know that he used to play professionally or that he used to actually charge for lessons. But he never took a cent from me, even when I was old enough to realize he should.

But more than that, Mr. Barrero showed me how the music makes everything else stop; how it slows life down, turning a whipping tornado into nothing more than a breeze.

The night of the talent show, my parents weren't the only ones watching me from the audience. He was there too.

As I squinted against the harsh spotlights, his fedora was the first thing I saw, and just below the brim, the giant smile on his face. Then the yelling started and when I was frozen to that spot, wet and cold and ashamed, he was the one who took my hand and led me down the steps.

"It's all right, Mia. Everything's going to be all right."

The sight of me in tears snapped my parents out of their rage, and they rushed me to the car. Mr. Barrero buckled me in while my father tried to apologize to him, while my mother tried to explain.

But then my father said something I couldn't quite make out. My mother got in his face again...and then she hit him.

I felt it too—struck in the chest, my heart stopped for a moment.

She'd never done it in front of us before, never made it any bigger than a sound. But this time I *saw* her hurt him. Mr. Barrero did too. And then I saw my father shrink, burning pink with shame. As small as I'd ever seen him.

When we got home they sent us to our rooms. I locked

myself inside and then I ran to the window. The light was still on across the street, Mr. Barrero's shadow moving back and forth across the kitchen window.

Something shattered on the other side of my bedroom door, their voices like flames. And that was the day I learned to run. Before my mother showed me how, I was already learning to escape.

I ran to Mr. Barrero's front door, trumpet case in hand, and he led me inside.

He placed his hand on my head and squeezed. "It's going to be okay, Mia."

He said it over and over and over again.

Even after she left.

Even after we found my father's body.

For almost ten years, he has promised only this: *it's going to be okay.*

At his kitchen table, I could still hear them, my eyes drawn to the darkness outside, wondering if I might see their friction casting sparks, if the world was ripping at the seams the way my heart was.

"Let's play," Mr. Barrero said.

Then he lifted his trumpet to his lips, motioning for me to do the same. He led me into the song I'd been practicing for the talent show, his lungs carrying me up to the notes that were too hard to reach. Until the sound was a cocoon. Until I was safe inside. Until I finally believed him when he said, *It's going to be okay.*

A few months later, I walked up his driveway and saw him with a shiny new trumpet.

"Do you like it?" he asked, smiling.

I traced the shape, examining my reflection in the brass. "Is it mine?"

"I think you've earned it."

I cradled it close, pretending it was something that needed to be taken care of. Something sleeping that, in the gentlest way, I was supposed to wake.

I sit across from Mr. Barrero now, that same trumpet perched on my knees. A lukewarm breeze rushes by the open garage, rocks skittering across the pavement.

"How was your audition?" he asks.

My silence gives it away. Last time I bailed on the audition, Mr. Barrero gave me this long pep talk about fear and courage and never giving up.

Today, he frowns. "It won't wait, you know."

"What won't wait?"

He uses an old toothbrush to clean the mouthpiece of his trumpet. "Your destiny."

I'm not sure if I should tell him I don't think I believe in *destiny* anymore. It was something I wished for back when I thought it would change things. But fear keeps things the same and it's all I know how to feel these days.

Instead, I respond the only way I know how. We've been working on "While My Guitar Gently Weeps," and I reach for the first note as I press my lips over the mouthpiece. He leans back, listening. When I slide up to the key change his lips curl into a smile. I smile too, the next note falling flat. But he just nods, feeling what I'm feeling, what I barely allow to come to the surface when I'm not holding my instrument.

I let the last note trail off and it seems to hang in the stale air of the garage, reminding me of everything I didn't leave on that stage last night.

In the silence, he asks, "Were you afraid they'd love it?"

My face feels hot. Because *it* is me and he knows it.

"Mia, I haven't given you notes in months. You've been practicing six hours a day since you were eight. Now you have to make a choice. About what it was all for."

My voice is so much smaller than my trumpet. "Can't it just be for me?"

"You think you were put here to play to your bedroom walls?" He leans forward, arms resting on his knees. "Playing for no one is not an option, Mia."

"But...what if I can't?"

"Then you forfeit your gift. You insult the Creator who gave it to you."

Mr. Barrero isn't Catholic like most of the people who live in our neighborhood. But he is a religious man, and every time he taught me something new about the trumpet he tried to teach me something new about the spirit. When I was a kid everything was like a fairy tale and God was as easy to believe in as magic. God *was* magic.

But then my mother left and my father was swallowed by his own grief.

There was no more magic in the world. There was no more God.

"Are you trying to warn me that He'll take it away?" I scoff, angry tears trying to come to the surface. "Like He took my parents?"

"You think God's a murderer?" He leans back. "A

thief?" He shakes his head. "He's an artist, Mia. And so are you. That's not the choice I'm asking you to make. I'm asking…what are you going to create? And not for yourself but for others."

I've caught a glimpse of the man Mr. Barrero used to be. In between his testimony he's let it slip that he used to tour in a band. That they used to get drunk and party with women whose names they didn't even know. That when he went on the road, he left a family behind. A son.

I've lived across the street from Mr. Barrero for seventeen years; I've spent every Saturday morning and Sunday afternoon in this very garage and I don't even know his son's name.

He's got demons. The kind that made a little boy grow up without his father. Now Mr. Barrero clings to his scripture because it's all he has left. He turns to God to be forgiven. And he plays the trumpet alone at his kitchen table in the middle of the night to remind himself what he needs to be forgiven for.

He talks to me about using my gift as if I'm the one who needs to atone for something. But I don't need forgiveness. I need answers to questions good Catholics aren't allowed to ask. Like why didn't God wake up my father? When my brothers and I needed him.

We *needed* him.

When I ask Mr. Barrero these questions, he never has an answer. He just tells me not to doubt. That doubting is a sin. But what about leaving three poor kids from the barrio to fend for themselves? If that's not a sin, what is?

"Let's try it again..." he offers.

I nod, relieved that we can get back to communicating in the language we know best.

"One...two..." He pats his knee, counting me in.

The next two hours pass in beats, but these days Mr. Barrero does less teaching and more listening. When I get tired of waiting for him to tell me what's wrong with me, I pack up my things and carry my trumpet back across the street.

"It won't wait, Mia!" he calls out.

I wave over my shoulder.

Grease pops on the kitchen stove as I crash through the screen door.

"¡Cuidado, Mia!" My brother Jazzy waves a filthy oven mitt in my face. "You're gonna break that door down. Again."

"Well, maybe we need a new door."

He huffs. "Add it to the list. Right next to the new toilet seat, the new window screen, and the new roof. Now, will that be cash or check?"

Andrés groans from the couch. "I told you I was going to YouTube it."

Jazzy puts his hands on his hips. "You're going to YouTube how to fix a leaky roof..."

"Yeah, and then I'm going to fix the leaky roof."

"You?"

"Yes, *me*, Jazzy!"

Jazzy whips out his cell phone, a few of his acrylics missing. "I'm calling Oscar. He's a *real* plumber."

I furrow my brow. "Plumbers don't fix leaky roofs."

"Fine, I'll tell him about the toilet seat and while he's here I'll just have him take a *look* at the roof."

My mouth quirks. "Take a look at the roof or at *you*?"

"If it gets our roof fixed, he can look, he can touch—I don't really give a shit."

"And that's exactly why he's not coming over to fix a goddamned thing," Andrés says.

I gather silverware while Jazzy grabs glasses. Andrés fills plates with arroz con pollo and carries them over to the kitchen table.

We bow our heads.

Andrés clears his throat. "Dear Dog, thank you for this food that smells like feet. Possess us good Englishman with our ghost bodies..."

When we were kids without a dinnertime—sometimes without dinner at all—we'd wander the block at sundown, watching our neighbors through their windows. They would always bow their heads before eating, talking to someone we couldn't see, who they couldn't see either. Not with their eyes closed at least.

We weren't expert lip readers, but after many weeks of intense study, we came up with a prayer that was as unnervingly true as it was seemingly nonsensical. But in a world that didn't often make much sense to begin with, it made perfect sense to us.

As Andrés recites it now, Jazzy smirking under his breath, I think about what Mr. Barrero said about God. That He or She or They... are an artist.

Like me.

"In your game, we play. Amen."

We cross ourselves, each of us tapping our left shoulder and drawing an X across our chest, pledging allegiance to our fellow mutants. *X-Men* was the only cartoon we could actually sit through as kids. But as soon as the credits rolled so did we, wrestling on the floor until one of us squealed for mercy.

Jazzy watches me. "¿Qué pasa? Are you still thinking about your audition?"

I fluff up the rice with my fork.

"Maybe she doesn't want to talk about it," Andrés says.

I exhale, staring at my plate. "Maybe that's the problem." I drop my fork. "Do you ever...?" Then I just shake my head, not sure if I can get the words out... or if I should.

"Do we ever *what*?" Jazzy asks, an eyebrow cocked.

The words crash on the tip of my tongue, like water trying to break through the cracks in a dam. I stare down at my plate again, summoning whatever strength I may have, and then I let them through. "Do you ever wonder if we're...afraid...because of Dad...?"

"Because he died?" Jazzy asks.

"Because he dreamed so big." I scrape my plate with my fork. "Because none of those dreams ever came true."

Andrés points his fork at me. "You were his dream." Then he motions to Jazzy. "The three of us."

"Gee, thanks," Jazzy says. "No pressure."

"Exactly." I look between them both. "What if *that's* why we're so afraid to make things and do things and *try*?"

Jazzy scrunches his brow. "*We*? I'm not the one who choked at her audition. Three times. In the same week."

Andrés crosses his arms. "No. But you are the one who broke up with Manny the day after he told you he loved you."

I keep my eyes down. "And Javi. The week of your one-year anniversary. And Germaine after he—"

"Okay!" Jazzy waves his hands. "I get it. I'm as messed up as the two of you."

"Hey"—now it's Andrés's turn to try to defend himself— "I actually meet with my poetry group on the regular."

"Yeah," Jazzy says, "while wearing a lucha libre mask that hides your identity."

"It's part of the poetry. People want Latinx caricatures, not human beings. So that's what I give them. All while making powerful commentary on exactly that. It's called irony, Jazzy."

"It's called being a coward."

Andrés grips the table. "What did you call—?"

It occurs to me that I have unraveled something delicate, something that has been holding us together since the day Andrés found our father's body and sat Jazzy and me on the stoop until the ambulance came so we wouldn't see.

But I *did* see. I saw every ugly, awful thing in his eyes, his entire body contracting against the pain. And all I could do to comfort him was to let him believe he was protecting me. Even though that day I realized that no one really could.

"I feel like one," I admit. "Like a coward. Like I'm suffocating under the weight of all the things I'll never do. Just like they did."

Andrés doesn't look at me as he asks, "Where is this coming from?"

"I graduate in a few weeks and I still don't know what I'm supposed to do with my life." It's not the whole truth, but it's all I can say considering I still haven't figured out what that is yet. "Maybe I'm just tired." I meet Andrés's eyes. Then Jazzy's. "Aren't you?"

Andrés takes his plate, chucking the last bit of food in the trash. He looks back at me and Jazzy. "We're not like them." Then he heads out to his truck, starting the engine and rolling onto the street.

And I know that whatever I've unraveled, I'm not going to be able to put it back together.

Jazzy picks at the chicken on his plate. "The only time Andrés doesn't see Dad is when he puts on that mask."

"I know…"

"So why are you trying to force him to take it off?"

"I wasn't. Besides, you're the one who brought it up *and* you're the one who called him a coward."

"Because the two of you called me one!"

"It was supposed to be about me," I lie, trying to backtrack now that I know I've hurt them both. "Not Andrés's mask."

"He raised you, Mia. He raised us both. You were so young when Mom left and then Dad…" He clenches his jaw, forcing back the memory. "Whatever demons you're wrestling with, they didn't all come from them."

"That's not what I was trying to say."

"Well, that's what he heard." He scratches the back of his neck, trying to get the next part right. "You don't remember them like Andrés and I do, Mia. Every fight, every breakdown, every time one of them ran away. This world isn't kind and they knew it, which is why they had no idea how to raise us in it. And..." He looks down as if staring deep into a well of memories we don't share. "After twenty-one years on this earth...I get it."

"Well, I don't." I get up from the table and the second I'm on my feet, I sense the nudge coming from deep down in that place Jazzy thinks I can't remember.

But I remember *everything*. My mother's makeup all over the bathroom counter, all over her face and mine. My parents dancing in the living room one second and my father's nose bleeding the next. The clink of beer bottles at 2:00 AM. The sound of sobs.

What I can't tell Jazzy is that I almost miss the chaos as much as I miss them. Like it was a person. A person I could always count on to show up and destroy. And there was comfort in that, safety in knowing that it would always be around.

Jazzy sighs. "Maybe this shit's just in our DNA."

I wonder what the difference is between DNA and destiny. They're both signatures, road maps, a way of marking where you've been and where you're going. But are they both things you're not allowed to choose?

I look out the window again, at the sky that is stretching just as gray over the Acadia School of Music as it is over our rotten hole-filled roof. And I could be *there*, somewhere, *anywhere*, if I would just reach for it.

Like my father begged me to. Because it carried him. The hope that I would matter; that I would build a life that mattered. A life that was nothing like his own—a cautionary tale about what happens when you *stop* hoping. Even though more and more my life is starting to feel like a cautionary tale of its own. Like every time I run from what scares me, I'm hurtling myself toward the edge of that same cliff.

"I don't want it." I shake my head. "*This* can't be my destiny."

Jazzy smirks, but it's another pained thing. "Mr. Barrero tell you music is your destiny?"

"Maybe it is." It feels silly to say it out loud and that's how I *know* it's brave.

Jazzy rolls his eyes and I think I've failed. But then he says, "And there's your problem, Mia. *Maybe.*" He looks me in the eye. "For those of us who have actually heard you play, we *know* it's your destiny."

His words are a serum, filling me up. I let them. Another act of bravery.

"You've got one too, you know." I come up behind him, gripping his shoulders.

"Yeah," he snorts, "it's keeping you two starving artists alive."

"You know it's more than that."

He shakes his head. "I don't." He exhales. "And it scares me just as much as your destiny scares you."

"We can try to be brave," I say. "We can do it together..."

"What about Andrés?" he asks.

We both turn to the window, wondering which direction Andrés's headlights are pointed; how many times he's thought about following the light, about running the way our mother did.

But he'll come back. He always does. And then he'll

put the mask back on, not just the one he wears to perform but also the one he wears every time he goes out into the world. The one he's mistaken for some kind of shield. He'll put on the mask and we won't say a thing. Because he's allowed to do whatever he has to in order to survive. He's earned it.

5

Aarón

MY ALARM GOES OFF, AND I SCRAPE MY NIGHT-
stand, searching for my phone so I can hit snooze.

Just five more minutes...

Except it isn't there.

"Looking for this?" the robot dangles the phone between
two fingers.

"Give it back."

"Why? So you can like another one of Mia Villanueva's
photos from six months ago?"

My stomach drops. "What are you talking about?"

He tosses me the phone, exasperated. "See for yourself."

The app's still open to Mia's profile. I barely remember scrolling through her photos until I finally dozed off.
But there it is—a heart over a photo of her, curly hair in
a messy bun, a bright pink straw between her lips as she

drinks a lime-green smoothie. And the robot was right. It's dated six months ago.

"Shit!"

"My thoughts exactly."

"She's going to think I'm some kind of stalker."

The robot peers at the screen over my shoulder. "So... unlike it."

"Are you kidding?" I pinch the skin between my eyes. "That would make it even worse."

I scroll back to the top of her profile, checking her latest post. Maybe she hasn't logged on in a while. Maybe she hasn't even seen the notification yet.

It's an album cover—*Before Love Came to Kill Us* by Jessie Reyez—with the caption: *today's soundtrack*. Posted today at 7:30 AM.

Today.

I toss my phone in my backpack like it's a grenade and try not to think about all of the ways this mistake might detonate. *What if Mia thinks I'm a creep? What if she blocks me? What if she tells her brothers about it and they want to kick my ass?*

The robot leans in the doorway, watching me brush my teeth. "You're being a bit dramatic, don't you think?"

I spit, hard, ignoring him.

Out in the hall, I can hear Miguel still snoring. He catches a ride to school with one of his asshole friends, which means he gets to sleep in forty-five minutes longer than I do.

But beneath the sound of his snoring, I hear something that stops my heart. Grips it hard.

I inch toward my father's bedroom door, the cadence familiar like the hum of an old lullaby. But not the kind that puts you to sleep. The kind that keeps you awake. *Waiting.* For her to walk through the front door. For her to walk out of the bathroom with her wet hair wrapped up in a towel.

For her to call out from the kitchen. "¡Están listas! Eat your migas before they get cold."

But *this* voice, the one my father is playing over and over and over again, isn't calling from the kitchen. It isn't calling from the present at all. It's from the past. When Mom wasn't dying. When our hearts weren't smashed to pieces.

I take another step closer, my mother's voice muffled like the phone is pressed to my father's ear. Loud enough that he can probably feel the vibrations against the side of his face. Her voice a buzzing apparition.

"I'm feeling so much better today. I think I'm going to take the boys to the park, maybe get some ice cream."

Every once in a while, I'll hear my father playing the voice mail behind a closed door or sense it by the look on his face as he idles in his truck. I always know when he gets to the end, when she says, "I wish you were here with us," because all of the color will drain from his face.

I wait to hear if he plays it again. I wait for his sadness to seep out from beneath the door.

He clears his throat. Silence. And I leave him in it just like he leaves me alone in mine. Even though we could carry it together. The loss of her. The emptiness that is the heaviest kind of nothing. It would be easier that way. More survivable. But I'm not sure if he wants to. Some days, I'm not sure if I want to survive it either.

But I lace up my shoes and shrug my backpack onto my shoulders, resisting the urge to give up with every step. Because I know that's what she would want—for me to survive this. So I try. By placing one foot in front of the other. By filling my lungs with air. Until someday maybe it won't feel like I'm trying or pretending or lying. It'll feel like being. Not *living*. But *being*. And maybe that will be enough.

⸳ ⸳ ⸳ ⸳ ⸳ ⸳ ⸳ ⸳ ⸳ ⸳

The bell chimes as I enter Speedy's and Speedy pops his head up from behind the counter. When he sees me, he gives me his signature hundred-watt smile before clearing his throat and belting out "El Rey" (Chente's version).

"Yo sé bieeeeeeeeeeeeeeeeeen…"

And he does this. every. single. time.

When I pop in for a pack of gum.

When I need a new set of batteries for my headphones.

When it's over a hundred degrees out and I'm so thirsty I could die.

He sees me and he sings.

All because Mr. V gave him one of my business cards and now he thinks I have the power to make people famous. As if I wouldn't have already used that power on myself if I did.

Lately, the robot has gotten in on the act, wearing a sombrero and shaking a pair of maracas.

"Hey, Speedy…" I wave a hand unenthusiastically.

His voice carries, following me around the store while I grab a bag of Takis and a Zero bar.

"Does he serenade you like that every morning?"

I jump at the sound of her voice, dropping the candy bar at her feet.

The robot snorts. "Real smooth, Romeo."

Mia smiles, picks it up.

"Uh…" I pull down the bill of my baseball cap, trying to hide my red face. "He thinks I'm going to make him a star or something."

She hands me the candy bar. "Too bad he's got the kind of voice only a mother could love."

My heart races, searching for signs that she's annoyed or creeped out; waiting for her to humiliate me in front of Speedy and an entire aisle of individually packaged breakfast foods. But she doesn't.

She's…*smiling*. Like the sun is rising in her eyes.

I smile back. "Just needs a little auto-tune. Speedy's real problem is that he's cheap. He said he'd only pay me *after* he becomes famous." I mimic the way he talks with his hands. "*It's a once-in-a-lifetime investment, güey.*"

Mia laughs, before grabbing a Big Texas Cinnamon Roll off the shelf. She tucks a loose curl behind her ear.

I adjust the strap of my backpack.

The robot chirps like a cricket again and I wish I could swat him like one.

"Well…I guess I'll see you later," Mia says.

"Yeah…later."

I watch her go until she's disappeared behind the cars parked at the pumps.

The robot deadpans. "You're sweating."

That's when I look down at the Zero bar in my hand and notice that it's melted.

"Shit..."

Speedy pops up in the next aisle, belting out the chorus again and almost giving me a heart attack.

"You're going to scare away the customers!" Speedy's wife, Mrs. Speedy, slaps him with the rag she was using to wipe down the counters. "You traumatize this poor kid every time he comes in here."

My cheeks burn as I slide my goods onto the counter, not wanting to hurt Speedy's feelings by agreeing but also not wanting him to burst into song again.

Speedy just laughs. "What you call traumatized, I call inspired. Why else would he keep coming back here?"

"Because you're the only convenience store in Monte Vista?"

The smile slips from Speedy's face. "I *was* the only convenience store in Monte Vista. Next month there will be at least two others."

I remember the construction signs. "Yeah, I saw them breaking ground a few months back."

Mrs. Speedy squeezes Speedy's arm. "They want to compete with us? Let them try." She gives him a sad smile. "Besides, we have something they never will."

"What's that?" Speedy asks.

"You." She nods to the entrance. "It's your name on that sign outside."

"If only I could cash in that reputation for a big fat check." He sighs. "Things are already tough. I don't need some corporate chain coming in and makings things worse. It would be one thing if they told us to our faces they want us out. But to buy up every inch of land, scooping up foreclosed homes at auction, pushing us out one by one..."

I didn't know Speedy was struggling, but lately, who isn't? I heard Dad complaining the other day about bills. Our trash is full of them, usually unopened. Another thing he probably never thought he'd have to figure out on his own.

Speedy pinches the bridge of his nose. "Mierda."

Gravel crunches, a black SUV parking right in front of the double doors.

"How many times are they going to come in here?" Mrs. Speedy hisses.

Noni, Speedy's oldest, appears from the back. "I'll take care of it," they say before pushing Speedy and Mrs. Speedy through the storage door.

"What's going on?" I ask.

Noni braces themself behind the counter. "Pinche pendejos."

Two men step inside, one of them pretending to browse while the other approaches Noni.

"Hi there. Is the owner here?"

"Nope." Noni doesn't break eye contact.

"Well, maybe you can answer some questions for us."

"Nope." Then they reach across him for my chips and candy before sliding them across the scanner. "That'll be five dollars and twenty-five cents."

I slide over the cash and Noni makes change, handing me back three quarters.

"See you later, Aarón."

At first I'm not sure if I should leave, but Noni's eyes are fierce. When a few more customers enter the store, I give Noni a small nod before turning to leave. On my way out I check the plates on the SUV. There are none, windows tinted so black I can't even see inside.

From the bus stop, I watch the two men finally exit Speedy's before easing back onto the street. The windows are rolled down as they pass, the man on the passenger side giving me a stiff wave. My stomach turns.

■ ■ ■ ■ ■ ■ ■ ■ ■ ■ ■

I'm not the only one who's noticed the unmarked cars hanging around Speedy's. In the hallway at school, I overhear someone mention seeing them outside Loco Lavado Laundromat, in the parking lot of the ER, even circling the public library.

"I heard they're putting Mr. Salazar on a plane back to Mexico tomorrow." A girl in my history class straddles the back of her chair, whispering to the guy behind her.

He leans in. "I heard they already did."

"Mr. Gomez, do you have a question?" Mr. Bullock stands at his desk, shooting daggers at them both.

A group of white girls have been chatting in the corner the entire class period, but Mr. Bullock only starts seeing red when the conversation's in Spanish. I don't know if he just hates the sound or the fact that he can't eavesdrop, but he always shuts it down the second he hears the first ¡oye!

"No." Gomez shakes his head. "Sorry."

The girl rolls her eyes and says under her breath, "Hijueputa…"

Gomez laughs and I can't help but crack a smile too.

Mr. Bullock gives me a look from across the room. I scribble on my paper just to appease him. When he turns his attention back to his computer I finally look down and read the instructions.

Choose an event from your own life that shaped you more than any other and explain its importance.

My jaw clenches. I wish teachers would stop using stupid prompts like this. I know they probably think it's interesting, but the truth is it's rude as hell because the moments that shape us usually aren't pretty and asking someone to tear open those old wounds for the sake of taking a grade with no first aid kit in sight means making a huge mess that no adult actually intends to help clean up.

So I don't spill my guts. I don't talk about Mom. I doodle. First, my father's cell phone. Then La Maquina. Mia's trumpet.

When the bell rings I still don't have any words on the page.

Mr. Bullock takes my paper, looks at it, and sighs before handing me a six-page final exam review. "Due next class."

He knows I don't fill out test reviews because I can still ace the tests without them. But he's happy to take one last opportunity to make me feel like shit for not being the kind of student who excels because he cares.

I might have if he'd cared first. If he'd tried to learn a little Spanish instead of asking his students to leave behind part of their identity every time they step through his classroom door. If he'd asked me why I skipped his class so much in the fall instead of assigning me detention, where I never had a single fucking second of privacy to cry when I needed to. If he'd actually been able to look me in the eye when the office aid handed him a pass for me and he knew it was about Mom. Because all the teachers knew.

■■■■■■■■■■■

It was a Friday and I got to the office before Miguel did.

The school secretary smiled like she wasn't delivering bad news. "Your father has signed you both out. He needs you to meet him. Do you understand?" She didn't want to say why, but I knew.

It was happening.

And it felt like running headfirst into a moving truck.

She's dying. She's dying. My mother is dying.

"Do you have transportation?" she asked.

"Yeah." Miguel pushed me toward the entrance like he couldn't stand to be there another second.

But I didn't want to hurry.

When we reached the crosswalk, Miguel punched the metal walk button. Then he punched it again and again.

"Miguel." I grabbed his fists.

Then he looked in my eyes like he was remembering for the first time that we were twins; that the pain would be split in half.

"This isn't real," he said, falling into me.

I held him. We held each other.

"It's not real, Aarón. Please. Tell me that it's not fucking real."

I couldn't. I could only keep my arms around him, not letting him detonate.

When we got to her hospice room, the chaplain was already there, speaking quietly to Dad, trying to prepare him for what was coming.

"Did you read the pamphlet?" he asked. "It goes through every step of the process. No surprises."

No surprises.

Every day of the past ten months had been a surprise, a shock to the system until I started feeling things I couldn't even name. Every second that ticked by, I was somewhere new. Deeper in the pain than I ever thought possible.

But maybe he wasn't talking about us. Maybe he knew there was no *process* for us. No ten-step plan back to normal.

After he left no one touched the pamphlet. We just sat around her bed, watching her breathe. Waiting for the breathing to stop; for the pain to finally crest so we could finally drown.

"Flowers." My father exhaled, leaning back against the window. "They want to know what kind."

Miguel stayed quiet, staring at Mom's feet under the blankets.

"Magnolias," I said without meeting their eyes. "She loves magnolias."

Dad scribbled something on a notepad. "Okay, music. They want to know her favorite song." He cleared his throat. "I wrote down 'God Only Knows.' I think she likes that one…"

" 'Como la Flor,' " Miguel added. "She started dancing every time it came on."

"I think you're right," Dad said.

"No." I finally looked up. "Her favorite song is 'Book of Love.' "

Miguel narrowed his eyes at me. "How are you so sure? You can't be allowed to pick out everything, Aarón."

I heard it, what had been bubbling beneath the surface ever since she got sick. Jealousy. And I wanted to scream. Because she tried so fucking hard with Miguel. To get him to watch a movie with us on the couch. To get him off his phone long enough to tell her how his day was at school.

Every time I chose her, he mocked me, and every time he chose his friends, he felt so fucking cool. But they weren't around. They hadn't been for weeks. And suddenly he was sad that he didn't know her favorite song?

I looked right at Miguel and said, "I know it's her favorite song because she told me. I know magnolias are her favorite flower because she told me. Because I asked. Because I fucking cared."

Then he swung.

I fell out of my chair, making him miss, and then Dad tackled him, dragging him out into the hall. And I couldn't look at her. Because she was dying and we were fighting and there was nothing I could do to change any of it. All I could do was exist in that brokenness, knowing that we'd be cutting ourselves on each other's sharp edges for the rest of our lives.

6

Mia

THE SECOND THE BUS PULLS UP MR. V IS ALREADY beaming. "Hey, Mia! How was your audition?"

I should have known that would be the first thing he would say when he saw me. Still, it stops me in my tracks. My face gets hot.

"Pobrecita..." He waves me over. "Ven aquí."

I can't look at him.

"Hey, keep that head up." He waits for me to meet his eyes. "Screw that fancy school. You're too good for them."

I don't mean to crack a smile, but for some reason it feels good.

"Say it, 'I'm too good for that fancy school.'"

"Mr. V..."

"I'm not moving this bus until you say it."

Some guy calls out from the back. "What's the holdup? I'm trying to get to work!"

Mr. V just raises an eyebrow.

I exhale. "Fine. I'm too good."

"'I'm too good for that fancy school,'" he says again.

"I'm too good for that fancy school."

He nods, satisfied.

The guy in the back grows more irritated. "Let's move it!"

"Ya, ya." Mr. V waves a hand. "Vamos."

As we roll through Monte Vista, past La Puerta Abierta, letters missing from the welcome sign, past the beat-up cars parked at Speedy's, and the middle school with its crumbling brick and broken chain-link fence, I'm not sure if I believe what I told Mr. V—that I'm "too good for that fancy school." Maybe that's part of the problem. I wasn't just afraid of failing, of being embarrassed. I was afraid that even if I did get in...I wouldn't actually deserve it.

Maybe if I had grown up on the west side of town things would be different. But I didn't. I grew up here. And even though I love my neighbors, *my home*, it can be hard to believe in your dreams, to give yourself permission to dream at all when you're surrounded by signs that it's pointless. That even if you get out of your old neighborhood, you always take a piece of it with you. A piece that other people can see, that they can judge.

When I get to the library there are more people than usual. There's a children's program going on, kids hugging stuffed animals while one of the librarians reads them a story about dragons. Parents whisper in the back by the big bay windows, some of them girls who used to go to my high school.

"Oh, thank God," Deb says when she sees me. "We're slammed."

Deb Casarez has worked at Monte Vista Public Library since I was a kid. I used to walk here after school and read by the bay windows until Jazzy got out at the middle school. Then he would come get me and we'd walk to the bus stop together.

One of the reasons I was so comfortable asking Mr. Barrero lots of questions was because Deb loved it when I asked questions. And I had a lot of them. *Why do we read books from left to right? How many hands have touched this book before mine? How do you say this word and this word and this word?*

Deb has an answer for everything, and in exchange for having taught me how to read (a debt, which, let's face it, can never fully be repaid), I help out a couple of times a month, shelving books, disinfecting computers, and basically doing whatever else needs to be done.

Deb sets a few books down on a display table for home renos before giving me a hug. "Sorry, should have said hi first."

I pick up one of the books on plumbing.

"Don't tell me Andrés has started another one of his DIY projects," she says, an eyebrow cocked.

"You mean DIY *disasters*?" She laughs and I shake my head. "Not yet, but it won't be long. He thinks we need a new roof."

She walks behind her desk and opens a drawer. It's full of business cards. She plucks one out and hands it to me. "These guys are good and they won't charge Andrés an arm and a leg."

"You know he hates spending money on stuff like that."

"And when it breaks down again, what does he do?"

"Swear that he can fix it himself. Pretty much the same thing over and over again."

"I think that's the definition of *insanity*."

I shrug. "Well, that's Andrés." Suddenly, a lump forms in my throat. "And me too, I guess..."

"What do you mean?"

I look at her, waiting for her to read what's there. It doesn't take her long.

She deflates. "Mia..."

"I know." My throat tightens. "Mr. V and Mr. Barrero have both been on me about it." My eyes plead with her not to lay into me too. "I know I have to get over this fear. I know I screwed up." My voice cracks and it's so unexpected, so sharp in this quiet place, that Deb just reaches for me.

"You didn't screw up. You tried and you failed and that's human, Mia." She looks me in the eye. "You're human and you can try again."

And this is who Deb is to me—a tight hug that lets me catch my breath, a soft place to bury my face so no one sees my tears, a quiet voice telling me it's okay to let them fall. Deb is not my mother, but just like Andrés and Mr. Barrero, and even Mr. V, she raised me. She still is.

I wipe my eyes as she leads me to the employee section in the back. A mountain of books sits under the return chute, instantly knocking me out of my feelings.

Deb's office is just as packed, a group of young people using her desk and the floor to decorate posters and tape signs to yardsticks.

"Coming through!" One of the library pages almost runs over my foot with a full cart of books.

"Hey, Deb, we're out of black paint." A girl with a sleeve of white roses tattooed on her right arm drops some empty paint tubes in the trash. "You got any more?"

"Storage closet," Deb says. "Third shelf on the right."

"What's going on back here?" I ask.

"We're organizing a demonstration at the end of the month at the capitol."

I examine the organizers' shirts more closely. They say things like: KEEP FAMILIES TOGETHER and RESIST and NO HUMAN IS ILLEGAL.

I turn back to Deb, my voice low. "I heard ICE has been rolling through Monte Vista lately."

"ICE has been showing up everywhere lately. In unmarked cars and plain clothes. They're harassing people at work and lying to get them out of their homes. Other times they just force themselves inside."

I shake my head. "But they can't do that. Don't they need a search warrant?"

"They can do whatever they want," the girl with the roses tattooed on her arm says when she returns. She's wearing a gold necklace that says *Esther*. I knew she looked familiar. She was in my US Government class last semester. "That's why we're demonstrating. Because there are no rules anymore and the laws are changing every day. They just removed protections for Dreamers and are stripping people of their green cards and visas. They're planning a mass expulsion right under our fucking noses."

"Not if we have anything to say about it." Deb squeezes Esther's shoulder, her eyes pained.

"Hey, Esther, we need your brain." The group in Deb's office looks in her direction.

"Coming." Esther gives Deb a sad smile before rejoining the other organizers.

Another library page, Ana, pushes an empty cart in my direction. She's got to be at least eighty and has worked at the library longer than Deb has. Usually, there's a couple more girls back here. No wonder they're backed up.

"Short-staffed today?" I ask.

Deb lowers her voice. "Estefanía..."

"They took that poor girl." Ana stops stacking books on her cart for a moment. Her lip trembles. "She wasn't hurting nobody."

"Wait, Estefanía was deported?"

"It all happened so fast." Deb's comforting Ana now. "They picked her up and said she could go to jail or leave voluntarily. She didn't try to get a lawyer. She didn't know she could."

Estefanía had started coming to the library about a year ago to learn English at one of the ESL classes Deb teaches. Eventually, she started working here. I didn't talk to her much, but I do remember that she had two kids, both of them still in diapers the last time I'd seen them.

"She was worried about her babies." Ana frowns. "She was worried they'd be separated so she did what they told her to do and left."

"Estefanía didn't have any family here like a lot of other people do."

"*We* were her family." Ana's eyes glisten with angry tears.

"I'm so sorry, Señora."

"She was working two jobs." She wipes her eyes. "She was a good mom."

"I know." Deb reaches for her. "We all miss her."

"It isn't fair..." I know it's worthless, but I don't know what else to say.

Ana shakes her head, still in disbelief. "When Nacho's was open they left us alone."

Deb tries to calm her. "But it wasn't the police, Ana. It was ICE."

"La policía. La Migra. Es lo mismo. They want us gone. That's it." Ana's anger has her in tears again. She waves a hand before forcing herself back to work.

"Mr. Salazar and then Estefanía." Deb sighs. "It's been a rough couple of weeks."

"Well, I'm happy to help," I say.

"Thanks. We could really use it today." Deb rolls an empty cart over before hurrying back to the front where patrons are lined up at her desk.

Ana took the chapter books before I could get to them, so

I'm stuck rolling a cart of sticky children's books down the row Q–R. Between the books I can still see the girls who graduated a few years ahead of me, tapping on their cell phones and snapping selfies like they're still in high school. Maybe there's a piece of them that still is, or wishes they were.

I can't wait to leave, but there's a part of me that's afraid I'll get stuck here too. The kids who *did* get into college have been wearing their school shirts all week. I could have gone. My grades were decent enough for community college, but I didn't want to put that financial pressure on Andrés. I wanted to figure it out on my own.

When I came to talk to Deb about it, to see if she could help me fill out the financial aid forms and actually get the process started, I saw the flyer for the auditions. I'm still not sure if I believe in signs, but it sure felt like one.

I spent the evening staring at it and doodling little stars around the words SCHOLARSHIPS AVAILABLE instead of doing my trig homework. It slipped out of my bag at school the next day, but it didn't matter. I'd already memorized all of the dates and times.

I thought I was ready to step into the spotlight, or at least out of the shadows, my life at Monte Vista High School all about being invisible. But that's a little hard to do when every other time I've become a spectacle was because of some tragedy. Like that stupid school talent show when my parents fought in front of everyone. Or after my father passed away and my classmates and teachers couldn't help but gawk, as if they couldn't believe I was still intact.

At some point, I realized that becoming invisible actually had nothing to do with disappearing, or hiding, or making myself small. It had to do with blending in, with staying the same. But there was a part of me that was getting sick of that too. In high school there's a level of safety in staying the same. But the world is so much bigger than Monte Vista High School. What if I'm supposed to be something bigger too?

What if getting into Acadia is supposed to be the beginning? Of my life. Of who Mia is supposed to be...

"Mia...?"

I look up at the sound. Ana has already emptied her first cart and refilled it with more books. I glance down at my cart and realize that I've barely made a dent.

"I'm sorry, Señora. I got a little distracted."

"It's okay, mija." She starts pulling books from my cart, deftly shoving them into place.

"Thanks." I slide to my knees, putting the books back on the lower shelves.

We work in tandem, emptying my cart first and then hers. In the quiet, I can't help but imagine how she and Estefanía must have worked together. I wonder what they talked about or if they worked in silence like we are now. The way Ana's face still looks so pained, they must have known each other well.

"Do you think she's going to be okay?" I finally ask.

I don't want to upset her again, but instead of her eyes welling up with tears, they narrow, like she's trying to see Estefanía's life now, the details slowly coming into focus.

"She's with her mother in Tapachula." The way she says the word *mother* I can tell that's what Ana was to her while she was here. That's what Ana's lost. Not just a coworker, a friend. But a daughter.

"What will she do now?" I ask.

"She wanted to be a nurse..." She shoves another book into place. "Now? Whatever work she can find." She looks down to meet my eyes. "I must have told her a million times to apply to school, that Deb and I would help her figure out how to pay for it. That once she was accepted she could apply for a student visa and then she wouldn't have to worry, looking over her shoulder all the time. But she kept hitting one roadblock after another and she was just so scared."

I think about the fears that must have kept Estefanía up at night. Fears I can't even fathom. Fears that totally eclipse my own worries about being seen. Spotlight on me, the worst that can happen is I humiliate myself and someone spreads a viral video of it for a few weeks. But I wouldn't lose my family. I wouldn't lose my home.

"But even a visa won't protect people anymore." Ana sighs. "They make the rules and then they change them. All so they don't have to say the truth. That we break the law the second we're born. That being brown is the only crime we have to commit."

"Not everyone thinks that, Señora."

She cups my cheek. "We'll see." She nods, turning back to her books. "On protest day, we'll see."

I work double time, helping Ana clear out the return chutes. When the back is clear, I grab my things and give Ana a quick hug before heading out toward the front.

"Hey!" I turn and Esther holds out a flyer. "It starts at noon if you want to join us."

I take it, nodding. "I'll be there."

7

Aarón

THE BUS SCREECHES TO A STOP, MR. V GRINNING
wide when he sees me come up the steps.

"Hey, Aarón. I think I'm going to need some more business cards from you soon. They're going like hotcakes."

The robot snorts. "I highly doubt that."

He's right. The business cards I had made are not, in
fact, "going like hotcakes." But every couple of days, like
clockwork, Mr. V claims he's fresh out and needs new
ones. I know he's only handing them out to the viejos who
ride back and forth from their doctors' appointments, but
even though it's a waste of money for him to keep handing
them out like he does, I get a small pang in my chest every
time he asks for more.

"I'll bring some tomorrow."

"Sounds good." He pats me on the back on my way to
one of the window seats.

I sit facing the glass and as the bus lurches forward, the sun glitters in streaks, stretching like oil. Making the neighborhood into new shapes.

But it's not just a trick of the eye. So many new buildings are going up. Nacho's Tacos is in the process of being rebuilt after the fire there a few months ago. There's Pen's Pastelería food truck next door and a new playground going in at La Puerta Abierta across the street. Someone bought the old strip club on Real and is turning it into a gastropub. A Whole Foods has broken ground near the interstate and a Korean taco joint opens in two weeks next to Pablo's Pawn shop.

Not everyone likes the changes. New businesses mean new people. New people who might have every intention of erasing the ones that were already here. Every time another house in Monte Vista is sold to some hipster for half a million dollars it feels like we already are.

An old mariachi song hums from the radio clipped to the bus's sun visor. Mr. V hums along, head swaying. He catches my eye in his giant rearview mirror and winks before letting out un grito that is so overdramatically sad and pitiful that it makes me laugh.

Javi, Mr. V's nephew, calls out, "Who's skinning a cat up there?"

"What are you talking about?" Mr. V glares at him in the rearview mirror. "I've got the voice of an angel."

"An angel having its wings ripped out." The robot covers his nonexistent ears.

Mr. V just keeps singing.

I put on my headphones and press play on my La

Maquina playlist as we roll to the next stop outside one of the old warehouses where they used to make textiles. The brick wall has been tagged from top to bottom, thick black lines running like the paint is still wet.

I have to lean back to see the whole thing, the way the lines wrap around themselves over and over and over again. Like the image is in motion. I carve out shaggy eyebrows and a pointed chin, and even though the portrait is crooked, and from a certain angle it just looks like a mess, it doesn't take me long to find his eyes.

Up close, they look tired. Like the artist wasn't trying to capture the twenty-year-old La Maquina who came on the scene a decade ago, but the man he's become. The warrior, weary from battle. The expression full of knowing—that he's not done fighting just yet.

La Maquina's portrait used to be all over Monte Vista. There was one of him eating a chihuahua sandwich behind Montoya's drive-in movie theater. Another of him throwing out the first pitch against the Flying Chanclas' Little League clubhouse. And my personal favorite—his sparkling white grin plastered wide over Bobby Guapo's Big Mouths dental practice.

Basically, if you owned a business in Monte Vista, La Maquina was probably your mascot at some point. Not only because his image guaranteed business but because he never gave anyone shit about paying to use it.

"And this is an outrageous abuse of that privilege. For the love of God..." The robot's eyes burn red. "Could they have picked a more unflattering image? I was *People en Español*'s Sexiest Man Alive. Twice!"

"It'll be painted over by tomorrow," I say, because as soon as new people started moving in, they changed that too. Painting over the graffiti art because they thought it was gang related. In reality, the criminals here are blue-collar ones. Los gabachos would know that if they bothered to ask before moving all their shit in. But I guess they prefer to call the cops now and ask questions later.

All I know is that white people couldn't wait to build a big-ass highway to keep all of the Black and brown people on the east side of Austin, and now all of a sudden they're obsessed with fucking horchata and espadrilles and moving into communities of color they don't actually give a shit about.

Scrubbing us from the signs and storefronts. Bulldozing our memories. Trying to take apart the soul of Monte Vista piece by piece.

That's what they really erased when they painted over the artwork.

Us.

But *this*...this paint is still fresh, the stark lines barely done bleeding. I snap a photo of it before we roll forward, using my fingers to zoom in and out.

"What's that?" the robot asks, pointing to the bottom corner of the painting.

There's a tight scribble and at first it just looks like a teardrop. But within the white space are letters. A signature.

Starfish.

I pull up La Maquina's latest album on my phone.

"Track number six." The robot leans back, listening too.

I press play and it's like being swallowed by a monster, or maybe God, the bass so heavy that it feels like my soul is being sucked out through my ears. And then there's silence. Eight seconds of it followed by eight gut-wrenching beeps like the sound from an EKG machine. Eight phantom heartbeats to match the eight bullets police lodged into Frankie Fernandez for rolling through a stop sign at 2:00 AM.

He worked nights restocking items at H-E-B. During the day he coached his son's Little League team. His daughter was about to have her quinceañera. His wife was going back to school to become a nurse. His elderly mother-in-law met him on the front porch with a cup of coffee every morning at the end of his shift.

He brought flowers from his own garden to my mother's funeral.

And then they just killed him. The center of so many people's universe...just gone.

But La Maquina refused to let him disappear. Not just because Frankie was his mother's favorite cousin or because he had a family or because he was kind in a way most people forget to be. But because he mattered. Regardless of who he was or what he had to give, he mattered. So La Maquina took that rage we were all choking on and he immortalized it all—the man and the void he left behind—in a song.

The notes crash into one another like a guttural scream

and I can't listen to it without that scream bubbling up inside me too. But that's not even the worst part. The worst part is not having somewhere to put it.

I can try pounding it into a song the way La Maquina did. But that doesn't bring Frankie back. That doesn't stop another brown body from being ripped to shreds.

"Aarón, it's your stop." The doors open and Mr. V looks back at me, waiting for me to get off.

I clutch the phone, my palms sweaty. That's when I realize the thoughts are coming as fast as they did at dinner last night. I wonder if Mr. V sees them racing behind my eyes the way my father and Miguel do.

"How could he not?" The robot fans at the smoke pouring from my ears. "Your brain's practically cooking inside your skull."

Mr. V whistles. "You feeling okay?"

"Uh…" I quickly grab my stuff, parting the smoke as I head to the front of the bus. "Yeah. Fine. Sorry."

Mr. V wags a finger at me. "One day you're gonna get lost in that head of yours, kid."

"*Too late*," the robot sings.

I push past him.

"Tell Mr. Barrero I said hi," Mr. V says.

"I will."

On the sidewalk, I zoom in on the photo one more time, another clue to add to my wall of evidence, and then I stuff the phone in my pocket before I'm late for work.

At least one of those business cards Mr. V passed out actually led to something. I got a call a few days ago from a local band in need of an audio engineer to help them record an album. I've never actually recorded an entire album before, but when Mr. Barrero said it was time sensitive and that my lack of experience was not a problem, I jumped at the chance.

I walk to the small house on the corner of Manzanito Drive, wind fluttering through chimes. The sound peters off, giving way to something else riding on the breeze. It's harmonious at first, different instruments rising and falling together. But then the sound splits in half like someone was a beat behind while someone else was two beats ahead. Suddenly, there's yelling.

"...está cabrón!"

"Cada puto tiempo."

I follow their voices by way of the wraparound porch before coming upon a small garage on the side of the house.

An old man in a crisp white fedora is hunched over his knees, a trumpet between his feet. Next to him, a scrawny mustached pirate-looking type very unenthusiastically holds a donkey's jawbone in one hand and a mallet in the other. Behind them both is an extremely short woman wearing cowboy boots and carrying an accordion that's almost twice her size. Center stage is a tall woman with purple hair on a steel guitar, and to her left is an old cholo hugging a Spanish guitar, a beat-up microphone within screaming distance.

"Hijo de la chingada. Who's *this* kid?"

"Watch your mouth." The man in the fedora stands. "This is Aarón." Then, even though we've only talked on the phone a few times, he grips my shoulder like we've known each other for years and says, "He's going to make us sound like a million bucks."

The others blink at me with wide eyes and then they all start laughing hysterically. The percussionist clutches his gut while the accordion player (and her accordion) start cackling wildly. Everyone is hunched over or throwing up their hands, falling all over themselves as if this is the funniest thing they've ever heard.

The woman with purple hair pokes at my backpack. "The kid's still in school."

"Actually, I graduate in a couple of weeks."

She ignores me, turning to Mr. Barrero. "Why didn't you just let me call my nephew? I told you he's a DJ—"

"He's a drunk," the pirate shoots back.

"Whatever, Osmin. You just didn't want to pay his twelve-hundred-dollar fee."

"Oh, perdón, Naomi, so he's an *expensive* drunk. Doubly useless." He turns to Mr. Barrero. "And the kid? How much is he charging you?"

"That's between us," Mr. Barrero says.

"You're being robbed, Marcelo."

"It's my money and I'll do what I want with it."

"What *you* want." Osmin examines him more closely. "What you want is a time machine. We're not kids anymore, Marcelo."

"Oh really?" Naomi crosses her arms. "Because you keep throwing tantrums like one. What happened to the cholo hanging out of the purple lowrider who couldn't wait to tell girls he was in a band?" She grabs the front of her jeans like she's grabbing a big shiny belt buckle and leans back. "¡A mamacita!" She whistles between her teeth. "Vente pa ca..."

"And what about you?" Osmin wriggles his eyebrows. "Those flat black eyebrows used to melt off your face every show." He circles her, snickering. "With those black lips and orange hair. You thought you were La Chola Reina."

She swats at him. "I'm still La Chola Reina."

"Then you're stuck in the past the same way Marcelo is. We were supposed to be meeting up on weekends, maybe cracking a few beers while we messed around on these old instruments that have just been collecting dust in our basements. But things changed, Marcelo, and now you've got us out here for hours. Sweating in this damn heat. Like we're twenty years old again. Like we're trying to make it or something." He shakes his head. "But we ain't in our twenties, Marcelo." Then he motions to the cholo with the guitar. "Gabriel's got gout." Then he motions to the woman with the accordion. "Gina's got hypertension." He goes down the list, naming everyone's ailments while they frown or blush. Then he takes a few steps closer to Mr. Barrero, hands clasped, pleading. "And we've got grandkids and spouses and jobs and—"

"Sí, Osmin, y yo tengo Parkinson's disease."

Osmin stops.

They all blink, staring at Mr. Barrero. But this time they don't laugh. Because they don't know. They *didn't* know.

"Marcelo..." Osmin reaches for his friend with both hands. "When?"

I take a step back, giving them space. Even the robot pretends to be distracted.

"About a month ago," Mr. Barrero says.

Something passes between them, ghosts only they can see. I watch the air get sucked out of that garage. I watch their eyes well up.

"When Deb asked us to play at the protest, it felt like a gift. Like that time machine you said I needed." Mr. Barrero leans against the wall. "And it reminded me what it was like sitting on my father's shoulders in a sea of signs. ¡SI SE PUEDE! ¡LA CAUSA ES LA LUCHA! All of us staring down a line of Texas Rangers that wanted nothing more than to beat the shit out of us. And then meeting at sundown at Raul's where my father's band sang about pride and revolution and carrying the struggle on our backs."

Gabriel nods, remembering. "I was there, Marcelo."

"We all were," Gina adds. "My parents were campesinos. They worked the land for years, my father coming home with blisters and all kinds of chemical burns. Like our bodies were disposable."

"Of course they were," Osmin says. "Do you remember how many of us came home in boxes during Vietnam?"

"Do you remember when we were standing in an empty garage just like this one learning the songs our parents used to sing?" Gabriel plucks a few strings on the guitar. "Some days, the music was the only thing that kept us all going."

"It was there when we needed it." Mr. Barrero stares down into the bell of his trumpet. "I'm not sure I've ever needed it more..." He meets their eyes. "But I'm not the only one. These kids"—he motions to me—"they need to know that we've been here before. They need to know that we have fought these battles and won. They *need* us to show them how. So I'm sorry I've been pushing." Mr. Barrero hangs his head. "But I know how the music keeps people in the fight and I have to keep playing for them with whatever fight I have left."

Osmin squeezes his arm, holding on to his friend like he refuses to let him be wrenched from this place. "It's our fight too. Por la raza y por ti." Then he takes his place back in the garage, everyone hoisting their instruments at the ready. "¿Por la raza?"

They all call back in unison, even me. "¡Por la raza!"

■ ■ ■ ■ ■ ■ ■ ■ ■ ■ ■

When I get home I head to my room and wake up my computer. I revisit every fan forum and type *Starfish* into the search field. There are old posts about a GoFundMe page for the Fernandez family and a protest at the state capitol. But nothing new in almost a year.

I remember how the city had erupted after Frankie's death. The marches and sit-ins and town halls filled wall to wall with people who were horrified. People who were afraid of being next. But then the police chief resigned and the rumble died down. Except it wasn't the Fernandez family that really won. It was exhaustion. A spiritual fatigue that forced people back into their normal lives, their daily routines a place to try to mend.

Machines 1. Humans 0.

That's all a government is really. A monster made of all these moving parts. One arm spinning webs while another is planting seeds. Feeding the people one day and starving them the next.

They starved the spirit right out of that movement before any of us could move forward at all. Even with Xavier López leading the way. I remember him addressing the protesters on the tenth day of demonstrations.

He screamed into a bullhorn while tears streamed down his face. "That man was our flesh. This *land* is our flesh."

I know the portrait of La Maquina popping up in Monte Vista can't be a coincidence. I *know* Starfish has something to do with where he is now.

I type the word *Starfish* again. Still no new results. I split the word in half. Nothing.

I try *Estrella de Mar.*

Zero results.

I google how to say *starfish* in Nahuatl and try that too.

Zero results.

Then I remember that the last time La Maquina made an appearance he wasn't speaking in words.

... - .- .-. ..-..........

I get a hit.

When I click on the link the forum is empty. No posts or comments. But in the top right-hand corner there is a small blinking user icon. A tiny robot.

"Is it...you?"

The robot looks at the screen over my shoulder. He grins. "There's only one way to find out."

"What do I say?" I look back at him. "What do I do?"

"The first thing you can do is stop sweating. It's starting to feel like a sauna in here."

I slowly begin to type a greeting: *Hi, I'm Aarón*.

"I'm an artistic genius. Do you really think I don't get emails from emo teenagers telling me how much they love me every single day?" The robot yawns. "Ugh, it's exhausting."

"How else am I supposed to start the conversation?"

The robot's eyes light up. "*Exactly*. It's a conversation. One that started the second you saw that portrait. That's what you should respond to."

I swallow, saliva scraping all the way down.

All of those late nights I spent laying down tracks, the notes side by side with La Maquina's music, I would dream about the day he might actually hear one of my songs. That he *might* actually like it.

But every time I sent him a message about players on a local sport's team dying their hair his signature blue or a restaurant introducing a new special named after one of his songs and I had the chance to add an attachment, I choked.

The robot nods. "It's a theme with you, for sure."

When I wrote my own version of "Starfish," I played the song sixteen times in a row, trying to recreate the sounds, rearranging them until it wasn't just noise anymore. But a thank-you.

"A love letter," the robot corrects me.

In a way, he's right. But it's one I never thought I'd actually send.

My hand hovers over the mouse, and then I immediately

feel the fear that trapped me on the bus, cold and filling me like a serum.

"What if it's not him?" I breathe.

"Eh, you're probably right." The way the robot says it, I know he's taunting me.

My mind drifts back to this afternoon, to Mr. Barrero telling his friends that he still has dreams; that as long as he can still play he wants to chase them.

What would have happened if they'd given up on him? What would have happened if he'd given up on himself?

I already gave up so many times this week. What would happen if I do it *again*?

I'll keep being the guy who can't play his music in front of people, who can't tell Mia Villanueva how he feels, who can't leave his father's house.

Unless I do something brave; do it without dying so I can finally hush the voices in my head.

Click.

I attach the file of the song I made in response to "Starfish." Three minutes and twenty-nine seconds of open wounds that whoever's listening can rub salt into. Then I attach the photograph along with a one-sentence description like I normally do.

Someone painted your portrait on the side of the old textile factory.

I take a deep breath. Let it out.

My brain screams: *It's going to hurt. Don't do it!*

The robot shrugs. "Everything hurts, kid."

My mouse hovers over the word *post*. I swallow glass.

Click.

I sit back, stunned. "I did it."

A few seconds later, just below that, I see a response.

To the right of the robot icon there are three lines of Morse code. I find an alpha generator and plug in the dots.

1107 Mesa Drive

5:00 AM

I read it again

1107 Mesa Drive

5:00 AM

And again. And again.

I stare until every letter is scorched into my skull. Until I ache with questions. Until I ache with *knowing*.

Knowing that the robot is right. *Knowing* that I might be about to jump straight off the deep end.

But also knowing, with more certainty than ever, that I am not alone.

■ ■ ■ ■ ■ ■ ■ ■ ■ ■

Several hours later, I'm carrying a Number 2 from Beto's Burgers to the dark corner where Mesa Drive and Monte Vista Boulevard meet. They weren't open, but when I tapped on the sliding window just like Xavier's message instructed me to do, Beto himself slid back the glass and handed me a greasy bag of takeout.

"You better hurry," Beto said. "She hates it when her food gets soggy."

Then he slid the window closed again before I could ask who exactly is *her?*

"Well, it's obviously not me," the robot says.

"But it *has* to be. Who else would be lurking around in

one of those forums and only responding in secret Morse code?"

"Oh, I don't know..." The robot shrugs. "Pathetic teenage boys with imaginary friends who resemble their favorite musical act? Why are you so certain it's me?"

"Because..." I shake my head, annoyed at myself for talking to him like he's real.

"Because?"

"Because none of your business."

"Unfortunately, you getting murdered is my business."

"And why's that?"

"Because the captain always goes down with the ship." He nudges me. "You're the ship in this scenario, by the way."

"Yeah, I got that," I grumble.

"Weren't you supposed to turn left here?"

I stop, examining the street signs before taking a left, without acknowledging the robot's help.

This irks him and he starts ranting again.

"Have you considered the fact that if my murderer knew you were conducting your own amateur investigation that they may use whatever means necessary to try to stop you?" He clunks along behind me. "You could be walking into a trap. What if this mysterious *her* is waiting around the next corner with an axe?"

I try to ignore him, but my steps still slow as I reach the end of the street. Whoever I'm supposed to meet should be just around the bend. With an empty stomach and, hopefully, *not* carrying an axe.

I readjust my baseball cap, wiping the sweat from my brow.

The robot stops. "Any last words?"

I hesitate too.

"Jesus Christ, really?"

At the sound of her voice, I jump, both feet coming up off the ground.

The girl groans, slapping her yellow baseball cap against her knee. It's covered in flecks of paint. "I told Xavier I was fine!"

I approach carefully, holding out the bag of food. "Hi, uh, I'm...I'm Aarón."

She snatches the bag. "This a Number Two?"

I nod fast. "With extra pickles."

She quirks her mouth, sighs. "I fell off the ladder once and now he's sending me a goddamned babysitter."

"I'm sorry?"

She backpedals, pulling us both out of the glow of the streetlight. That's when I finally look up. The entire south wall of the building is covered in a giant mural just like the one I saw from the bus.

"You...*you* did this?" I ask.

"Don't get too close. Paint's still wet."

She yanks me back before I even realize I've been drifting, getting lost in the swirl of colors, of the faces I recognize from the six o'clock news. Jacob Jimenez, shot by police with a "nonlethal" projectile on his way home from work in the midst of a Black Lives Matter protest. He was sixteen and unarmed. Mike Sucedo, shot by police in the front seat of his car after a routine traffic stop. He was twenty-one and also unarmed.

My eyes travel to the center of the mural and right there is Frankie Fernandez, yellow marigolds bursting from his torso like his soul is in bloom.

"It's beautiful," I breathe.

The sun burns pink, barely peeking up from the horizon at the end of the street. As it bleeds in our direction, cutting shadows across the girl's face, I notice the tears in her eyes. I notice the dimple on her chin. Just like Frankie's.

"Are you Nina Fernandez?" I ask.

"To you?" She shrugs. "Sure..."

"And to everyone else?"

She walks to the edge of her canvas and points out the same, almost imperceptible, signature that was on the first painting I saw. *Starfish*.

"Did Xavier ask you to do this?"

"Not exactly. But paint doesn't come cheap." She scans her finished piece. "Especially when there are three hundred and eighty-two walls in Monte Vista that could use a new coat."

"You're not seriously going to paint all of those, are you?"

"I've got seven more planned before the protest at the end of the month." She juts out her chin, suddenly serious. "So don't blow my cover until then, got it?"

"I won't tell anyone."

"Good." She scarfs down the rest of her burger. "But... while you're here..." She leads me to a ladder propped up against the side of the building. "Hold this steady, will you?"

8

Mia

THE COURTYARD IS ALREADY PACKED FOR THE senior picnic. There's games like cornhole and bocce ball set up and hammocks strung between columns, people lounging on beach towels while J. Balvin and Cardi B compete from cell phone speakers.

I'm only outside for two seconds before the humidity wreaks havoc on my hair. But it's not the only thing I can't stand about being here. There's also the noise, every senior devolved back to kindergarten for one last moment of freedom before adulthood snatches their joy.

I try to remember when the world was only as big as Monte Vista Boulevard; when I wasn't constantly worried about that world being destroyed. Wading through those memories is like watching the sunlight pierce a dark canopy of leaves, brief joyful flashes made of sound.

Which is why, instead of getting in line for food or to

pelt Principal Judd in the face with a pie, I cross the court-yard and escape into the empty band hall.

I find a chair right in the center of the room and sit, cold brass pressed to my lips as I take a deep breath. Some-times I don't even know what I'm feeling until I hear it.

Today, the sound bouncing off the walls is a little bit of everything. I hear the questions that keep me up at night about what comes next. I hear the ache for something more even if I don't know what that is yet.

The music doesn't always give me answers, but some-times the notes against my lips is enough, my lungs con-tracting, my spine straightening, all of it forcing me in motion even when I'm too scared to move.

The door creaks and I let go of the sound.

"Sorry…"

When I turn, Aarón Medrano is staring, mouth ajar like he's just seen a ghost.

"It's okay," I say.

"It was…you were…" He tugs on his baseball cap, blushing. "It sounded really good."

I try to say thank you, but nothing comes out, my hands sweating like it's not Aarón in the doorway but the sun. He bites back his smile and I feel a rush of heat—a solar flare I want to run straight into.

The Medrano brothers are the only other people my age I know who have also lost a parent and I don't even really know them. Just that Aarón likes La Maquina and the X-Men and that we've had thirty-seven classes together since the first grade. And that he has the most symmetrical dimples I have ever seen.

When I saw him on the bus on my way to the audition, I forgot for a second why I was there. Like I was looking at him through the lens of a camera, everything outside the frame going dark. And then again at Speedy's when he was being serenaded and his face turned the most adorable shade of pink.

And now, with his bottom lip pinched between his teeth, that same blush spreading all the way to his ears.

I've seen him a thousand times. In the hallways at school. At block parties. At church back when our parents were still alive and worried about our salvation.

But that day on the bus was different. Because he was scared. We both were and it was like looking at each other under a microscope.

That's exactly what it feels like now. Like we're millimeters apart. Like it's supposed to be that way.

"You know there's only one more night of auditions," I say.

"Yeah," he sighs. "I..." His voice shrinks. "I don't know why I can't get off the bus."

"Maybe it's the same reason why I can't get up on that stage."

"What reason is that?" he asks.

I look down. "Because if I do, every cell in my body will spontaneously combust."

He grimaces. "That sounds painful."

"Exactly."

"But..." He finally steps into the band hall, giving his voice a slight echo. "What if we *don't* spontaneously combust?"

My brow furrows. "You think something else happens?"

He shrugs. "Something . . . or maybe nothing?"

"Nothing." I bite my lip. "Wouldn't nothing be worse?"

I hadn't realized before that ever since my dad died, this is how I've been navigating the world, how I've made every decision. *Does it hurt?* As if it's a setting I can dial down by doing all the right things. But where has it gotten me?

"What if we could help each other?" I say.

"How?"

"You don't let me run and I won't let you either. Not this time."

He takes a step closer. "Are you sure?"

"Sure that I want to try again. Not sure if it'll actually work." I reach out my pinky. "You in?"

He smiles. "The pinky promise is sacred."

"The *most* sacred."

We lock eyes, then fingers.

"Swear?" I ask.

He nods. "Swear."

We hold on for half a second more, then another. Staring at each other until my body is the Fourth of July. Until he's grinning again, both our faces flushed.

"Are we really going to do this?" he asks, inching closer.

I lean in too. "We're *really* going to do this."

■ ■ ■ ■ ■ ■ ■ ■ ■ ■ ■

Back outside, the sun is still blazing. We stop at the edge of the courtyard, looking out at all of the faces that used to be our entire universe. How much time had I spent trying to find a place to fit in? How many times did I fail before I realized that none of it even mattered? High school. Being popular. Being in the top 10 percent of my class. It was all bullshit.

But this…me and Aarón and Acadia. This feels real. This feels *right*. But it also feels terrifying.

And I wish we were still touching, pinkies still locked in a promise. Because the world felt safe there…and I'd almost forgotten it could be.

"What are you thinking?" he asks, examining my face.

I brush my hair back, searching for words. I don't tell him about the fireworks. Not until I know he feels them too.

I dab at the sweat on my brow. "Just thinking you had the right idea about wearing a hat."

He flips off his cap and rests it on my head. It smells like sandalwood and mint.

"It's a little big," he says, tapping the blue bill.

I laugh. "I'm swimming in it." I tug it lower. "But I…I like it."

"Looks good on you," he says.

"You too." I shake my head, flushed again. "I mean *looked*. Before you gave it to me. You looked good too."

He laughs. "Oh, uh…thanks."

I pinch the bridge of my nose, trying to breathe, to figure out how to change the subject. I turn to him. "Do you have a dollar?"

"Yeah, what for?"

"I…um…" I exhale. *Get it together, Mia.* "I think I know the perfect way to celebrate our new pact."

He raises an eyebrow before reaching into his wallet and pulling out the cash.

I snatch it, smiling, and then I lead him across the courtyard to where Principal Judd is perched and waiting to be pelted in the face with a pie.

⬛⬛⬛⬛⬛⬛⬛⬛⬛⬛⬛

I skip last period and take the long way home, knocked back by the citrus smell wafting from Loco Lavado before I even pass the entrance. It's still hot out and the doors are propped open, samba music blaring, box fans blowing the scent of cafecito and Cubanos being pressed against a flat-top grill—the laundromat hiding the gem of a café just on the other side of the washing machines.

Around the next corner, Doña Josefa sells tortas topped with the creamiest guacamole and the crispiest carne asada. But instead of inhaling the smell of fresh bolillos over a sizzling slab of butter, I choke on the smell of fresh paint.

On the side of the building a girl in a yellow baseball cap is whitewashing the brick. To her right, there's an explosion of flowers—Mexican sage, marigolds, hot pink cosmos, and bright red sunflowers. A frame for the woman inside—Virginia Regia, her arms full of the most beautiful conchas I've ever seen. Pink and orange and yellow.

The artist captured every detail—her dimples and deep forehead wrinkles. She's wearing her favorite yellow apron, a bit of flour dusted on her shirt. She laughs and I can almost hear it.

"It's bullshit what they did to her panadería." The girl stops for a moment, readjusting her ponytail.

"I remember the day they knocked it down," I say. "Virginia Regia had chained herself to the front door. Her cat Chocó refused to leave too."

The girl laughs. "Yeah, it took three cops to shoo him away."

My stomach knots. "Then they took off Virginia's chains and replaced them with handcuffs."

I think about all the times Andrés stopped by Virginia's on his way home from work, my stomach growling the second I saw him carrying in that box full of bright pink conchas, cuernitos, and pan fino that always gave me a sparkly cinnamon mustache. Her pan was the centerpiece at every local restaurant and café, her son making the rounds on Sunday evenings in a box truck that made the entire neighborhood smell like warm yeast.

She kept a giant black-and-white photo on the wall of the panadería the Regias used to own in Jalisco. Next to that there were notches marking every inch her children had grown over the years. That bakery was their home; a home she'd spent decades building. A dream she'd planted on American soil, that she'd tended to, that she'd raised from the earth with her own two hands.

And then they just took it away.

"If they're not trying to run people out by closing down their businesses, they're dragging them out of their homes late at night, arresting them for bullshit they didn't even do." The girl's face darkens. "No one's safe."

Maybe we never were, I think.

Maybe that's what makes our dreams so defiant; what makes the people who dream them so strong. That we carry them without knowing if we'll ever find soil safe enough for them to bloom. That we tend to them even though someone else might come along and yank them up by the roots.

We do it anyway.

We dream and we hope and we fight.

All promises I made to my father. All promises I made to myself.

And there's only one way to keep them. To make my life mean something. To make his mean something too.

I have to keep *dreaming*.

I have to keep *hoping*.

I have to keep *fighting*.

When Mr. Barrero sees me coming up the driveway, he motions for me to follow him inside. Like he knew I'd just had some kind of epiphany and would soon show up for confirmation that auditioning is the right choice.

A small fan blows from where it sits on the windowsill, ruffling a stack of papers on the kitchen table. Mr. Barrero pours two glasses of lemonade.

I've had his great-aunt Judy's juice before. It always makes my ears itch, so instead of taking a sip I clutch the glass while working up the courage to say, "I've made a decision."

He eyes me from across the table. "And what's that?"

"I'm going to audition. For real this time."

He smiles, but his eyes are sad. "That's great news, Mia."

"What's wrong?" I say.

He waves a hand, tries to force the smile to reach his eyes this time. But again, it doesn't quite get there.

I set the glass down and suddenly I don't know what to do with my hands. "Mr. Barrero...?"

"You know, the day my mother died she was more alive than ever." He slips into his storytelling voice. The one that demands patience, that can needle its way into even the darkest corners of me, making me listen. *Really* listen. "I heard her voice around five AM, singing." He laughs. "And not with the voice of a woman on her deathbed. But with the voice I remembered, crooning over my crib, loud and joyful next to me in a church pew. When my mother sang, her heart was outside her chest." He closes his eyes, savoring a sound only he can hear. "She auditioned for the church choir every year and every year they just so happened to fill up."

"Why didn't they let her join the choir?"

He slaps his knee, guffaws. "Because she was terrible. She was always off-key and a beat behind. As a kid, I hated sitting next to her in church. The looks we'd get..." He whistles. "She embarrassed me every day of my life and she knew it too. When she'd catch me squirming in my shiny shoes, cheeks bright red, she'd just sing louder."

"She was trying to teach you a lesson."

"That she was. A lesson about bein' brave and bein' you. You can't be one without the other."

"That's what you keep telling me." I tap my fingers against the glass, the condensation cool.

Mr. Barrero is quiet and for a long time he just stares at me. Like he's trying to paint a picture of my face in his mind. Like he's looking for something important.

"Will you do an old man a favor and play me your audition piece one more time?"

I nod. "Sure." Then I take a half-hearted breath and lean into the song—"Pièce en Forme de Habanera."

I try to remember how excited I'd been the day I chose it. I thought it was perfect, that mastering it would change everything. Now it feels stale and silly and my lips fall off the mouthpiece as soon as I reach the end.

But Mr. Barrero is smiling, his eyes closed like it's the most beautiful thing he's ever heard. Still listening with his whole body even though I've stopped playing.

"Well...?" I finally say, waiting for his admonishment.

He opens his eyes. "You *need* me to say something."

"That's why I'm here, isn't it? So you can teach me?"

He sighs. "Mia, I haven't taught you a goddamned thing in years. The second you learned how to put two notes together you didn't need me anymore. And yet you keep coming here for praise. For reassurance." He looks down. "I've given you too much of it over the years."

"What do you mean you've given me 'too much'?"

"I mean I've praised you so much you don't know how to praise yourself. I've been believing in you for the both of us."

"But you're my teacher."

He nods, slow. "And now it's time for me to teach you what you need to know. By not being your teacher anymore."

I stand, the panic painting my face more like anger. "You can't do that."

He lowers his voice. "Mia…it's what's best."

"For who? You?" I'm crying now and it feels so foreign, so infantile, so stupid. But I don't know how to stop.

Mr. Barrero steps past me, reaching for his reading glasses before turning his attention to the pages scattered on the table.

I stand there, shaking, afraid to move, afraid that if I do, everything will change. Maybe it already has. Maybe it's supposed to. Or maybe Mr. Barrero is wrong and I can't do this by myself. *I can't do this by myself.*

"Please…" The word is weak and cuts me open on the way out.

He doesn't look up. And I can't help but think about my parents. I can't help but think about his *son*. The boy he left behind.

I grab my trumpet, clutching the cold metal. Then I look right at him and say, "You're just like them."

I storm out and he doesn't follow. I stand on the sidewalk, waiting for him to come to the window. For a long time I watch the sun glint against the glass, sweat starting to bead at my hairline. But I can't even feel the heat. All I feel is alone.

Back home, I stuff my trumpet inside its case, angry at all the questions it's forced me to ask, at all the times it made me believe in something more. It's what started all of this. The rift between Jazzy and Andrés. The rift between my head and my heart.

I shove the case into the hall closet and slam the door. In the silence, the sound ricochets, striking me like a bullet.

And suddenly I remember.

Slamming doors and rattling doorknobs. My father banging, banging. *Let me in. Let me in.* Spanish insults snapping back and forth from slingshot mouths.

I pinch my eyes shut, but it only drags the memory closer to the surface.

My father's work boots are sitting by the front door. My mother stands next to them. The moon on the other side of the window is a giant flame. She can't take her eyes off it.

"What do you mean, you 'met someone'?" My father can't look at her.

"I didn't come here just to have your children, Germán."

His voice is small. "We came here to have a better life."

"That's why I'm leaving."

"But the kids…"

Her lip quivers. She bites it hard. And then she walks out the door, carrying nothing.

She doesn't want to remember us.

My father stands at the window, watching her go. For a long time he just stares at the empty street. Then he goes to the kitchen, grabs a beer, the top popping off with a hiss. He takes a drink and then he disappears too.

I don't know where this memory's been hidden. I thought my mother had vanished like one of those women in the telenovelas she used to watch. Here one minute, gone the next. An incessant plot twist I'd given up on trying to unravel. But all of a sudden I remember watching her go. I remember her words, her reason why.

Because she *wanted* something—to stop being a mother, to run and never look back—and she got it. She got what she wanted.

It's the part of her that made it impossible for her to be my mother, and yet, it's the only part of her I want to inherit. Not her selfishness but her stubbornness. *Her devotion.* She broke our hearts, our family, but she didn't give up. Regardless of the destruction it caused.

And I don't want to destroy anything—including myself—but I want to *want* something as powerfully as she did. I want it to drag me into the future the way it dragged her out of mine. Even though I hate her, I want to be her.

9

Aaron

MY HANDS FUMBLE WITH THE KNOT OF MY TIE.

"Are you trying to get dressed or are you trying to strangle yourself?" the robot asks.

I hit play on the YouTube video, watching how some guy with a man bun loops the tie's tongue perfectly. I stretch it out, trying again. But it smells like magnolias and old lady perfume, and suddenly it's hanging limp around my neck while I grip both sides of the sink.

The day we buried my mother, my father had tied it too tight, until it felt like it was slowly choking the life out of me. As they lowered her down, down, I wanted it to. Through every prayer and hymn and impromptu speech, I stared at the darkness beneath her casket, begging it to swallow me.

Please.

Take me with you.

Please, Mom.

And then I felt her—a hand on my shoulder, her breath by my ear like I was showing her a new song. Both of us staring at the sound waves like they were bits of my DNA. Like they were dancing just for her.

"It was beautiful, Pepito." She'd ruffle my hair. "Play it again."

And I would. Every night it was me and my keyboard. Me and my drum set. Me and my beat-up guitar. Writing song after song. Waiting for her to come in my room in the morning so I could show her what I'd made.

"She was your mother. She had to tell you your songs were good." The robot laughs. "You know how many parents lie to their kids and tell them they're geniuses? Or lie to themselves about it?" He uses a metal finger to pull the curtains back so he can look out the window in disgust. "Then they unleash those cocky little beasts on the world." He whines, *"I'm special. I'm important."*

"My mom wasn't like that," I say, remembering how she used to always tell me that we weren't better than anyone. That everyone deserved respect.

The robot adjusts my tie. "Well, I guess we'll find out tonight."

My heart pounds in my chest, and I try to imagine myself ripping it out and leaving it bleeding on that stage, sharing this mess inside me and calling it art. In front of strangers. In front of Mia...

"I never thought you could actually die from stage

fright." The robot examines the sweat on my forehead. "But you look well on your way to being the first." He smirks. "And I know a thing or two about being—"

"Don't." I turn to face him. "What's your sick obsession with being a ghost?"

"Leaving behind a ghost would require having a soul. I'm a machine." He steps to my computer, waking the screen with the tap of a key. La Maquina's song "Mamá" begins to play. "*This* is a ghost."

The sound slinks between us and he's right about it having a soul. Maybe that's why I can never listen to it all the way through. Because of the way it comes alive, like Xavier's mother isn't dead but dancing between the notes.

I thought saying goodbye to my mother would be the hard part. But I was wrong. Because even if the person is gone, the feelings you have about them aren't. *Feelings*… they have a way of sticking around. In songs. In the creases of an old tie.

But every time I get caught up in them, all I have to do is put on my headphones and crank up the sound. And that's why I have to find him. Because his music is my life raft on days when I'm drowning and my mirror on days when I'm scared to be alone.

"*Alone*…?" The robot places a hand on my shoulder. I feel his breath by my ear. "Trust me, you're never alone."

"Mamá" ends and in the silence all I can do is bleed. In the places that should have healed by now but that I know never will. Raw in all the same ways Xavier was when he first wrote it. And I let myself wonder for a second if maybe that's why the Universe is trying to bring us together, our mothers conspiring from the other side.

"Do you realize how sick that sounds?" The robot stares at the frozen sound waves on my computer screen. "You're a seventeen-year-old superfan who thinks the onstage persona of a semisuccessful recording artist is your imaginary friend. The 'Universe' has nothing to do with it."

My heartbeat skips. The robot's been calling me crazy for months, but this is the first time he's called me a child. I realize that that's why my stomach sinks every time I wake up and he's still here. Because he doesn't just make me feel like I'm losing it. He makes me feel weak.

I glare at him as I head for the door. "*Don't* follow me."

On my way to the bus stop he clanks a few yards behind. Little good it did slamming the door in his face. This is not the time for his words to be rattling around inside my head. *Superfan. Imaginary Friend. Loser. Loser. Loser.* That's what he meant. And he's not wrong.

I don't know why I can see him, why I talk to someone I know isn't there. Maybe because I understand what it feels like to be treated like you're invisible. That still doesn't make it okay…make *me* okay. Something is wrong with me, and I don't know if finding Xavier in the real world will finally cure me or only make everything worse.

But I have to try.

Because he's saved me. *So* many times. And I have to tell him before it's too late.

■ ■ ■ ■ ■ ■ ■ ■ ■ ■ ■

Mia is sitting at the back of the bus. For a second I just stand there, wondering if she's a glitch in the matrix, a hallucination like the robot.

But then she spots me, waving me over, and I lug all of my equipment to the empty seat next to her.

She's wearing a new performance dress, black velvet. But the same pearls she had on last time.

"You nervous?" Mia asks quietly.

I exhale. "Yeah..."

"Me too."

Then we're both quiet. The robot nudges me.

"Well...I, uh...I think you look nice."

Mia smiles. "So do you." Then she hesitates, scanning the other passengers before lowering her voice and saying, "Is the tag showing?"

"What?"

"The dress. My brother Jazzy has to return it first thing tomorrow morning. Can you see the tag poking out from the neckline?" Slowly, she turns her back to me.

I see a piece of plastic edging out from the neck of her dress, and she waits for me to slip it back inside the fabric. But that would require touching her.

She sits still, holding up her hair.

I inhale, fingers trembling as I tuck the tag inside her dress, the nail of my index finger barely grazing her skin. But *barely* is enough to burn, the heat rushing up the rest of my arm until I'm sweating.

She turns to face me, just in time to see the sweat dripping from my hairline. Without a word, she reaches into her purse and pulls out a tissue, handing it to me. Instead of staring at the way I'm silently freaking out, Mia turns to the window where city lights rush past in giant streaks.

The neighborhood is a different thing at night. Neon and buzzing. We ease to a stop at a red light. Down below, old muscle cars with new rims idle outside Speedy's. Music blares while girls in tube tops bite the ends off bright red Twizzlers. People pass around bottles of Modelo and young guys covered in ink bump chests.

A patrol car eases into the parking lot, but the cop doesn't get out.

This is the version of our neighborhood packaged into a ten-second sound bite for the evening news. They have no idea that just around the corner, Mrs. Lulu's toddler dance studio is open late, tiny girls in tutus twirling in circles.

As we pass, Mia leans forward, wistful. "I danced for Mrs. Lulu for a summer before I found the trumpet. I was terrible. Like, absolutely horrid. But it was so much fun." She picks at the hem of her dress. "I wish I could get that feeling back."

I think about my mother, about how much I loved playing my songs for her. Even though, according to the robot, they were probably terrible.

"Oh, they were definitely terrible," he whispers.

I ignore him, turning to Mia to say, "I know what you mean."

The bus rolls forward and I see her shoulders tense.

I pull out my phone. "Do you remember what song it was? That you danced to?"

She bites her lip. "Something like…" And then she hums.

It's just five notes, but something clicks.

I hand her an earbud, the thin white cord dangling between us, and then I pull up "El Son de la Negra." It's the same game I play at every quince and graduation party when I'm fishing for that one song guaranteed to drag even the most miserable person onto the dance floor.

Then I press play, the song forcing an inhale like she's finally coming up for air. The nerves evaporating for a moment. The space between us warm.

She laughs. "You're good."

I smile back. "I try."

Suddenly, the bus pulls to a stop.

Mr. V waves us forward. "Vamos, you don't got much time."

I cut the music, stuffing the phone and headphones back in my pocket.

Mia goes pale and I worry that she's about to be sick… or worse. What if she gives up again?

"Isn't that why you're here?" the robot says. "To make sure she doesn't?"

In that moment, I forget that I'm in my funeral tie. I forget that I'm about to take the same stage Mia is. Instead, all I can think about is getting her off this bus and into that auditorium.

"Mia…"

She looks back at me, startled by my voice, or maybe the fact that she hasn't moved.

"If you make a mistake it will still be better than any-one else who's auditioned."

"You don't know that."

"Neither do you."

"I can't."

Mr. V honks his horn. "A la uno...A las dos..."

I straighten, letting Mia see where the hem of my pants rise too high above my dress socks. "This is the suit I wore to my mother's funeral."

Her eyes widen.

"I never thought I'd wear it again. I never wanted to wear it again."

"I'm so sorry, Aarón..."

"Don't be sorry. Be brave."

I follow her off the bus, the two of us looking like a 1960s version of Antonia La Singla and Diego Vargas. As we make our way up the steps of the auditorium, I desperately cling to whatever courage hijacked me on the bus, but as we break through the doors, the lights of the stage seeming to reach all the way into the entrance, it starts to lose its grip.

Someone pins a number to Mia's chest. Mia pins one on me. Her hand rests there for a beat and I hope she can't feel the rioting underneath.

A group of other freshly pinned performers head for the auditorium and we're swept up in their current. On the other side of the double doors the first performer is already waiting in the wings.

The houselights dim, people taking their seats. Mia and I find two near the end of an aisle.

A guy wearing suspenders and a fedora clutches a guitar. The face is scuffed, but the strings are new. He taps the underside of the wood, shifting from foot to foot.

Mia suddenly breaks from her stupor. "I know him. I mean, not really. But I've seen him outside Pen's Pastelería."

I follow her stare back to the guy onstage and finally get a good look at his face.

"Joaquín."

He's been playing outside Pen's food truck a few nights a week, looking to get a spot once the new patio at Nacho's is finished. He's not the best singer, but the waitresses don't seem to mind. I wonder if his good looks will help him here.

Joaquín pulls something from his pocket, dabs at his hairline. One of the program directors comes up from behind and I read his lips as he asks Joaquín if he's ready. Joaquín nods. He hasn't even started playing yet and he looks electric.

But then Mia breathes. "He won't get in."

"How do you know?"

She stares at him, terrified. *Of* him or *for* him. Maybe both.

"Because," she says, "he's not perfect."

As Joaquín takes the stage, head hanging as he conjures something from the mouth of his guitar, I don't see what Mia does.

He's not perfect.

I don't know what that means. I wonder if Mia really does either.

Joaquín's fingers rush down the strings like a spider spooling a web. He falls off a note, not enough air. But the groan that comes after is so earnest. I can hear what he wants. The audience can too, bodies leaning forward.

And as he fills the auditorium with the sound of the things inside him, no one winces at his fingers letting go of the strings too soon or of the stray note he couldn't hide in time.

They don't want him to hide.

Instead, they are stricken by this beautifully ordinary thing because he isn't. He isn't hiding and that's what Mia is so afraid of.

So afraid that she can't even sit and watch.

I follow her as she heads back toward the double doors. Light peeks through, feigning a blankness on the other side that I know she wants to run straight into.

"Mia..."

"Don't follow me." She looks back at the stage, at Joaquín taking a bow. "If I run, don't follow me."

"You're not going to run."

It comes out like more of a challenge than I mean it to be. But it's the implication of a test that makes Mia finally take a deep breath. I follow her back to our seats just as the next performer takes the stage. And then we sit. Through twelve more acts while Mia traces nervous shapes in her velvet dress—squiggles and sharp lines. Flames like her insides are on fire.

There are only two more performers and then it's her turn. Then mine.

While we wait, I let my mind wander to the conspiracy theory that La Maquina was the anonymous donor. If he was gonna show, tonight could be the night.

The robot nods. "Just to make sure I'm happy with the way my money's being spent. Especially after these assholes didn't even let me into their fancy school." He sneers. "Who knew all I had to do was dangle a little money over their heads? With some stipulations of course. But they took the bait." The robot conjures a stack of hundred-dollar bills, fans them out. "¿Quieres el dinero? Then you gotta let in kids from every color of the goddamned rainbow." He tosses the money like he's in a music video.

I ignore him, scanning the balcony for Xavier. It's mostly empty now that they're nearing the last of the night's auditions, save for a couple making out at the very top and a family of four near the railing. There's an old man in a bowtie and two guys in Acadia shirts.

I swivel in my seat, examining the faces behind us. People in black tie, parents with video cameras, more students in spirit wear. I spot a guy in a beanie, face tucked into his hand. Goatee. Sunglasses.

The robot taps me on the shoulder. "Is that…?"

I hold my breath and Mia notices, tensing next to me.

The guy sneezes into his elbow, moving just enough for me to see that…it's not him.

"Maybe I wasn't the anonymous donor after all." The robot now has a bag of popcorn. He tosses back a few kernels, nonchalant. Then he nudges me. "She looks a little pale, doesn't she? Maybe she could use some water."

Mia looks even more afraid than she did while watching Joaquín. Her face isn't just pale. It's almost green.

I ease out of my seat and Mia's hand clamps down onto my arm.

I stare down at her fingers, waiting for us to flinch or break apart.

When we don't, I squeeze back. "Water," I say, and she lets out a deep breath. "I'll be right back." I leave behind my equipment so she knows I'm telling the truth.

There's no line for the concession stand. I hand the girl behind the counter two dollars and she hands me two bottles of water.

"Have you gone up yet?" she asks.

I shake my head before cracking open the lid on one of the bottles and taking a drink.

She leans across the counter and lowers her voice. "Just so you know, I heard there's only one spot left."

My throat's suddenly dry again. "Uh, thanks."

"So, you gonna throw it?"

I look back at the robot "What?"

"Your audition. Are you gonna throw it as part of some big romantic gesture so Mia can get into her dream school?"

"I'm not trying to make a big romantic gesture."

"Oh, so then just lots of little ones that you're hoping to amass into..."

"Mia and I are..." I stop. I don't know what we *are*. A few days ago we were just two kids who've grown up in the same neighborhood with the same fucked-up experience of losing someone we love way too soon. Now we're not exactly friends, but we're not *not* friends.

"Are you really trying to lie to someone who lives inside your head? I know your deepest darkest secrets, Aarón. I'm one of them."

"Whatever." I glare at him. "I have to pee."

The bathroom is just as empty as the concession area. My shoes echo off the tile floor. It reminds me of all those lunch periods I spent in a stall, watching La Maquina music videos until the bell rang. For so long, I was done with school. I couldn't wait for that bell to ring for the last time.

But the closer we get to graduation, the more I think about the *nothing* that will come after. I think about how I hate home so much more than I ever hated school. That's why when I found the flyer, I told myself it was a sign. That he'd left it for me.

Now I'm here and he's not.

I shake my hands off in the sink before staring at my reflection. "*Where* are you?"

The robot appears beside me. "I think the more important question is, *where* is Mia?"

I rush back through the auditorium doors. Number fifteen is leaving the stage and Mia isn't in her seat.

She's . . .

"There," the robot whispers, a sharp metal finger pointing to center stage.

Mia steps beneath the spotlight and even from this far away I can see that she's shaking, which means that so can everyone else. She closes her eyes, her fear palpable as people whisper and shift in their seats. Someone laughs from the back row.

I don't know what to do. Part of me wants to throw myself in front of her, to drag her offstage, to pull the fire alarm so this moment can be over.

But I made a promise.

Mia finally opens her eyes again. She can barely get her hands around her trumpet.

You've made it this far, Mia.

She doesn't see me, the lights too bright as she blinks against the glare.

Mia.

Everyone is waiting. For her to get control of herself. For her to blow them away.

Mia, you can do this.

For a long moment she just breathes, and I think she knows it's true. But then she grits her teeth and shakes her head and then she does what she warned me she would— she runs.

I grab my backpack, hoisting it over my shoulder, and then I'm running too.

The robot clanks behind me. "But you're up next!"

His words only make me run faster and it feels good to flee, to use Mia as an excuse to save myself. But save myself from what? No school means no leaving home, no getting away from my father and Miguel.

I slow, looking from the street back in the direction of the auditorium. My stomach sinks.

"Well, you're too late now." The robot puts his hands on his hips, panting.

"You don't even have lungs," I say.

"And you don't have a future."

"That was harsh."

"Because it's true?"

He's right. It is true. But it isn't any more true than it was two hours ago when Mia and I first got off the bus. Because even then there was something inside me that knew I was never going to get on that stage. What I didn't know was that I was going to end up chasing Mia down three city blocks.

"Where do you think she would go?"

The robot looks down at me, amused. "Glad you're finally acknowledging I'm the smart one." He looks from one end of the dark street to the other. "What was the last thing she said before the nerves took over?"

"That she was going to run..."

"Before that. On the bus."

I remember her smile as she stared out at the tiny ballerinas.

When we reach Mrs. Lulu's the lights are still on, little girls in full costume as they dance in circles around the instructor. I expect to see Mia, hands pressed to the glass, remembering. But she isn't here.

"I guess I was wrong."

The robot points. "No, you weren't."

I catch sight of Mia just as she turns the corner. When I reach the alley she's halfway up the fire escape.

"Mia!" I call out.

She looks down, startled, and then she just keeps climbing. When she reaches the top she disappears.

"Yikes," the robot says. "So much for that big romantic gesture."

"Psst!" Mia peers over the edge of the roof. "You coming?"

I climb the fire escape and find Mia sitting against one of the air vents. A lamp with a dim bulb is fastened to one of the doors leading down into the building. But she's chosen a spot in the dark. Still hiding.

I slide next to her, being careful to leave some space between us.

She presses the heels of her hands to her eyes. "I told you I would run."

"It's okay..."

"You missed your audition." Her face twists. "You shouldn't have followed me. Why did you?"

"I don't know."

It's not the whole truth, but telling Mia that I'd follow her anywhere feels even scarier than facing that crowd of people.

Mia hangs her head back. "Do you remember that game hot lava?"

"The one where you climb onto things to keep from being burned by imaginary lava?"

"That's the one. My brothers and I used to play from this very rooftop all the way to the church."

"Is that even possible?"

"Oh, it's possible. But it's also incredibly dangerous and incredibly stupid. Back then we were both."

"It sounds like you were pretty fearless."

"Temporarily." From the strain on her face, I sense another memory coming to the surface, this one much darker. "Until I learned to be afraid."

I try to remember the exact moment I learned to be afraid, but the farther back I go, the more it dawns on me that I can't remember *not* being afraid. Like something whispered it to me in the womb. *The world is not a good place. It will not take care of you.*

Night sounds grow louder. The music from the dance studio wafts from the air vents, the teacher's voice echoing like she's right behind us.

"I was going to be brave." Mia chucks a rock and it tumbles over the edge of the roof. Then she whispers, more to herself than to me, "I *promised*."

"You're trying."

"And failing." Mia stares into the night sky. There are no stars, just the pulsing red of an airplane descending to the south. "My dad…all he wanted was for me and my brothers to have the kind of life he only dreamed about. He said those dreams carried him and now they're the only pieces of him I have left. Like I'm living for the both of us."

"And you don't know if you're doing it right…"

She looks at me. "Exactly. And every time I get up onstage, I don't just see the boy he was—the boy who read about roads paved in gold, never knowing where they'd actually lead. I see the man too. I see how he and my mother raged at each other. I see how those dreams rotted away. How they poisoned everything they touched."

"Because they never came true."

She nods. "So I know the cost. Of hoping *too* much." She presses a fist to her chest. "So I keep it right here, not letting anyone see, not pouring it out onstage. Because I don't want the world to break me like it broke him. And I don't want him to see me broken. Wherever he is, if he's watching, that's not who I want him to see."

I cup her fist in my hand, hold it tight, feeling all the

things I've been lugging around too. "Who would you want him to see?"

She hugs her knees and I can tell she's wrestling with something. But then she reaches for her trumpet, slowly bringing it to her lips. She closes her eyes, takes a deep breath, and then she forces out a sound that scales my arms like vines.

Mia's eyes flicker behind her eyelids and I want to know what she sees, if the sounds dredge up old memories, if they paint for her something new. The piece swells, growing and growing until the knife stab of the peak, a crescendo dragging the blade back down again. The notes untangle themselves, drifting off.

It's quiet again.

She takes a few deep breaths, as if waiting for the world to fall apart. When it doesn't she pushes out another note, loud and strong, making the night sounds scatter like birds.

Suddenly, Mia spreads her wings too.

Cars with their windows down begin to slow, people on the street searching for the sound.

Tiny footsteps patter on the sidewalk below, the ballerinas getting out of their dance rehearsal. A girl clutches her mother's hand and looks up, listening. Another little girl jumps on her toes as she tries to see where the sound is coming from.

I wait for the attention to make Mia stop, retreating into herself again. But her eyes are still closed.

I take her arm, pulling her to her feet. I lead her to the light she'd been avoiding. She hesitates, goosebumps trailing her arms.

Down below, the little ballerinas begin to dance. It moves something in me too. But Mia still isn't looking.

Suddenly, she inhales, readying for something magic. I can see in her muscles the moment she harnesses it and then she lets go. This beautiful, bottom of the ocean thing. She flings it into the night, waves crashing, making everything clean.

"Mia . . ." I breathe, "open your eyes."

She looks out, awestruck. Like she's forgotten where she is or that she's not alone.

Cars are stopped in front of green lights. Kids stare up, Takis pinched between red fingers. The ballerinas still on tiptoes as they marvel at what's glowing beneath the light.

Mia stares back, just as stricken. And I decide in that moment that there is only one thing she could possibly be afraid of—how incredibly powerful she is.

10

Mia

THERE ARE EYES EVERYWHERE AND ALL I WANT IS to peel them from my skin. To hide. To disappear.

I pinch my own eyes shut, waiting to be swept up and away. To fall to pieces.

"Mia..."

I can't look at him. I *can't* look.

The first claps create the faintest echo and then the sound is a raucous cheerful thing. Down on the street, people whoop and holler. *¡Otra! ¡Otra!* A man hangs out of a car window and whistles. One of the ballerinas clutches her tutu and curtsies. People watch from the adjacent apartment building. Some smile and wave from their small terraces, from the fire escape.

There's Mrs. Medina raising her watering can in salud, flowers that will soon be in her shop swaying in the breeze. Mr. Vasquez from the carcinería, with his elbows hanging over the railing, puffing a cigar. Señora Sanchez has her granddaughter on her lap, taking her two hands to show her how to clap. Two kids still holding their gaming controllers stand next to their mom, wide-eyed.

Everyone...looking right at me.

Sweat paints the back of my neck and I feel like I might pass out. But I'm also smiling so much it hurts. And then Aarón takes my hand, motioning with the other for me to take a bow, and suddenly I'm laughing. I'm laughing and it feels strange and scary and wonderful.

I think about what Mr. Barrero said—that playing only for myself was not an option; that eventually I was going to have to decide what it was all for. The years and years of practice. The music itself. I didn't understand the stakes before. Because I didn't know my music could do *this*.

That it could summon an entire neighborhood. That it could *move* other people the way it moves me. That when the sound travels between us we are bound by some invisible grace, connected in a way I usually run from. Because it's vulnerable and overwhelming and reminds me that being human hurts.

But music...music is the salve to it all. The answer to Mr. Barrero's question about what it's all for. It's for *this*. This moment. This *feeling*. Isn't it?

Until it's cut short.

Aarón hears it before I do, his hand pulling me away from the roof's ledge.

Tires squeal up the street and the sound of growling engines disperses the crowd. One of the mothers snatches her daughter off the pavement just as a black SUV skids to a stop in front of the apartment complex.

The man who'd whistled at me earlier speeds off. Others follow fast on foot. The little girl who was almost run over sobs into her mother's shoulder as they race to the bus stop.

I feel myself backing up too, even though I know they're not here for me. It doesn't matter. I still feel like prey.

I can tell Aarón does too. Because he's backing up in the same direction. Because he hasn't let go of my hand.

Boots hit the pavement, spotlights trained on the windows of the apartment building.

I think about all of the other people who live in that building. Mrs. Fuentes, her aloe vera overgrown and hanging over the side of her terrace. Mr. Ramirez and his vanilla-scented pipe tobacco that you can smell all the way to Speedy's. *Speedy*. His family is somewhere on the third floor. On cool nights, they keep their window open, Tejano music wafting out along with the smell of Mrs. Speedy's caldo rojo.

I could name every person in every apartment, the movies they watch on Saturday nights, the meals they cook on Sunday afternoons, their favorite songs, the sounds they make when they're celebrating a birthday, a christening, a graduation; when they're grieving someone they love, fighting with them too.

In the dark, in this moment that feels a thousand years long, I can hear those sounds, scrambled like they've been put through a blender.

"Is it a raid?" Aarón breathes.

I try to imagine the men in Kevlar maneuvering down tight hallways, kicking down doors. Dragging people out one by one. My knees almost buckle beneath me.

"I don't know."

I wait for it to be over. Like the seconds are bullets. Like time is a ticking bomb.

Then light comes pouring through the entrance to the building, a flood of flashlights barreling down like a moving train. But there's only one passenger.

Handcuffed, head down, Mr. V is led to one of the SUVs.

"No . . ." Aarón's voice is miles away.

It's swallowed by the sound of people exiting the building, of people on the street, stunned and screaming for them to let Mr. V go.

Then he's swallowed too, trapped behind tinted windows, monsters glistening in the sheen. They growl, a warning, before the car speeds off again.

Slowly, more people edge out of the shadows. When Mrs. V appears, everyone falls quiet. She steps off the curb, staring at the taillights as they disappear, clutching herself with one hand, reaching for the space and time unraveling between her and her husband with the other. But he's gone.

He's gone.

She wails and it is a sharp knife through the silence.

The numbness wears off and suddenly I can feel Aarón's hand still in mine. I squeeze, needing to feel his flesh and blood. But then I can't stop squeezing, digging my nails in, the anger trying to claw its way out. He squeezes back. Then I hear him sniffle.

I remember Mr. V keeping the bus in park until I declared to him and every other passenger that I was too good for Acadia. He made me say it again and again. Until he could feel me starting to believe. Maybe I did…*just* for a second. But only because he believed it first.

When Aarón and I finally make our way back down to the street, there are more faces in windows, more hands gripping Mrs. V and holding her up.

More people tearing things down.

"Fuck this shit!" Mr. V's nephew Javier slams his hands on the hood of a parked car. The alarm goes off, the flashing light cutting him into shards.

A couple of young guys join him, kicking at garbage cans, smashing bottles in the street, breaking things the way their family just was.

"He was a person!" Javi screams. "He was a goddamned father!"

Beneath the sound of more things breaking, Aarón breathes, "He was my friend."

My throat clenches. I squeeze his hand again.

"Why him?" I whisper.

Javi loses steam, head hanging. "His visa expired. Two days ago." He grimaces. "I've heard about others. Denied their renewal. Picked up after just a few days. They're trying to make us an example because Austin's a sanctuary city."

Not anymore, I think.

Javi's face twists and I watch this moment chew him

up. While the rest of us walk in circles. While we cry. While the world feasts on us. While we lose ourselves, bit by bit.

Down the street more lights flash on, people peering out of the fancy new high-rise right across from where they're planning to build the Whole Foods. I remember when they first broke ground. They had to demolish a millinery shop first. I remember when they posted the cost of rent. More than Andrés and Jazzy made in a month combined. I remember when the first family from our neighborhood applied for a lease. They were denied.

Someone lights a match, tossing it into the trash strewn in the street. The flame catches.

I can't see the faces behind those windows, but I know they're watching it burn. Probably wondering if they're next. Thinking this is about them. Always thinking it's about them.

Some kids Aarón and I go to school with join the people yelling at passing cars, at the moon, at God. Some are singing; others chanting. Where Mrs. V sits, palms pressed to her back and forming a makeshift shield, I hear only prayers.

"We're not going to let them get away with this, Señora." Esther is there in her homemade T-shirt, clutching Mrs. V's hands. "I promise."

"You want to arrest me too?" Javi spits, raging again, arms raised at the people in those high-rise apartments. "Go ahead! I'm right here!" He flings himself at nothing. "I'm fucking *right here*. . . ."

"Javi…" I'm not even sure that I've said his name out loud, but then he turns around.

"It's not safe out here, Mia."

He uses that same big brother voice he used to use when he and Jazzy were dating. When he used to bring me a sour pickle and some Lucas salt any time he picked Jazzy up for a date.

They used to be inseparable. Until Javi wanted Jazzy to spend more time with his family, to be his plus-one at every wedding and quinceañera and birthday party. Because nothing meant more to Javi. And it terrified Jazzy to belong to something bigger than just the three of us. For him to stretch his heart around so many people. As if that somehow made it weaker, easier to bruise.

As Javi falls to his knees in the middle of the street, his big heart completely shattered, I understand Jazzy's fear. But as Esther and Mrs. V and Speedy and Noni wrap their arms around him, helping him back to his feet, I understand Javi too. Because even though big hearts may be more easily broken, there are so many more people there to help you put it back together.

"What do you think they're saying?" Javi's still staring at those faces looking down at us.

Behind sheer curtains in darkened rooms, they stare back.

"Do they think we're even human?"

I turn to glare at them too, wishing my stare was as sharp as a knife.

"It doesn't matter what they think," Aarón says.

"Oh, it matters." Javi says, his skin awash in the fire-light that's beginning to spread. "If they want us dead, it fucking matters."

The faint sound of sirens swells a few streets over.

"You should go," Javi says. "Jazzy will be worried."

I wish I could say, *He'll be worried about you too,* but I don't know if Jazzy will ever be that honest. If he'll ever admit to himself, let alone Javi, that he's still in love with him.

The sirens' wail moves closer.

"He's right," Aarón says.

I squeeze Javi's hand, but before we go I have to look one more time. At Mrs. V crying into her hands. And then at the faces in those high-rise windows, looking back, making sure the police have come to do their jobs. Because the police work for them, not us.

So maybe it *is* about them. About their need to control the people down below, the people who only live here because our separation used to be the law.

For a while, we'd all gotten good at pretending that things had changed. That we could live in the same neighborhoods and shop at the same supermarkets. That Aarón and I could attend a school like Acadia without it being negotiated into some contract, our last names satisfying some quota.

But things never changed.

Mr. V drove a bus.

He *drove* a bus.

He wasn't a criminal.

But...I guess he didn't have to be.

He just had to be vulnerable. He just had to be an easy target. He just had to be a "stranger" in a country where fear is a weapon. Where whiteness is a bulletproof vest.

A local news van hops the curb, and Aarón and I slip into the shadows again, racing back down the alley. Lights swell as one of the cruisers comes at us head-on.

A police officer calls out for us to stop. We don't.

When the block ignites like this, it's like shooting fish in a barrel. The police arrest everyone in sight, innocent bystander or not. In Monte Vista there's no such thing as an innocent bystander. No such thing as innocent at all until proven guilty. You're just guilty for being alive.

"Wait." Aarón throws an arm in front of me.

An ambulance races past the mouth of the alley. We round the corner, pressing ourselves against a storefront window.

"Ready?" Aarón asks.

Then we bolt the second we see more lights. Because we're not bulletproof. We never will be.

The darkness breaks, but we don't stop running. Behind us there's smoke, the fires drenched. I wonder if Javi made it out or if he wanted to be found. If he wanted *them* to see him handcuffed.

Suddenly, the alley opens up right in front of the church and it stops me in my tracks.

I see the spire, moonlight glinting off the gold paint, and between us, an ocean of grass, waves cresting in the shapes of tombstones.

From here, the cemetery looks endless, the night stretching it in all directions. Like the darkness has finally given the dead room to breathe. As the breeze cuts across my face, thick and lukewarm, I feel their wanting exhales while mine stays bottled up. While my lungs scream the same way they did the day we buried him.

"My father..."

I shiver, afraid for a second that I've woken him. That he'll see me here and wonder where I've been. But nothing moves except the shadows.

The darkness peels away one layer at a time, objects winking back at me as the clouds shift overhead. Picture frames and flower vases and stones stacked in neat piles. From here I see a sports medal and to the right of it a folded cap and gown.

Details I never let myself notice.

Even though I've walked by it a thousand times; ridden past it on the bus every time I meet Jazzy at the hair salon or take the long way home from school. But my eyes are always to the ground, my cheek turned from the window, my hands on my cell phone scrolling through social media until I forget.

That this is where my father sleeps now.

I wait for more sirens and flashing lights, for the things that chased us here to keep spurring my steps. But I can't move.

Neither can Aarón. I feel him tense next to me, but neither one of us can make a sound. Suddenly, my eyes are drawn to the far end of the cemetery. To the darkness that is not my father but still feels like him anyway.

I smell whiskey and Pine-Sol and red beans burning on the stove. I feel Jazzy shaking and stroking my hair, rocking us both as if staying in motion made it harder for the moment to stick. I hear Andrés sobbing behind his bedroom door on our first night alone.

Aarón brushes my arm and the memory loosens its grip. But when I look over at him, he's stoic, and I realize it must have been an accident. Sweat paints his upper lip, something awful racing behind his eyes.

"Aarón?"

I remember when he was pulled out of class last semester during US Government. I sat two rows over. Everyone at school knew Mrs. Medrano was sick. But no one really knew how bad it was. Until I saw the look on Aarón's face when Mr. Bullock called his name.

It was the same look the school counselor had given me when I showed up like normal the day after it happened. It was unusual, she said. Didn't I want to be at home? With my family?

I didn't.

I didn't want to be in that house with my father's things. With his fingerprints on every fucking surface. His pocketknife on the nightstand. His reading glasses on top of the TV. His house shoes by the back door. His favorite hot sauce in the middle of the kitchen table.

Everything we had. Everything we'd done. All of the memories piling on top of me until I couldn't breathe.

I shook my head, told her I wanted to stay at school. That I was fine. *I'm fine. I'm fine.*

And that was good enough for her. All the reassurance she needed to mark my name off her to-do list. She didn't know our mother was gone too, that Andrés was only sixteen, that when you're the children of undocumented immigrants no one cares where you end up. All we had to do was keep showing up to school. No failing grades. No pink slips. Jazzy learned how to forge our mother's signature. Andrés learned how to sound like an adult on the phone.

I learned how to lie with a straight face.

I'm fine was the first.

But I wasn't fine. Neither is Aarón.

Beside me, he shakes his head, mouth open just slightly like he's about to speak. But then he stops himself. Like it's pointless. Like there's nothing I can do. But there is one thing. I can get us both out of here. Before the memories take root. Before they strangle us.

"Come on." I try to ease him off the curb. "Aarón?"

His shoe grazes where the grass meets the sidewalk and then he grabs my arm like he's about to be sick.

"Aarón, I'm right here."

His jaw clamps tight. He tries to breathe.

"Aarón, it's okay." I pull him away from the cemetery and each step in the opposite direction seems to disentangle him from the panic.

I ask him if that's what it is. "Are you having a panic attack?"

He just nods. And then, "I'm sorry, Mia."

I stop us outside my house. "No. No, Aarón, don't be sorry. You don't have anything to be sorry for. Okay?"

He nods again, but I'm not sure if he's really listening.

"I get it, Aarón. It's been a long time since I've visited my father's grave too. It's... *rough*."

Suddenly Aarón's face falls. "I've...never been back to see her." He pinches his eyes shut. "Ever."

Then I see what's dripping off him. Shame.

Like every time he walked past the cemetery, he was walking past *her*. Ignoring her. Rejecting her. Leaving her behind.

"She's not there, Aarón." I take his hands. "So you don't have to feel bad about not visiting a patch of dirt and a tombstone with her name on it."

"Is that what you believe?"

My mouth suddenly feels dry and I chew my lip, trying to figure out how to explain without sounding like a total asshole. I can tell Aarón needs reassurance, but maybe someone who's also lost a parent is actually the worst person to offer advice.

It's hardened me in places that used to be soft; made me see truth when lies are so much safer.

But then I remember how every adult I interacted with after my father's death had tried to comfort me. With religious bullshit and false promises. The lies made me sick.

So I won't do that to him. I can't.

"To me, it's just a body." I clench my jaw. "I wish there was more. . . . I wish I knew it for a fact. But I don't."

"I know you're right." He runs a hand down his face. "I know she isn't *really* there. But I just feel so shitty every time I think about all the people who bring flowers once a week, who decorate their family members' plot for every holiday. She deserves that. Doesn't she?"

His words sting. Because I know what he means. That there could still be a piece of my father in the world, if I would just remember him. If I would just *let myself* remember him.

But it hurts. Dragging myself to a place where he isn't. Pretending like he can hear me. *It hurts.*

"Just because that's how other people want to honor their loved ones doesn't mean you have to do the same thing," I tell him. "It's more for the living anyway."

"How do you do it?" he asks, so earnest that my heart wedges itself into my throat.

I stare down at the space between us that's slowly been closing centimeters at a time. "I think I'm still trying to figure it out."

"I guess I am too..." He exhales. "But it's so fucking hard."

I erase those final few centimeters and wrap my arms around his neck, feeling the way his heart pounds beneath his shirt. Knowing that if they were notes, the ache inside us would be in perfect harmony. "I know." I say. "It's so *fucking* hard."

He leans back a little, letting me see his eyes. "I'm sorry."

My stare hovers at his lips. "Me too."

The porch light flicks on and we break apart.

Aarón shrugs his backpack. "I uh...I should probably get home."

"Yeah..."

He looks down and I take a step closer.

"You know we don't have to conquer all of our fears in a single night," I say.

"Maybe just one." Aarón leans down and then he brushes his lips against my cheek. "Good night, Mia."

"Good night, Aarón."

As I watch him walk away, I feel those notes again— the vibrations before they've even become a sound. Like when I'm breathing into the mouthpiece of my trumpet. The song just on the edge of my lips. Just about to begin...

11

Aaron

I CAN'T BELIEVE I KISSED HER LAST NIGHT.

The robot deadpans, "It was on the cheek."

"So?"

"*So* that's how you kiss your grandmother, not your secret crush."

Is the secret out now? Does she wish it wasn't?

I search my memory of her face for any sign of disgust. But all I remember is her leaning in. Her eyes lighting up. The soft smile on her lips as I turned to walk away.

Or maybe I'm wrong. Maybe she only felt bad for me and let me kiss her out of pity.

"Now you're thinking logically," the robot says.

I'm so consumed by the memory that I forget my panic attack from the night before. I forget everything rotten from the last twenty-four hours.

And it isn't until the bus pulls up to my stop that I finally remember.

Mr. V.

He won't be driving the bus today.

Or tomorrow.

Or ever.

I'm never going to see him again.

The doors screech open and I freeze. As the new driver looks me up and down, I'm hijacked by last night's fears all over again. But he doesn't swing or bite or call me a name. He just stares, his blue eyes piercing, his bottom lip stretched out like it's usually full of dip.

He finally jerks his head, motioning for me to get on the bus.

I'm surprised when I see that it's full. The other riders are quieter than usual. No chatter. No music humming from Mr. V's radio. Because there's no Mr. V.

Mr. V is gone. He's gone and he's not coming back.

The bus lurches forward, almost tossing me into one of the empty seats.

The old ladies who volunteer at the church are bunched in the back, rolling rosary beads. Mr. and Mrs. Molina are sitting by the window, carrying canvas bags for their trip to the grocery store. Flyers for local childcare and people selling home remedies are still pinned to the ceiling. The hearts and initials of kids who think they're in love are still etched in permanent marker on the seat backs.

Everything about the bus is exactly the same except for who's driving it.

I can't stop looking at him, at the buzz cut beneath his baseball cap, at the wrinkles on his forehead that are all I can make out in the oversized rearview mirror. Until he looks up, catching me staring. His eyes don't stray, sizing me up too. My heartbeat ticks faster.

He winks.

I exhale.

At the next stop, our collective silence is interrupted by a guy and a girl boarding the bus carrying stacks of flyers.

"Don't make eye contact." The robot snaps open the biggest newspaper I've ever seen and pretends to read.

The guy tries to hand me one. "Are you free on the twenty-eighth?"

A guy in grease-stained coveralls groans. "Great. Traffic's gonna be shit that day."

Mr. Molina shakes his head. "You take the bus, pendejo. Why would you be worried about the traffic?" He snatches a flyer from the guy dressed like a hipster, scans it before holding it out and scanning it again. He nudges Mrs. Molina. "¿Qué es eso?"

She answers back in Spanish, building a wall between us and the front of the bus where the new driver glances back in his rearview mirror. "It's a protest."

The hipster switches to Spanish too, drawing wide eyes from the other riders. "It's about the raids and the police working with ICE."

"They're not supposed to do that in a sanctuary city," the girl with him says.

I recognize her voice instantly. *Esther Pineda*. We had

US Government together last semester. She raised her hand constantly, always picking fights with the male students, with Mr. Bullock. She was smarter than all of them. I heard she got a scholarship to a big university.

"I'll be working a double." Coveralls hands back the flyer he's holding. "It's fucked up what happened to Mr. V, but I can't lose the hours."

"We understand," Esther says. Then a little quieter, she adds, "They'd pay you more if you had papers."

His brow furrows, agitated, maybe even a little afraid. "I got papers. Besides, some little walk around the block ain't gonna change a goddamned thing. You know that, right?"

Downtown, there are protests every other week, guilt usually dragging out every twentysomething with an affinity for breakfast tacos or boba or any other slightly "ethnic" food. The fact that they call it "ethnic" food is all the proof I need to know that their alliance is as fragile as their egos. But they do it for the gram. For the free T-shirt. For the good night's sleep.

As I watch Esther and her hipster boyfriend handing out flyers, I wonder what they think will be different this time.

"It'll change things all right," Mr. Molina says. "For the worse. Life around here's already hell for most people and now you're just gonna go and—"

"Enough!" Mrs. Molina swats at him. "If the kids want to go and protest, that's their right."

He huffs at her, "You want ICE knocking on our door in the middle of the night?"

Coveralls rolls his eyes. "You think they'll actually have the decency to knock?"

"That's why we're marching." Esther looks between them both. "I'm tired of lying awake at night too. I'm tired of being afraid. Which is why I'm going to march right up to one of those police officers, show him I'm flesh and blood just like he is, that I'm a human being. And if he wants to arrest me in front of all of those people, I won't stop him. I won't run or hide. I can't do it anymore."

I didn't know Esther was undocumented. I've known her since we were in kindergarten, which means her parents must have brought her here when she was even younger, probably still a baby. If ICE sent her back to Mexico, would she even know anyone? Would her hipster boyfriend go with her? What would happen to her scholarship?

I can tell by the hard look in her eyes that she's thought about all of these things, that printing these flyers, handing them out, organizing this protest is her way of trying to answer these questions before someone else answers them for her.

I think about the questions I should be answering: Where was I when they took Mr. V? What did I do about it? What *should* I be doing about it?

Maybe Mr. Molina and Coveralls are right and this protest won't change a thing, or worse, it'll make things even harder than they were before. But if we do nothing, if we don't even try, things will definitely get worse.

Last night, I was relieved when I could use chasing after Mia as an excuse not to go through with my audition. What's at stake if I make excuses now?

Esther glances in my direction, just for a second, but it's long enough for me to decide that I don't want to make excuses anymore. It's long enough for me to say, "I'll be there."

"Thanks," she says.

The bus slows to another stop. Mr. and Mrs. Molina head for the doors with their grocery bags. But not before Mrs. Molina squeezes Esther's arm. "I'll pray for you."

Esther squeezes her hand. "Gracias, Señora."

■■■■■■■■■■■

Mr. Barrero's trumpet begins to wail like he's leading them all into battle. Then Gabriel jumps in on the Spanish guitar. The notes are like two birds in flight, soaring before swooping straight down. Then comes the accordion, Gabriel letting out un grito while Gina muscles the instrument in and out. Naomi on the steel guitar comes in next while Osmin smooths it all out with percussion. They sway back and forth, totally vibing—even the robot can't help but move his hips—but just when I think the chorus is coming, the sound evaporates.

"Hey"—the robot throws up his hands—"I was dancing to that!"

"What happened?" I say, switching off the record button. "That was incredible."

Osmin's face goes red. Then he throws down his güiro and mallet. "Naomi, how many times are you going to come in late?"

Naomi glares at him. "I can't keep time if Gabriel won't."

"Me?" Gabriel huffs. "Gina's right in my ear. I can barely hear Marcelo!"

"Enough!" I wave my hands in the air, trying to get their attention. "Y'all sound ridiculous!"

"See?" Osmin gestures to me. "He agrees. We sound terrible."

"No." I shake my head. "No, I meant the fighting. Y'all sound ridiculous because that song was...it was incredible." I dig the flyer that Esther gave me out of my backpack, holding it up for them to see. "Two organizers had a giant stack of these on the bus. I saw them taped to lampposts on my way here."

Gina snatches it, reads the small print. "There's a lot of performers on this list."

I nod. "Poets, politicians...it's a big deal."

Gabriel rips off his hat, slapping it against his knee. "You really think that many people will show up?"

"I don't know," I say. "There were mixed reviews. Some people don't think it will do any good."

"Been there," Osmin says. "I'm in my seventies and the world still doesn't look like I hoped it would."

"But it's better," Mr. Barrero says.

Gina jumps in, still staring at the flyer. "*Better*'s not good enough. They might not be forcing our kids to learn in a one-room shack or to change their names to something that's easier for their white teachers to pronounce..."

"Or repatriating us by the thousands," Naomi adds.

Gabriel nods. "Or lynching us in the town square."

"Ya." Osmin raises a hand. "The list goes on."

"Exactly," Gina says. "And every year they add more cruelty to the list. So things aren't better. Just different."

"And so are we." Mr. Barrero holds out his trumpet, examining the scuffs and scratches. "Like Osmin said, we're not those young kids anymore who were so certain their music would change the world. But we keep trying to sound like them."

"I thought that's what we were doing," Osmin says. "Trying to re-create the past, right down to the garage turned recording studio."

Mr. Barrero stares at an oil spot on the concrete, thinking. "Maybe that's not the way."

Gina raises an eyebrow. "So now it's okay if we sound like shit?"

Naomi snorts. "If that's the goal, Gabriel is definitely in the lead."

"¡Chinga!" Gabriel laughs. "I'm no rustier than you. How many acrylic nails have you lost since we started practicing?"

"At least my fingers can still keep up. Those sausages on your hands are going to pop a string right into Osmin's face. He's going to be sporting an eye patch at the protest."

Gina shrugs. "Sounds like an improvement to me."

"And it'll complete the pirate look," the robot adds.

They all erupt in laughter, Gabriel clutching his chest while his face turns as red as a tomato, Gina crossing her legs and gasping that she's about to pee her pants.

Osmin howls, "You're going to make me throw out my back."

"Okay, basta..." Mr. Barrero shakes his head. "Osmin's bones are too brittle for this."

This just makes them laugh harder, Naomi's mascara running down her face while Osmin hangs an arm on Gabriel's shoulder, trying to hold himself up.

"Mierda"—he throws his head back, gasping for air. "We're old."

"And if people hear that when we play," Mr. Barrero says, "that's okay. Because it's the truth."

Gina nods. "We can remember the past without going back there."

"That's what the music's supposed to be for, right?" Gabriel plucks a few strings on his guitar. "To make sure people don't forget."

Mr. Barrero riffs on his horn. "Where they come from."

Gina tickles the keys on her accordion. "The cost of leaving."

Osmin tosses his egg shaker from one hand to the other. "Who they want to be."

Gabriel lightly strums. "From the top?"

Osmin nods. "Listos."

◾ ◾ ◾ ◾ ◾ ◾ ◾ ◾ ◾ ◾ ◾

I've never been inside the county jail before today, but it looks exactly like I thought it would—gray walls, gray floors, gray cells. A hallway of them recedes from behind the front desk. A woman with thick glasses smacks on a piece of bright green gum while she types, an eyebrow raised in my direction as I sit there, trying to take up as little space as possible.

"You make yourself small in a place like this, you'll be the first to go." The robot feigns the sound of bones breaking and it turns my stomach.

"Are you Aarón?" A man in a crisp suit and bowtie reaches out a hand.

I reach back. "Yeah…"

"Seems we have a mutual friend."

A swarm of butterflies erupts in my stomach at the word *friend*. Once again, Xavier gave me nothing but an address and vague instructions—*Give him their names.*

"Seems there was a raid last night."

I swallow. *Shit. Am I being arrested?*

The robot groans. "Jesus, I've got to teach you how to keep a straight face."

The man lowers his voice, cleans his glasses. "To which you were an eyewitness, is that right?"

I can't speak, too afraid of saying the wrong thing and ending up in one of those cells too. Mia and I ran before the arrests started so I have no idea how many people they rounded up.

"Relax. I'm here to bail them out. I just need you to tell me who."

I exhale, nodding fast. "I can do that."

He approaches the receptionist. "I'm here to see Officer Solis." He turns to me. "Another friend of our mutual friend."

Really? Xavier and Officer Solis?

I've known Officer Solis since as long as I can remember. He grew up here and he's the only police officer anyone feels safe enough to report a crime to these days. Not just because he speaks our language but because his parents are immigrants too.

He comes down the long hallway of cells, looking very unamused. "Apparently, I've been summoned."

The lawyer gives him a crooked smile before dropping a duffel bag onto the counter.

Officer Solis unzips it. It's full of cash.

"Xavier sends his best."

Officer Solis riffles through the bills. "And he had to send it in ones?"

"In his words, he loves you like a brother, but you're still a cop."

The robot cackles. "Man, I'm hilarious."

Officer Solis deadpans, "Got it."

The secretary takes the duffel bag of cash and starts counting while the lawyer and I go through all of the mug shots taken from the night before. Officer Solis even lets us see the outtakes. Javi vogues like he's on *RuPaul's Drag Race*. There's his brother Juice flipping the bird, teeth gritted so his gold fronts sparkle. Noni winks right at the camera, tongue out.

I point out everyone I recognize, and the lawyer writes down their names and booking numbers. It isn't long before they're all filing out with trash bags of their belongings, whatever tech or jewelry they were stripped of on the way in.

But no one's voguing or winking or even smiling. They're wide-eyed but exhausted; dazed and disheveled.

Because they were scared. They still teem with it. Like the night isn't over. Like it never will be.

And there's Officer Solis, head down as they pass, like he's reliving something too.

Javi turns to him. "You better hold tight to that fucking badge." Then a little quieter. "It's not just us they want to get their hands on."

"I think I can take it from here, Aarón." The lawyer shakes my hand again. "Thanks for your help."

The secretary shoves the empty duffel bag over to the lawyer with a grunt. "I believe this is yours."

"Thank you."

"Oh, and this." She holds up a large silver key. "It was in the bag too."

"Actually, that's not mine," the lawyer says.

"Then whose is it?" I ask.

He tips his chin at me. "It's yours."

■ ■ ■ ■ ■ ■ ■ ■ ■ ■ ■

The key is embossed with an address just a few blocks from the county jail. When I arrive, Virginia Regia and her cat, Chocó, are sitting in the alcove of the small stucco building sandwiched between the Loco Lavado Laundromat and Doña Josefa's café.

"You're late," she says, beating her skirt as she gets to her feet.

"Am I?"

She waves a hand, hurrying me to the door. "Well, go ahead. I don't have all day."

I hold up the key and smile like I know what I'm doing and why we're here. But I don't. Even as I slide in the key, teeth fitting perfectly, and push the door open to reveal a dark dusty space on the other side, I'm still not sure.

Until Señora Regia flips on the lights.

"Ay Dios." She grabs my arm, almost falling over. "Chocó, venga, venga. ¡Ay cielos!"

Sunlight streams through the windows and lands on the empty glass display case. It's backlit and glowing, just waiting for Señora Regia's pink and orange conchas. Behind it is a tall counter with a cash register. She presses a button on the screen, and the money drawer pops out with a ding. It's full of cash and she fans the bills, pressing them to her face.

She drops them when she sees the commercial ovens. Sparkling and silver, they make it look like we're inside a spaceship. There's an entire counter topped with bright red mixers and a refrigerator that's bigger than us both. Chocó jumps up onto a tall pan rack as Señora Regia rushes to check out the pantry. It's fully stocked, and she holds on to the door frame to keep herself upright, wrecked with laughter and then sobs.

"Es maravilloso." She cups my face before clasping her hands in prayer. "Gracias a Dios."

Suddenly, my body wants to come apart and it's so unfamiliar that I almost think I'm about to be sick. But then I close my eyes, letting the feeling come to the surface. Pulling it toward the light so I can see it up close.

Joy.

None of this was my doing. I don't deserve her

gratitude. And yet, it feels like I helped manufacture some kind of miracle.

"And that's not all." The robot stands next to an exit door, holding a microphone and doing his best Game Show Host impersonation. "It's time to guess what's behind door number two. Could it be a trip to Hawaii? Or what about a brand...new...car?"

Señora Regia opens the door to a concrete patio, small metal tables lined up against the wall outside. And on that wall, in colors so bright they burn my eyes, is her face.

She marvels at the eight-foot portrait, the defiant smile drawing tears. She presses a hand to the paint. "They think they can do whatever they want to us because we're invisible..." She cups my face again. "But we *see* each other."

Señora Regia is right, and the longer I look the more I find. The past. The present. The future. I see it all in Señora Regia's eyes and I know she sees the same in mine. Because I carry all of it with me in every moment.

But only because people like her and Mr. Barrero carried it first.

When I finally turn to go, there's a small crowd gathered, people celebrating with Señora Regia, crying with her too.

I slip back inside and the robot's still dressed in his Game Show Host getup. "There's still one more prize for you too," he says.

That's when I spot the envelope on the counter. My name is on the front and I trace the handwriting, ink slightly raised. I slide my finger in, ripping it open, and out clanks another key.

12

Mia

"IT'S TOO TIGHT, JAZZY! YOU'RE GONNA CUT OFF the circulation."

I find Jazzy and Andrés in the living room. When they see me, Jazzy's fingers slip off the strings of Andrés's luchador mask, the one he shamed him for wearing because he said it made him a coward.

"You can at least wait to put it on after you've gotten to the club," I say.

"Ruins the mystery. Someone might see me."

Someone might see me. I want to ask him, as earnestly as possible, what's so terrible about that, and not because I want to give him a hard time again but because I *need* to know: Why can't I do it? Why can't I play if I know people are watching? Why can't he do it either?

Jazzy examines me more closely. "We missed you last night. How did your...?"

"It didn't." I slump down on the couch, arms crossed like a child. Like the little girl who used to jump off the armrest and body-slam Andrés while he sat on the floor watching WWE. When he was honest about his luchador mask being a costume. When we were honest about everything.

Andrés sits down next to me. "I'm sorry it didn't go like you planned." I know he means it and I know it hurts him that this is a problem he can't fix for me. Not like the bills he works so hard to pay or the house that constantly needs repairing.

Jazzy throws on an apron. "Sopapillas coming right up. Then we'll watch Selena and cry it all out."

"It's not just the audition." The previous night starts to play in reverse. The panic pressed against my ribs at the edge of the cemetery. The fire in the street. Mr. V being dragged out of his home. "I saw them take Mr. V."

Jazzy comes to sit on the other side of me. "I heard from the girls at the salon. Everyone's still in shock."

"Yeah, well they shouldn't be." Andrés rests his forearms on his knees. "It was only a matter of time before they started going after people with papers. Because it was never about that." He straightens, arms outstretched the same way Javi's were when he was letting himself become a target. Begging the people behind those windows to take their shot. "It's about this. About this body. About the fact that it doesn't belong to them."

"Is that why you and your poetry group are going out tonight?" Jazzy asks. "You're not a superhero, Andrés. With or without the mask."

Andrés looks down, whatever resolve that had him digging that mask out of his sock drawer slowly waning. But then he shakes his head. "No, not them." He locks eyes with me. "Us. *We're* going out."

" 'We?' " Jazzy wags a finger between the three of us. "*We're* going out *together?*"

Andrés's eyes are still locked on me and they glisten with an apology, with apprehension. Then he says, "There's something I have to show you."

■ ■ ■ ■ ■ ■ ■ ■ ■ ■ ■

When we get to Spider House Ballroom the place is already packed. Stepping over the threshold is like stepping inside a womb. The walls are draped in red, the color ricocheting off the metal tiles stamped to the ceiling. There are chandeliers and disco balls and Christmas lights, synthetic stars vomited into every corner of the place.

For some reason it makes the crowd feel even more dense or maybe I'm just absorbing Andrés's fear. Maybe I'm still drenched in my own from last night. Andrés is just as drenched, sweat already pouring through his luchador mask.

"Andrés!" A Black woman waves from a circular booth in the back. "You slamming tonight?" She squeals as we approach.

Andrés just nods, his eyes darting from one corner of the room to the other. He looks like prey searching for the scope of a rifle.

"Have a seat." The woman and the mustached man next to her scoot over to make room. "You look like you need a drink."

"Or ten," Jazzy adds, tossing his purse into the booth. "He almost turned the car around three times."

But he *didn't*. For some reason my brother is choosing to endure this agony. I scan the growing crowd, people filling seats near a small stage. I don't want to think about what'll happen when he actually goes up in front of them.

"Just relax." The woman squeezes his arm before reaching out a hand to me. "I'm Celeste."

"Mia." Her hand is cold from her mixed drink. "Nice to meet you."

"Andrés says you're a performer too."

I shift uncomfortably in my seat. "Oh, no..."

"She means she's not a poet," Jazzy corrects me. "She plays the trumpet."

The mustached man quirks an eyebrow. "Jazz or classical?"

"Both," I say coolly.

He nods. "Dope."

"I'd love to hear you play sometime," Celeste says.

The crowd erupts in applause, someone taking the stage. I don't hear what he says next, I'm too busy staring at Andrés who is also not listening. I can tell because he's sweating even more than he was before, his eyes glassy like he's just ridden the world's highest roller coaster. Or maybe he's about to, the massive drop just inches away.

Celeste waves a hand in front of his face.

Jazzy dabs at the eyeholes of his mask with a napkin, trying to mop up the sweat.

The clapping starts to peter out, bodies turning as everyone searches the room. They're waiting for the opening act and when Andrés can barely open his mouth, when he can barely move at all, I know it's him.

My stomach sinks, nerves buzzing. He faces me and I try to stop my eyes from telling him to run. I know he wants to. When he finally stands, I think he might. But then he squeezes my shoulder, grimacing against the fear, and then he heads for the stage.

And I remember his words: *There's something I have to show you.*

Andrés steps in front of the microphone and makes the mistake of looking out at the crowd. It's practically impossible not to, the first row of chairs pulled right up to the stage.

He breathes against the microphone. "Test."

Someone from the crowd yells, "The emcee just used it!"

Someone else calls out, "What's with the mask?"

I hear someone grumble, "Maybe what's underneath is worse."

I thought that when people became adults their insults would mature as well, but suddenly I'm having flashbacks to the middle school cafeteria, a place I loathed with such ferocity that I snuck off campus every lunch period to eat with Andrés in the bed of his pickup truck. He showed up every day at 11:45 AM with two avocado sandwiches on white bread, crusts cut off.

As I watch him, still frozen in front of that microphone, I realize that it was then, in the bed of his pickup truck, him shielding me from the monsters of my middle school cafeteria, that we began to cling to the fear as fiercely as we clung to each other. That we began to hide and make excuses. That we began to give up. Together.

I can't let him give up.

Suddenly, I'm standing beneath a slowly turning disco ball.

I lock eyes with Andrés. *Show me. Please.*

He inhales and then, "They say..." There is no punch, the words just hanging there. He stutters out the next line: "Y-you must p-pay with the tongues of your children."

And I know in an instant. It's about our parents. About the cost of coming here. All they had to shed.

*Chew you up and then spit you out
So, baby, don't open your mouth
You don't know what you're talking about*

They say

Speak English or get the fuck out

They say

*It's the land of the free if you listen
It's the land of the free if you're with them
So you'll never be free if you're different*

*You must pay with the tongues of your children
Cut them out and hope they don't miss them*

I try to imagine what our parents would think of us now. Desperately trying to make things. Trying to wrestle our emotions into a poem or a song or a kiss. Would they warn us that it's dangerous? That no matter what we do, what we think we're made of, the world will break us the same way it broke them?

Or would they be proud? Would they watch us in wonder? Would we remind them of who they used to be?

All of a sudden I need to *know*. I need to know that they would understand. That maybe that's why they left us. Because they tried to make something—a future, a family—and they couldn't do it. They couldn't make what they imagined and it killed them.

What if I let this thing inside me do the same?

But you can't stop the bleeding

Walking wounds that can't say what the pain is
Name what the shame is

Your Name, they take that shit too
Give you something shiny and new
Until you're more them
than you are you

People shift forward in their seats, gripping their knees like Andrés is taking them on a ride.

He is.

Right up until the last line. Until there's nothing coming through the speakers but the sound of his breathing.

And as his voice disintegrates, suddenly there are cheers, the sound ricocheting off the walls.

Andrés steps offstage, shaking and still sweating but also brimming with something...*else*. Something that has him chasing his breath. And hugging me. He pulls me against his chest and then we're laughing, Jazzy squealing as he reaches his arms around us both.

"What was that!" Jazzy squeezes tighter. "*Who* are you?"

Andrés is grinning from ear to ear and then all of a sudden he lets go of us, stumbling back. He clutches his stomach, face pale. Then he rushes for the bathroom and from behind the small door I hear him retch.

"He was great," Celeste says, cackling. "Wait"—she bangs on the door to the bathroom—"are you puking in there?"

Andrés waddles back out.

I catch him by the shoulders. "You did it."

He hugs me again, breathing into my hair. "I had to show you."

My throat aches. "*Thank you.*"

Cheers for the next slam poet follow us outside. We sit beneath another mess of lights, someone playing the guitar and singing softly on the platform between the club and the adjacent café.

"You were incredible," Celeste says. "I've got a spot open for you in a couple of weeks. Just say the word."

"What's happening in a couple of weeks?" Jazzy asks.

"A bunch of local artists are gathering downtown for a peaceful demonstration," Celeste explains.

Jazzy raises an eyebrow. "You mean a protest..."

"We can't just sit back and do nothing," I say, remembering Esther and the other organizers at the library. "Not after they took Mr. V."

"Andrés told us about your neighbor," Celeste says. "I'm so sorry about that." She exhales. "But sorry's not good enough anymore. We've got to start making some noise or else Austin won't be a sanctuary city anymore."

"So what?" Jazzy shrugs. "You guys are going to read a couple of poems and then...?"

I elbow Jazzy in the side. "Rude much?"

Celeste nods to the Mustache. "James is printing flyers with tons of action items to help people engage in their own personal protest. But the most important thing is for people to come together and see that they're not alone." She squeezes Andrés's forearm. "That's why I hope you'll consider performing. You have something to say. Something people need to hear."

"Do you...?" I'm not sure how to ask, so I just do. "Do you really think it makes a difference?"

"The protesting?" Celeste asks.

"The poetry," I clarify. "Do you really think it can help people?"

She wrinkles her nose, examining me more closely. "Let me guess. Stage fright runs in the family?"

"Oh, you're good," Jazzy says.

Celeste laughs. "Andrés may have mentioned it."

My face reddens. "What else did he mention?"

"That you've all been through a lot. I can't help but

think that your art played a big part in pulling you out of it."

Out.

Out implies going *through*, but I don't feel like I'm on the other side of anything. Not when seeing my brother tremble onstage only reminds me of how afraid we both are of getting hurt. But does his poetry temper it somehow, make it easier to swallow? I don't know if playing music has saved me from anything. All I know is that when I'm not playing, I'm not me.

"I'm not saying that art can heal all wounds," Celeste says. "But it can make you forget you have them for a little while."

"Or it can help you remember," Jazzy adds.

I know he's thinking about what Andrés said about our parents. How many times has he summoned their ghosts to paint them with words?

Sometimes when I've been practicing for hours, time fluid within my four bedroom walls, the notes will slip into something my mother used to love. My ears will finally register the melody and then my lips will fall off the mouthpiece. As if I'd been breathing with her lungs instead of my own. And in those moments, I remember everything.

But it hurts to remember, to sense her in pieces. It feels like grasping at glass.

"That too," Celeste says. "But hopefully, in that remembering, we're reminded that there's beauty in the pain. That it happens to all of us." She turns to me. "How long have you been playing the trumpet?"

"Since I was eight."

"She's amazing," Jazzy says matter-of-factly, eyes signaling that I'm not allowed to argue.

"Sounds like you've got a gift."

I stare at my shoes. "I don't know. . . ."

"Andrés said the same thing the first time I asked him if he'd like to read something. He could have said no, but instead he left himself a trap door. A way through when he finally felt ready." She leans closer. "It's okay not to know things, Mia. It's okay to be unsure, to doubt yourself. But one day you'll grow tired of the uncertainty. That's when you'll remember the trap door and finally step through it."

13

Aarón

THE SECOND KEY WAS ATTACHED TO A POST OFFICE box and inside were more than a dozen envelopes. I didn't realize they were full of cash until Deb Casarez opened the first one and immediately burst into tears.

But she isn't the last person to hug me. I'm assaulted by them practically everywhere I go—when I drop off an envelope of cash to Speedy and his family, another to Carlos Montoya who organizes Monte Vista's Little League baseball tournament, and then to Casa Marianella, and La Puerta Abierta. I drop off money to business owners and community organizers and single moms. All of them in shock. All of them grateful.

I get so many hugs. But in the middle of each embrace I can't help but deflate, knowing that Xavier's out there somewhere, orchestrating all of this from a distance. Why isn't he the one doing all of these good deeds?

"Maybe they're not just good deeds," the robot says.

"What do you mean?"

"I mean falling off the grid for almost a year and then suddenly popping up out of nowhere to redistribute my wealth doesn't seem like something a normal person would do, does it?"

"Xavier's always been generous," I argue.

"Not like this…"

I don't know why Xavier chose now. I don't know why he chose me. But what I do know is this to-do list has to be the key to finding him and if I just keep following these breadcrumbs, it'll eventually all make sense. Me. Him. *Everything*. It will finally all make sense.

I step past the robot and through the entrance of my next destination. It smells like sawdust and hot coals, men with masks holding blue flames over metal sculptures.

"How can I help you?" An old man with hands like two leather baseball mitts leans over the counter.

"I'm here to pick up a package," I say.

He looks me up and down and nods once before slipping behind a curtain to the back of the store. He must know why I'm here.

He comes back out and sets a heavy box down on the counter between us.

"What is it?" I ask.

He shrugs.

I lug the box out of the store and all the way home before letting myself take a peek inside. I toss it on my bed, the mattress bouncing under the weight. Then I lift the lid and realize why it was so heavy. It's full of stones.

"Let me guess," the robots says. "He wants you to break out someone's windows."

"We interacted with a criminal *one time*," I groan, "and she wasn't even really a criminal. She was an artist."

He huffs. "Same thing."

"Also, why are you so happy to take the credit when Xavier does something cool like bail people out of the county jail with a bunch of one-dollar bills and then when he does something you don't like, suddenly you're speaking in the third person?"

"Because my relationship with myself is complicated, all right? You should be able to understand that more than anybody."

"Well, it's confusing as hell."

"*You're* confusing as hell."

"Whatever."

"Whatever." He mimics me in a whiny voice.

I ignore him, rotating the box to see that there are coordinates written on the underside of the lid. I plug them into my phone and zoom in on the satellite image.

"Oh, hell no," the robot says, looking over my shoulder. "You are *not* dragging me through that cemetery."

My mouth goes dry. "Why does he want me to go to the cemetery?"

"He doesn't." The robot slams the lid closed. "*I don't*. It's a mistake."

"It's not a mistake.... It can't be...."

My skin feels hot. I remember the other night when Mia had to drag me away from the cemetery's edge. We weren't even on the grounds. I couldn't even see my mother's tombstone, and yet I felt my throat closing up anyway.

But there's no way Xavier López could know that I'm terrified of stepping foot in that place.

"Have you stopped to consider that he still doesn't even know who you are? You're running errands for him. This is not a two-way exchange. You're not slowly becoming best friends with a complete stranger." The robot's talking too fast. Almost frantic. "Face it, Aarón. You're nobody and he's using you."

"Will you just shut up for once?" I grip my scalp, trying to concentrate, trying to figure out *how* I'm going to do this without having another panic attack.

As soon as I think the words, my body is already buzzing, the vertigo slowly creeping in. I close my eyes, breathing deep through my nose.

"Suit yourself." The robot still hovers over my shoulder. "If you want to be the one to discover my body in an unmarked grave, be my guest."

"What are you talking about?"

The robot shakes his head, stiff, like he's angry. "It's only going to upset you."

"All you do is upset me."

"True." He picks up one of the stones, tosses it to himself. "You know, I'm not the only voice in your head..." He looks me in my eyes. "There are others. Much quieter voices. More like whispers." He shrugs. "Maybe Xavier hears them too."

I step back, creating space between us.

As I stare at him, my skin crawls. Like he's some insect

that's needled its way inside me. And not just the parts of me shrouded in grief. But to the darkness underneath.

And I want to tell him: They're *not* voices. They're not *anything*.

But lying to him...would mean lying to myself. About how the sadness is a wave, pulling me under. How in that deep black darkness, I sometimes feel a nudge that makes me shudder. That sometimes it holds me beneath the surface...and I let it.

"You don't know what you're talking about." Another nudge. Another attempt at drowning out the truth. That sometimes I want to be with my mother more than I want to be in my own body.

"When it comes to you, I'm an expert," the robot says. "And my expert opinion is that you are so far down this rabbit hole that you can no longer see a way out."

We're caught in a silent standoff, the robot waiting for me to admit that he's right while I wait for the strength to prove that he's not. Maybe that's why Xavier's sending me to the cemetery—to get the proof I need, to do what I couldn't the night I bailed on my audition.

Or maybe the robot's right and Xavier's lost in that same darkness, waiting to see if I'll join him.

"You're playing with fire." The robot holds up his middle finger, the tip a small flame.

"I don't have time for this." I stuff the box of stones in my backpack and toss it over my shoulder.

"I'm sorry," the robot laughs. "You don't have *time* for a psychotic break? Well, I've got news for you, kid. You've been stuck in one since your mom died."

My throat is full of glass. I shove him, but he barely moves.

"That's not how you get rid of me."

I'm inches from his chest plate, the metal warping my reflection. All I can recognize are my eyes, wet and staring back at me.

"Look, kid, I didn't mean to make you cry."

I don't think. I rear back my fist, ramming it into his metal frame. The pain is instant. I groan, falling onto the bed.

"Whoa, whoa…take it easy. I told you, that's *not* how you get rid of me."

"Leave!" I scream.

He's confused. "Kid, I—" He doesn't move.

"Fine, then I'll leave." I grab my house keys and head for the front door.

I get to the cemetery a lot quicker than I was expecting. Mostly because I wasn't thinking about anything except putting one foot in front of the other. I didn't even wait for the bus. I just kept walking, kept pulling myself toward the impossible.

When I get there it's midday. The sun is shining and with the headstones blocked by the view of the church, it almost looks like a bunch of families enjoying a beautiful day at the park. But beneath their feet are bodies.

I duck behind a nearby tree, waiting for the mourners to leave their flowers and go. Another family enters the cemetery, children laughing and racing between the headstones with flowers gripped in their fists. And it doesn't make sense how they can carry any joy at all into this place while I cower behind a tree feeling sick.

The robot finally catches up to me. "Trying to outrun me is also *not* how you get rid of me."

I glance back down at my phone, measuring the distance between me and the coordinates. Then I force myself beyond the gate before walking down the third row, getting closer. Closer.

I stop, my body perfectly in line with the coordinates Xavier sent. I look down at the tombstone and read:

ILIANA LÓPEZ
1970-1998
MOTHER, DAUGHTER, FRIEND

Mother.

His mother.

Bile burns the back of my throat. I smell the thick medicinal lotion the nurses rubbed on my mother's rough hands. I hear doors opening and closing, never knowing if it was the doctor, if he was going to show his face that day, if he was going to tell us *It's soon.* I see her body, all sharp edges. I see her eyes, the fear in them that she tried to blink away every time we were looking. I see her in pieces. I see her in pain.

She was in *so much* pain.

And she couldn't run from it.

But in this moment, I can.

I can run from her pain. I can run from my own. And that's exactly what I do.

I grip my backpack tight and then I take off running.

"What about the stones?" The robot clanks behind me. "Where are you going?"

I don't know.

I don't know.

I don't know.

"Hey!" he calls after me. "Are you even *listening?*"

I am, because he's in my head, even though I desperately don't want him to be. I just want him to be quiet. To disappear. To go away.

Go away.

Go away.

Go away.

Go away!

I don't realize I'm on the ground until there's a shadow pouring over me. I don't realize I'm curled into a ball until the person taps me on the shoulder.

I look up. It's Officer Solis.

I don't realize I'm crying until he asks, "Are you all right?"

I scrape at my wet face and grip the brick wall behind me to hoist myself up.

"Aarón?"

"I'm fine," I say.

"Do you need a ride home?" he asks.

I just nod.

On the way back to my house, I can feel Officer Solis glancing over at me, but I keep my eyes on the street, trying not to catch a glimpse of my reflection in the window.

When he asks me, "You and Miguel getting along these days?" I realize he was probably searching me for bruises.

"We've never gotten along," I say.

"Brothers can be tough. I never had one, but I had plenty

of cousins. They always used to gang up on me because I was the youngest. That's probably one of the reasons I became a cop."

"So you could arrest them as revenge?" I ask.

He laughs. "No. I guess it was less about them and more about me. I knew what it felt like to be helpless, to be bullied. It made me more empathetic to other people going through the same thing."

We hit a red light and Officer Solis's gaze tightens on my La Maquina T-shirt.

Behind me, the robot's eyes light up, amused that someone besides me knows that he exists.

"So, uh, what exactly were you doing with Xavier's lawyer the other day?"

My body tenses like I'm being baited. Like I did something wrong.

"Have you spoken to Xavier?" he asks.

My mouth is dry. "Well, uh..."

He sighs. "Look, I've known Xavier a long time. We grew up together."

"Really?"

He nods. "Our parents were cousins. My father was protective of his mother, Iliana. I feel the same way about Xavier." He's quiet for a moment and in the silence I read the worry all over his body.

"I *think*...it's him."

He raises an eyebrow, waits for me to go on.

"We've only talked online, but he's been asking me to do things. Deliveries mostly."

"What kind of deliveries?"

"Gifts? The key to a new bakery for Virginia Regia. Envelopes full of cash..."

"How much cash?"

"A lot."

He shakes his head. "Has he told you where he is?"

"No. All he gives me is an address and I just sort of figure it out from there." My face gets hot. "It...it might not even be him."

Officer Solis takes the next turn slow. "No. It's him."

"How do you know?" I ask.

"Because this isn't the first time he's tried to unload his life."

"What do you mean?"

He glances over at me. "Nothing. Don't worry about it. Just...if he tells you where he is, if he asks you to do anything else, let me know."

"Do you think it's bad if he does? Asks me to do something else, I mean."

"Depends on what it is. He had demons." Officer Solis clenches his jaw. "*Has.*"

"I can hear it," I admit. "Maybe that's why I love his music so much. It's honest."

"He's nothing if not that." He examines my shirt again and it ignites a small smile. "You know, I remember when he came up with that whole persona. Xavier used to have the worst stage fright." He pinches one eye closed, remembering. "But it was right around the time when all these DJs were comin' out with these crazy costumes. That robot used to sit on the shelf above his bed. His father gave it to him."

"I thought Xavier didn't have a father."

"Everyone has a father. He just didn't have one for long."

"That's why he winds him up at the beginning of each show," I say. "Like a toy. It *was* a toy."

He nods. "And that's where the music comes from. Not from the man. From the boy." He stares at the faded robot on my T-shirt as if it might come to life right now, something in his memories winding it up like La Maquina used to do at the beginning of a show. "From that little lonely boy."

I feel like I know that little lonely boy. Or maybe he knows me. Maybe that's what I'm really hearing when I listen to his songs. An echo.

"Can you think of anywhere he might have gone?" I ask.

He pauses. "I've got a few ideas. Just let me know the next time he gets in touch. And if he starts trying to give away something...more sentimental than cash. All right?"

The robot taps the plastic barrier between me and the back seat, his voice muffled. "'Sentimental' as in stones for his mother's grave?"

I go cold, suddenly understanding what he meant by Xavier having demons. Suddenly understanding that more messages from Xavier aren't actually something to get excited about. Because they're not signs that we're connected, soulmates finding each other in the same digital universe. They're signs that he's hurting. Signs that he's trying to figure out how to make that hurting stop.

Officer Solis makes the turn down my street, the house coming into view.

Up ahead, my father's truck is in the driveway even though it's not supposed to be.

Officer Solis barely puts the car in park before I open the door.

"You've got my number," he says.

I nod. "Thanks for the ride."

My father steps out onto the front porch, eyes pinned to Officer Solis's cruiser as it turns the corner. "What was that about?"

"Nothing. He just gave me a ride home."

"He's not your friend, Aarón." He lowers his voice. "He chose his side. Do you understand?"

"He's not like the others." The second I say it, I know I shouldn't have.

"Do you think that's what they say about us? That some of us aren't so bad?"

"I don't know."

"That's right. You *don't* know."

Neither do you, I almost snap back, even though it's not true. My father *does* know. Because he has to. Because when the president puts a target on your back, everyone becomes a hunter. Because when the world is hunting you, knowing your enemy is the only safe way to walk among them.

"You should get inside," he suddenly says. "There's someone here to see you."

When I step inside, Mia is sitting on the couch. She smiles, gives me an awkward wave. My father attempts a smile that is just as awkward, and as he looks between the two of us, I know exactly what he's feeling. Relief.

Here is a pretty girl my age who has shown up on our doorstep specifically to see me, which means that whatever defects I may have now have the hope of being mended. Mia is hope. That I'm not irrevocably broken. That I'm normal. That I'm a man.

Miguel steps into the living room, yawning and rubbing the sleep from his eyes. At first, he doesn't even notice Mia.

Then our father says, "Grab your shoes, Miguel."

"But we practiced this morning."

"And now we're gonna practice again." He picks up the basketball by the door, heaves it at Miguel. "You think your teammates are sitting on their asses on a Saturday afternoon?"

Suddenly, it clicks and Miguel looks from me to Mia. My father's trying to leave us alone together.

"But—"

"No buts. Grab your stuff."

Miguel stomps off, snatching his basketball shoes off the floor.

My father takes Mia's hand, more delicate than I've ever seen him. "It was nice to meet you, Mia."

"Nice to meet you too," she says.

My father heads out to his truck, whistling for Miguel to hurry up.

Miguel storms back through the living room. He stops, scowling at me. Then he shifts his glare to Mia. "He won't even know what to do with you." Then he throws open the door and jogs out to the truck.

Mia stares after him. "*Charming.*"

I let out a nervous laugh. "Yeah, well that's Miguel."

I try to appear less uncomfortable, but I can't stop staring at her hands—remembering her beneath that spotlight, our proximity to the stars, to each other—igniting their own sparks.

Then, Mia's voice a half whisper, she asks, "Is it okay that I came?"

"Of course it's okay."

"She's not just here to see you, Romeo." The robot nudges the coffee table.

Beneath it, I see Mia's trumpet case. My heart sinks a little.

She looks down at it too. "I thought...well, I was wondering if I could record something."

"Like music?"

"Uh..." she laughs a little. "Yeah, like music."

My face flushes. "Um, well, my recording equipment is in my room." I stare at the hall, at the shadow of my bedroom door, but I can't bring myself to get up.

Mia notices. "Are you not allowed to have girls in your room?"

"My father just dragged Miguel to the gym with him so we'd be alone. I don't think he'll mind if we go in my room."

"Well?" She pulls her trumpet case into her lap, waiting for me to lead the way.

"Uh...give me two minutes."

My room is already semiclean, just a few dirty clothes on the floor. I toss them into the hamper and then I spin in a circle, trying to assess the potential damage. What will

Mia think when she sees the lights? Or the clues connected with string. Or the La Maquina memorabilia.

The robot leans against the wall, as smug as ever. "I think the bigger question is, what will she think when she finds out about me?"

"She isn't going to find out about you because I'm going to get rid of you."

"All right," he raises both hands, "as long as you've got a plan."

I don't have a plan and he knows it. But I'll figure one out.

"Aarón?" Mia knocks, the door pushing open a few inches. "Did you say something?"

"What?"

The robot whispers in my ear, "Busted."

I back up, letting Mia inside. "No, I didn't say any-thing." I sit down in front of my computer. "Let me open the program."

As I suspected, she's not looking at me. She's looking at the lights, strung from one corner of the room to the other, at the photographs and news clippings. She is sitting inside my brain, taking inventory, and I have no idea what she's thinking.

"Wow." She smiles. "You know, this is not what I expected...but it should have been. Everything's so..."

I cringe. "Weird?"

She meets my eyes. "Honestly, it's not weird enough." She moves to get a closer look at the photographs, her pointer finger grazing the string connecting them to one another. "I heard no one's seen him in months."

"Eleven. It's been eleven months."

She looks back at me. "And these are clues? You're trying to find him?"

I don't know how to explain it in a way that doesn't make me seem like a total stalker. "People are worried about him. I am too. . . ."

"What do you mean?"

As Mia's eyes flit from one clue to the next, she doesn't look on with pity or disgust. She looks on . . . in wonder. Like she can see the way I'm trying to make the pieces fit. Like she doesn't think I'm ridiculous for trying to put the puzzle together in the first place.

So I tell her. About Xavier and the money and the murals and the protest. I tell her about Frankie Fernandez and how La Maquina's song "Starfish" changed my life. I tell her about my own songs, all the love letters I never thought I'd send. And somehow, I even tell her about the way we are connected. How Xavier's mom died when he was just a kid like me.

I don't mention the robot or my breakdown at the cemetery.

But I do muster up enough courage to say, "I see myself in him. Not just in the music. But in the way he's disappeared. Some days, I want to disappear too."

Mia moves closer, her eyes glistening and sad. "Please don't." She swallows, looks down. "We have more auditions to blow." She bites back a smile, blushing. "More promises to make."

"Like what?"

She tugs on the bill of my baseball cap. "I don't know

yet. All I know is that wherever I'm going...you're supposed to be there too."

"I'd like that," I say.

We are inches from each other and all my body wants to do is reach for her. Like it already knows how we fit.

Mia looks up at me. She leans in. Our noses touch and then she laughs, going red again.

"It looks like mistletoe." She turns in circles beneath a knot of lights. "What are these for exactly?"

For a minute, I just stand there, reeling from her proximity, from our lips almost crashing into each other. She blinks, waiting for me to answer, and I rush to turn on my keyboard. I hold down a G and watch her face as the lights blink on. Then I press down on an F-sharp, switching back and forth.

"It's amazing," she breathes. She unlocks her trumpet case and plugs a cable into her recorder. "Will it work if I...?"

I nod, taking the other end and plugging it into the converter box.

She rests her lips on the mouthpiece, inhales, and then she lets out a spirally riff. The lights dance. She laughs, losing hold of the mouthpiece.

"It's like magic."

"It's not magic," the robot corrects her. "It's electricity and ones and zeros."

I flash him a look. Because I can see in her eyes that she needs something to believe in.

"Do you know what you want to record?" I ask.

She grows still. "At first...I thought maybe my audition piece. I thought that if I recorded it and played it back,

I might hear what everyone else does. You know, instead of the mistakes."

"But you changed your mind?"

"I'm trying to. Right now my mind feels like this part of myself I can't control. I try to tell it to do something and it does the opposite. I try to tell it not to be afraid and it forces me to run three blocks and climb a fire escape."

"Sounds familiar," the robot muses. "Hey, maybe you *should* tell her about me. Maybe she's got an imaginary friend too."

"What's wrong?" Mia asks.

I realize I've been glaring at the robot she can't see. I shake my head. "Nothing. I just...I think I know what you mean."

"So, you don't think I'm crazy...?"

"Not at all."

She grows quiet, her gaze down. "I guess that's why I'm really here. Looking for proof."

"That you're not crazy?" I ask.

"That I *am*. That I'm crazy for thinking my music sucks. I need to know that the little voice inside my head is lying to me."

I look from her to my computer screen. "Want me to count you in?"

She nods but it's more like a grimace.

"Okay, I'm recording in one...two..." I motion for her to begin playing.

She grips her trumpet. She rests her lips on the mouthpiece. But she doesn't make a sound.

I wait and slowly her lungs summon something silksmooth, like pouring honey down my insides.

She guides the sound in and out, knowing exactly where to let the notes break, where to tie them into knots. She finesses them into tight spaces and blows them up like a balloon. The sounds are big and small and breathtaking.

They swell around me and now I'm sitting inside *her* brain. Taking inventory the same way she did when she stepped inside my room. The sound reaches a crescendo, waves crashing down over our heads. I let myself drown.

When Mia finally comes up for air, a smile cuts into her cheeks, as if she's still vibrating with the thing she just made. She breathes deep and I sense the vibrations too, the feeling rippling off me like raindrops over a still pond.

"That felt good," she finally says.

I adjust the lights, brightening the room.

"That's what I want to record," she says. "No more performance pieces. *That* feeling. That's what I want to make."

I look at her, earnest. "I don't think you have a choice."

"Maybe I don't," she says. "Or maybe it's no longer a choice between playing and not playing. It's a choice about why."

I look up at the lights again, thinking about all of the things that end and die and change. That leave behind questions the size of black holes. And I realize that "Maybe that's all life is." I meet Mia's eyes again. "Figuring out the why."

She asks, "Have you found yours?"

My first instinct is to say no. But the longer I stare at her, the closer I feel to answering *all* of my questions. The closer I feel to truth.

Mia's not just the girl I've been in love with since

second grade, but she's the feeling I've been chasing since my mother died. She's the promises I've been too afraid to make. She's the remedy to this black-and-white world. She's the North Star my mother used to point out in the night sky.

"You're never lost," she would say. "Not *really*."

That's how Mia makes me feel.

Found.

"I know I don't have a great track record when it comes to making promises," she says. "But I think we should make another one. One we can't break no matter what."

"What's that?"

She cradles her trumpet. "To help each other find our why."

"Deal," I say, desperate for something else to bind us together. Something that might be too strong for my delusions to break.

Mia begins to play again, not bothering to watch the notes as they manifest on my computer screen. She keeps her eyes closed for the next two hours, feeling her way through an ocean dark and deep. I'm submerged in it too, watching her float in a sea of sound. And it's the most beautiful thing I've ever heard. Because it's true. Every note, every flaw, every breath. Mia is turned inside out and she is beautiful.

■ ■ ■ ■ ■ ■ ■ ■ ■ ■ ■

"You'll send it to me tonight?" she asks as she packs up her trumpet.

"It shouldn't take me too long to mix."

"Okay, good."

"*Good* is right," the robot says. "Now I can finally get some peace and quiet."

Mia looks past me, eyes narrowed. My heart stops. *Can she see him?*

Then she looks down at my hands.

I didn't notice the scabs before, knuckles pink, blood barely dry. I look behind me and see the hole.

Gaping. Staring right at me.

No. No. I didn't—I couldn't—

I flex my fingers, sore now that I can see the wounds.

I'd been aiming for the robot, for metal. Instead, my hand had gone through plaster.

Because he isn't real.

Because he isn't *real.*

Mia takes my hand in hers, careful as she examines the cuts. And I wish she would just say the thing behind her eyes. I wish she would just say, "You're broken and I can't fix you." But she doesn't.

"Aarón…"

I feel like one of those people who march themselves into the ER, demanding to have a part of their body cut off because they're certain it doesn't belong to them. These scars…they don't belong to me.

"I'm fine." I can't meet her eyes.

Her phone starts buzzing.

"You should get that," I say.

"Not if you need me."

I do, I want to say. *So much.* But that wouldn't be fair. I have to figure this shit out myself. *I* have to. I *have* to.

But how?

"I need to be at work soon anyway." I can't tell if she knows I'm lying, but when her phone starts ringing again she doesn't argue.

"What time do you get off?" she asks.

"Late," I say, another lie to buy myself some time.

"You can call me if you want. You can always call me," she says.

"Okay."

"Okay." She stares into my eyes, searching. When they start to well up I worry about what she's found. "Text me as soon as you get off?"

She tries to smile, but I still can't find the right words. When I finally hear the front door close, I turn to the robot.

"Tell me," I say.

He looks down. "What?"

"Tell me how to get rid of you."

14

Mia

OUR NEIGHBOR, MRS. NGUYEN, LEAVES ME THREE voice mails.

"Uh, Mia, are you home? I hear yelling."

Beep.

"Mia, if you're home and you need help just come next door. I hear furniture sliding around. And still yelling. Lots of yelling."

Beep.

"Mia, I'm starting to think you're not home. But you should get home. Right away. Your brothers are going at it. I'm afraid someone's going to call the cops on them soon."

Mrs. Nguyen is right about the yelling. I hear it all the way to the curb.

She steps out on her front porch when she sees me, one hand still holding her phone. "I tried calling."

I wave. "I got it! Thanks, Mrs. Nguyen."

This time I slam the front door on purpose. "Mrs. Nguyen is about to call the police."

They ignore me.

"And you think you'll be able to go up there, recite your little poem, and then, what, go get brunch after?" Jazzy flings his hands, endangering the few nails he has left. He points one of them right at Andrés. "They're going to see it as antagonistic. They're going to find out where you live. Where *we* live."

"You really think I would do something that would put you and Mia in danger? It's a peaceful protest." Andrés's voice is anything but peaceful.

"'Peaceful' my ass!" Jazzy yells. "You think you're vigilantes. And it's not just me or Mia I'm worried about. It's you."

I drop my trumpet case on the floor, unbuckle the locks, and pull it free.

Andrés fumes. "Don't go there, Jazzy. It's not about me."

"It is, goddamnit." Jazzy's voice falters. "Tell *her* that it is."

"Stop it!" A chair scrapes across the floor. "Someone has to do something. That's what it's about."

Jazzy slams a hand down on the counter. "Why does it have to be *you*?"

The mouthpiece is to my lips before I know it. Jazzy and Andrés stare at me as I drown out the sound of their yelling.

In those months after our mother left, Andrés and our father's voices igniting a 2:00 AM tornado, I would creep out of bed and play until they heard me and stopped. Now it's Jazzy who's ready to explode, hands on his hips. Andrés tips the chair back upright before slumping into it. I let the last note trail off.

"Let me guess." Jazzy looks me up and down as if searching for the same stranger that's hijacked Andrés. "Now you've got something to say too?"

Something. Do I have something to say? It felt like I did this afternoon, sitting cross-legged on Aarón's bed, that *something* pouring out of me like an ocean. Maybe I don't have a name for it yet. Maybe I'm still trying to work out what that *something* is…but I know Andrés is right about the protest.

Some people might think it's just noise, but it's better than staying silent.

"I think Andrés should do it," I finally say.

Jazzy rolls his eyes. "A lot of good that little performance did, Andrés. Now she's as delusional as you."

Is that all bravery is? I wonder. *Delusion?* A mask I can slip on when I need to believe I can do impossible things.

"I'd rather be delusional than hopeless," Andrés says. "Right now, a lot of people are. This *protest* is more about them than it is about ICE."

"Then go door-to-door with cookies for Christ's sake. Don't make *yourself* a target by criticizing the government." There's something in Jazzy's voice I don't quite recognize— panic ringing at an unfamiliar pitch. He slumps down in the chair across from Andrés. "You're not shining a light on something with your peaceful protest, Andrés. You're stoking the flame."

It feels like we're in the eye of a storm, waiting for the winds to move us one way or the other. Jazzy wants to wait it out, but Andrés is too busy staring at the horizon, at the silver lining where sun meets infinity.

He is busy hoping while Jazzy is busy being afraid.

And as I stand between them, I'm both—afraid of what will happen if Andrés or anyone else shows their face at that protest and afraid of what will happen to the people in this neighborhood if they don't.

"Just tell me you'll think about it," Jazzy pleads.

Andrés's jaw is tight. He doesn't want to lie to Jazzy. "Mia's right. We can't stay scared. We can't be—"

"Don't go there, Andrés." Jazzy looks away.

I can see in the strain of Andrés's mouth how badly he wants the pain out of his chest. How badly he wants it out in the open, to rip it off like a limb, to show us we can still survive without it.

Jazzy's eyes are wet and I wait for him to say he chooses us. Over the fear. Over the past. But he doesn't say anything at all. He just gets up from the kitchen table and walks out the front door. Andrés gets up too, staring after him.

"I'm the one who brought all of this stuff up." I shake my head, tears prickly at the back of my throat. "I thought it would make things better."

"It will."

I look up, surprised. "But first they're going to get worse?"

He gives me a sad smile. "But first they're going to get

worse." He squeezes my shoulder. "Don't wait up." Then he heads out to his truck and off to work.

My phone vibrates and I look down to find an email from Aarón. He's finished mixing the song.

I hold my phone to my chest for a long time. *Just do it.* Then I close my eyes and swipe, letting the sound swell as I grit my teeth.

The first note stings more than I'd hoped.

Listen. *Just* listen.

I try to count the notes like I'm counting sheep, letting them manifest one at a time as I mumble the letters. But this is not my audition piece or anything else I've memorized through hours of practice. Soon the notes I think are coming next, don't. What I hear instead is something I'd give anything not to recognize. Something sad. Messy.

I leap from one note to the next and my heartbeat ticks up, waiting for the girl I know to take control. To tighten it up, smooth it out.

But the sound is scribbles and screams and broken things.

And I can't.

I can't do it.

I pull out my headphones, chucking the phone. It bounces off the couch, hitting the wall with a thud.

The walls. I remember the jagged hole in Aarón's bedroom wall, the evidence of his fist ramming through the plaster all over his knuckles. I hadn't noticed at first. I was too busy trying to psych myself up to actually play something in front of him, something unplanned and unrehearsed.

Now I realize the sounds I'd summoned were coming from the same place his fist was. That's probably why it ended up sounding like such a mess. Maybe it was supposed to. If I went back and cleaned it up, cutting and rearranging the notes, it would be a different song. Not what I'd been feeling in the moment.

But it's dangerous to let yourself get caught up in feelings like that. You end up hurting yourself. You end up hurting others. Like my mother's last words. Like my father's addiction. Like Aarón's bloody fist.

I can't let myself wade too deep in those waters where the current is out of my control. I have to swim back to shore. Even if land feels light-years away.

I close the MP3 file on my phone and open Spotify. In less than ten minutes I've fashioned myself a life raft. Jessie Reyez. Gina Chavez. Jorja Smith. Lido Pimienta. Ibeyi. Girl Ultra.

Songs that make me feel brave.

I'm still listening to them on repeat an hour later, thumb warm from scrolling through Aarón's posts on social media.

There's a photo of him with his headphones on, eyes closed; another boastful shot of a chorizo-and-egg breakfast burrito from Speedy's covered in habanero sauce. The latest is of a mural—La Virgen blooming from a cactus while campesinos pick jewels at her feet. The fields around them seem to go on forever, the hands tilling the land transforming until we get a glimpse of our ancestors, far off in the distance, praying for rain.

I wonder if it was painted by the same girl I saw white-washing the brick outside Loco Lavado. It must have taken days. And why on the west side? That paint will be bleached white by the sun within the year, another brown space gentrified. That's when I remember what's across the street. Those high-rise apartments overlooking Mrs. Lulu's dance studio.

The mural is probably the first thing the tenants see when they look out their windows. So she *had* to paint it on quicksand. Because pressing it hard into their memories is what matters most.

It doesn't mean they'll stop trying to make us disappear, but maybe it means we'll haunt them when they do.

"What are you looking at?" Jazzy plops himself down on the edge of my bed.

I hold out my phone, letting him see.

"It's pretty."

"I didn't hear you come back," I say.

"It's my catlike reflexes." He paws at the air with his remaining nails. "I just needed to clear my head."

I prop myself up on my elbows. "Same."

"But driving up and down MoPac didn't really work."

I smile. "My attempts have also been unsuccessful."

He narrows his eyes at me, thinking. "Want to try something else?"

"Together?"

He yanks on one of my curls. "Isn't that how we do everything?"

■ ■ ■ ■ ■ ■ ■ ■ ■ ■

We park on a dark street, flashing neon signs bleeding out of an alleyway so narrow you probably wouldn't notice it if you were just driving by. We come to an iron gate overgrown with vines and Jazzy gently pushes it open. I smell flames and smoke. Red light washes the gravel in front of us, the drumbeat making the pebbles bounce.

The space opens up to a mass of swirling bodies, people swishing their hips to a sharp cowbell. My heartbeat immediately latches onto the sound. My parents used to fold up the kitchen table on Saturday nights, lit cigarettes in their hands while they danced to Ray Barretto.

There was something about the music that made them forget, at least for a little while, that they hated each other, that they had ever not been in love.

That's what I see pulsing from the people on the dance floor. It pours from them and the hairs on my arms stand up, my body afraid of getting swept up in it.

Jazzy's lips are right by my ear. "We're not just here to watch."

Watching is all I've been doing for the past week of Acadia auditions. For my entire life, really. And where has it gotten me? What would happen if I let myself take up space? Maybe people wouldn't even notice. Or maybe I could learn not to care either way.

Jazzy takes my hand and then we're in the middle of the mess, people's sweaty bodies bumping into me, making me warm. At first I just sway, laughing as Jazzy shimmies in a circle around me. The light catches his glitter eyeshadow and he's the most beautiful person I've ever seen.

"Your turn!" he shouts, raising my hand in the air to guide me into a spin.

The first thing I do is glance around, noticing faces I hadn't before. Wondering if they're noticing me too. Suddenly, I'm sweating as much as they are even though I can barely move.

"No one's looking at you," he promises. "That's not why they're here."

I close my eyes, letting the tambour swallow the sound of my own heartbeat. Then I move—first my feet, then my hips.

Jazzy squeezes my hand. I open my eyes and then I let myself be led, my hair swinging around and slapping me in the face. I laugh, strands sticking to my lips. We dance as one song bleeds into the next, the whining horns winding me up like a clock. It feels good to be made of sound, to paint it with my whole body for once instead of just my lungs.

A few hours later and we're drenched, my dress sticking to me until my body is a different thing entirely. I stretch it out in front of the bathroom sink, the mirrors foggy from the dancers waiting in line outside the stalls. I swipe the fog away with my hands, face framed. My curly hair is wild, sweat sticking it to my face. My mascara is running and my cheeks are as red as clay.

At first, I want to panic, worried that everyone else is as startled by my disheveled appearance as I am. But they're not looking at me. Some are leaning against the cool tiled walls, laughing with other people in line. Some are still swaying their hips or peering into hand mirrors while they apply more lipstick.

Just a few days ago I might have wanted to hide in here, but the second Bad Bunny's baritone voice comes out low and gritty through the speakers, Jazzy and I grab each other and scream. We rush back to the dance floor and sweat it out to a dozen more songs until my shoes are dangling from one hand and my calves are screaming.

But it doesn't hurt. For the first time in a long time… nothing does.

●●●●●●●●●●●

Jazzy is still cha-chaing all the way back to the car, both of us still sweating, still laughing, and light as air.

"Head cleared yet?" Jazzy asks.

"Temporarily." I wrap an arm around his waist. "Thank you."

"You're welcome." He kisses me on the head. "I know it's not as earth-shattering as Andrés's performance but don't forget that those old souls y'all are lugging around also have bodies. Moving them can be medicine too."

The air feels thick and suddenly I smell fresh paint wafting from the mouth of the adjacent alley. We reach the opening and moonlight washes over the girl's yellow baseball cap. The same girl that painted the portrait of Virginia Regia. Only this time she's moving fast and barely making a sound; glancing over her shoulder to see if anyone's coming.

Jazzy tugs on my wrist. "Shit!"

I spin back toward the street. There's a cop car up ahead.

"Nina!" Jazzy hisses.

"You know her?" I say.

"We graduated together."

As the headlights approach we throw ourselves against the alley wall.

Nina drops her paint cans and presses herself to the shadows too. "I swear to God if they paint over this I'm going to cut someone."

Jazzy shushes her.

I hold my breath.

Suddenly, the headlights disappear, but I still hear the crunch of tires on gravel. On glass. The cruiser pulls forward and then it turns into the alley, slowing to a stop right in front of us.

I hear the flick of a pocketknife.

"Oh, hell no," Jazzy mumbles. "I'm not going to be an accessory to—"

"¡Cállate, Jazzy!" Nina hisses.

Sweat drips cold down my neck. Jazzy's knees are bent like he's ready to break into a run. Nina clenches her fists, more pissed than scared.

The headlights flash on again, illuminating the three of us as we stand beneath Nina's mural. I dare to glance up. This one is of Marianella García Villas. The local women's shelter's namesake.

"¡Pinche cabrón!" Nina kicks one of her empty paint cans.

That's when I see who's behind the wheel. Officer Solis.

He steps out of the car holding a bag of takeout. "Your mom said you didn't come home for dinner."

"Yeah, well, I don't need a babysitter." She groans. "How many grown men do I have to explain that to?"

Officer Solis smacks his lips. "Whatever. You know I was the best babysitter you ever had."

"They know each other?" I whisper to Jazzy.

Nina and Officer Solis both answer at the same time. "We're cousins."

Jazzy laughs. "So that's why no one's arrested your ass yet."

Officer Solis leans against the hood of his car. "I've been trying to catch her in the act." He gives an overdramatic shoulder shrug. "But she's always finished by the time I show up." He sighs. "Seriously, though, you know what you're doing is dangerous, Nina. Even though it's righteous and all that, I'm not the only one out here patrolling."

"Yeah, yeah." Nina's still eyeing the takeout bag he's holding. "That a number two?"

He winks. "With extra pickles."

She pulls the burger out of the bag and takes a giant bite before turning back to admire her work, still illuminated by Officer Solis's headlights.

The rest of us stop to admire it too, my eyes tracing the chains around Marianella García Villas's arms and wrists. She's shackled, but she's smiling, her hands cupped and carrying water while a swarm of hummingbirds float down to drink. Their flexed pink wings bleed into one another, shimmers smeared like a newborn galaxy. Like a future she is just imagining.

"What number is this?" Officer Solis asks.

Nina answers with her mouth full. "Seventeen."

"Damn, Nina." Jazzy shakes his head. "When do you sleep?"

"I'll sleep when I'm dead, I guess." She burps before handing the empty sack to Officer Solis. "Thanks for the burger."

"Anytime. You want a ride home?"

"Sure." She grabs a satchel off the ground and stuffs it with her paint cans.

"What about you two?" he asks.

"We're good," Jazzy says, batting his false lashes that are now hanging on for dear life. "But thanks for the offer."

After they drive away, the mural washed in shadow once again, Jazzy asks, "She was a lawyer, wasn't she?"

I nod, remembering learning about her from one of my Spanish teachers. "She tried to stop human rights violations in her country. The Salvadoran army tortured and killed her. She was only thirty-four."

It's too dark to see her smile, the portrait now just a shadow of swirling shapes, barely sharpening even as my eyes adjust. Like it's no longer a thing in this world. But the memory of it. Thanks to people like Nina, we might actually be able to hold on to those memories.

I think about the sixteen other murals she's painted. All those blank spaces she's breathed life back into. Spaces some people probably want to tear down. As if they don't hold memories. As if they weren't alive once. As alive as me and Jazzy.

I think about the paint fumes burning the back of Nina's throat. Of her pointer finger sore as it holds down the spray valve. Of her flicking open her switchblade every time she hears footsteps.

I think about how tired she must be and not just of the work but of lugging around all that it means.

I didn't know her father, Frankie. But when he died, I felt like I *knew* Nina. What she must have been feeling. How grief is a bed of hot coals. How you rake yourself over them until every inch of you is an open wound. Just to get to the other side.

Time has passed for both of us and as I stare at her painting, I search for all the ways we're still the same. But we're not. Because Nina knows her *why*. Because Nina isn't afraid to show the world who she really is. What she cares about. Who she loves.

It's all there, in every stroke.

I see who she is.

I see who I *want* to be.

■ ■ ■ ■ ■ ■ ■ ■ ■ ■

Back in the car, Jazzy unplugs his XLR cable from his cell phone and passes it to me. "Your turn."

I plug my phone in. And then I hesitate.

"Go on," he says. "Surprise me."

I surprise myself instead and press play on the song I recorded at Aarón's. The first notes almost make me fall apart again, and I squeeze my eyes shut, too afraid of looking at him, of even catching his reaction in the corner of my eye.

He's quiet for a long time, just listening, and I almost think I'm dreaming. That I never actually hit play.

But then he gasps. "Mia..."

I peek one eye open. "Is it terrible?"

We jerk to a stop and I fly forward, my hands landing on the dash.

"Mia!"

I glance behind us, but the street's empty.

"Mia, look at me."

I meet his eyes.

"Mia, it's incredible."

I sink into the seat, burying my face in my hands. "Really?"

He pulls them away from my face, clasps them tight. "Really. Trust me. I would *not* bullshit you about this."

"But it's... it's unrehearsed and..."

"It's perfect."

As I close my eyes and force myself to *really* listen, I can hear what's buried beneath the notes. A story about my mother. My father. Me.

Threads from the past tangled up in knots that every breath, every note, was trying to unravel. And suddenly it's not as much of a mess as I thought. There's rhythm and meaning and *so many memories*.

I'm not sure if I would call it incredible. But I *would* call it true.

For once, my music is telling me the truth....

Or maybe it always has. Maybe this is just the first time I'm actually willing to hear it.

15

Aarón

I MAKE MY WAY TO THE EVENT CENTER, BLEARY-eyed, and almost forgetting that I was just there a few hours ago, holding the ladder while Nina put the finishing touches on her mural of the Chicana Brown Berets. They stand tall in their military jackets and bandoliers, fists raised. Some of their faces are hidden behind black bandanas, eyes fierce. Others are pursing bright red lips, their aviator sunglasses sparkling like gunmetal.

Behind them stand Las Soldaderas, the female soldiers who fought alongside men during the Mexican Revolution. They're carrying rifles, knives strapped to their hips, while their long skirts fan out in the colors of the Mexican flag.

"I think this one's my favorite." Nina comes up behind me and I jump.

"What are you doing here?" I ask.

"It's my cousin's quince."

"Is *everyone* in Monte Vista your cousin?"

Nina shrugs. "Everyone except you."

Last night I learned that Officer Solis is *also* Nina's cousin. I wish she would have mentioned it when we saw his cruiser pull up. Instead, I nearly pissed myself thinking we were going to be arrested. Until he handed us *both* a Number 2 from Beto's Burgers this time. With extra pickles.

But when he asked again about Xavier, I told him I hadn't heard from him. Even though I'd been sending him photos of all of Nina's murals and relaying the messages of thanks from all of the people he's helped, I hadn't heard from him all week. It was as if the closer we got to the protest, the more he faded into the background.

"Which is *so* not my style," the robot says. "Speaking of style, when's the last time you washed that baseball cap? It smells like moldy cotija."

"Shut up..." I flip off my cap, sniff it.

"You registered?"

I look up to see Esther and her hipster boyfriend with a group of volunteers in purple Jolt T-shirts setting up tables under the awning next to the entrance. There's a photo booth with a glittery backdrop that says THE FUTURE IS PODEROSA.

I've seen them set up at other quinceañeras, the money from the dollar dances going toward community organizing, and the birthday girls giving speeches about the importance of civic engagement.

I put my cap back on. "I'm not eighteen yet."

Esther hands me a form. "If your eighteenth birthday is in the next two months, you can register early. And in exchange you'll get a free T-shirt." She holds one up by the sleeves. "We're asking everyone to wear them to the protest next Saturday. We'll have a registration booth set up there too. So bring your friends."

"Should we tell her you don't have any?" The robot strikes a pose in front of the photo booth. "Or let it be a surprise?"

"Oh, and here's a pen."

Esther eyes me eagerly as I fill out the voter registration form and it dawns on me that she can't do the same. Even though she'd probably know every issue on the ballot by heart, even though she gives up every hour of her free time to educate people on those same issues, she can't cast her vote on any of them. All she can do is this—volunteer and organize and educate and hope that every person who registers to vote knows what it means to have that privilege. To have a voice.

I hand the form back to her.

"Thank you."

"I should be thanking you," I admit. "I know Nina doesn't sleep. Seems like you don't get much either."

She laughs and then the smile slips from her face. "An activist's work is never done, I guess."

I hear car doors slamming behind me, guests starting to arrive. Esther waves them over, going into her spiel again while I finally head inside to set up my gear.

I look for the birthday girl's mom. They're usually easy to spot, in sparkly dresses and fancy updos almost as extravagant as their daughters'. But the ballroom's empty, save for the caterers setting out aluminum trays full of picadillo, enchiladas, and rice and beans. I smell the warm tortillas from across the room and my stomach growls.

Light pours through a doorway at the far end of the ballroom, laughter trickling out. I follow the sound to an explosion of glitter and tulle, the damas snacking on hot Cheetos while people do their hair and makeup; the chambelanes lounging on couches and sharing headphones, laughing at whatever's on their cell phone screens.

I choke on a cloud of hairspray and then out of the mist, a couple of bobby pins between her teeth, is Mia.

"Uh, hi…" I raise a hand, accidentally knocking over a bunch of hair products on the counter next to me. "Oh shit."

Mia spits out the bobby pins. "Here, let me…" She kneels to help scoop them up and we bump heads.

"I'm so sorry…." Instinctively, I take her face in my hands the way my mom used to when Miguel and I would knock skulls pretending we were luchadores.

She looks up. Our noses touch.

Like when we were standing under the lights in my bedroom.

When we almost…

Suddenly the damas and chambelanes are *oohing* and *aahing.* Someone starts singing "Bésame Mucho," everyone making kissing sounds.

One of the chambelanes reaches for the guy next to him. "Podría perderme en tus ojos…"

I pull my cap down, blushing hard.

"Mia…a little help over here." Mia's brother Jazzy shakes the spray bottle he's holding.

"Coming," she says.

"Finally, the DJ's here." A woman in a sparkly purple dress and curly updo leans into the doorway before wagging a finger at me. "You can set up over here."

I follow her, relieved to be rescued, but as I set up my equipment, I can't help but glance back at the dressing room, hoping for another glimpse of Mia. But then the lights dim, my signal to start the music—traditional mariachi is up first, ushering people inside, low beneath the buzz as people fill their plates.

"How's your head?" Mia slides behind my setup.

My whole body vibrates.

"Okay," I laugh. "How about yours?"

"You left a bruise." She moves closer, letting me see.

I graze her hairline. "Where...?"

She leans in, staring into my eyes. "Look closer."

I feel the breath moving between her lips. I smell her vanilla-scented Chapstick.

The robot fans the air. "Which means she can probably smell your moldy cotija hat."

"Dancers are ready!" Birthday girl's mom rushes past.

Mia and I break apart and then I queue up the Billie Eilish and Selena Gomez mash-up for the quince court's big dance. It starts out as a soft waltz before "Taki Taki" has the lights flickering like we're in a nightclub.

"So, you do a lot of these?" Mia nods to the full dance floor.

"Most weekends. You do a lot of hairstyling?"

"I play assistant when Jazzy needs one."

"Did you have one?" I ask. "A quince...?"

She shakes her head. "Not like this." Then she looks down. "My birthday's in December, so my brothers and I drive out to one of the rich neighborhoods to look at Christmas lights. Then pancakes for dinner. It's sort of a tradition."

"Breakfast for dinner is our birthday tradition too," I say. "My mom made these giant cinnamon rolls. Seriously, bigger than your face." I smile, just for a split second, before reality rips straight through.

"Hey," Mia says, noticing; trying to change the subject, "so how does all of this work." She motions to my setup.

I explain the software, point out the cables running from my laptop to the speakers. "And this is the song queue. I move tracks in and out, depending on the mood, what people seem to be enjoying."

"You care about that?" she asks.

"Well, I mean it's my job to make sure people have a good time." I shrug. "And it's sort of a game I like to play with myself. I notice someone on the sidelines and then I try to figure out the perfect song to get them on their feet."

Mia crosses her arms, amused. "Show me."

"All right..." I point to one of the tables. "Okay, there."

An old woman in a blue wig that perfectly matches her blue pantyhose sits alone. I load "Cumbia Sampuesana" and press play.

The sound of the accordion wrenches the woman onto her feet. She turns in tight circles at the edge of the dance floor. Mia's mouth falls open.

"Whoa, whoa, whoa...how do we know that wasn't a fluke?"

"Okay." I give her a nod. "You choose this time."

"Hmm…" She scans the crowd. Then she points out a little boy in a bowtie and cowboy boots, probably no older than two. He's sitting on top of one of the tables, playing with a plastic dinosaur.

I smack my lips. "Oh, little kids are easy."

"But this one's preoccupied."

"No sweat." I load the next song, "Cumbia Sampuesana" fading out as the *dun-dun-dun-dun-dun-dun-dun* of "El Baile del Gorila" gives way to the sharp cowbell and funky guitar.

The little boy jumps off the table, almost tripping over his cowboy boots as he races after the other kids heading to the dance floor. When it gets to the chorus, they throw their hands in the air and then hang them down low como el gorila.

Mia's eyes widen. "Guao!"

"So did I pass the test?"

She bites her lip. "Not quite…"

She keeps going, pointing out people who are standing against the wall, sitting alone in the shadows, waiting to be asked to dance. A man with a handlebar mustache leaps up at the sound of el grito at the beginning of "No Tengo Dinero." A girl with green hair and bright pink lipstick finally lets another girl pull her onto the dance floor when I hit play on "Azúcar," the Kumbia Kings obviously a family favorite.

For the next two hours I play El Dusty and Daddy Yankee and Selena and Grupo Kual and Don Omar until no one's left sitting alone at a table; every person on their feet.

Until I finally get Mia to admit, "Okay, that's pretty unbelievable."

"I told you. Everyone's got a song."

She narrows her eyes at me. "What's yours?"

I back away from my laptop, shrug.

"Okay," she says, "challenge accepted." She rests her finger on the mousepad and starts scrolling.

She goes for a few classics first—"Tao Tao," "Mi Cucu"—and the crowd loves them. But as she looks me up and down, she knows she's not on the right track.

"I think I'm gonna need a hint."

"That's cheating," the robot interjects.

"Okay, one hint." I scroll through my music library, back to the beginning.

"It starts with the letter *A*?"

I nod.

While Mia scrolls through each song title, I look out on the dance floor, my eyes drawn to a young mom in a blue dress with her baby boy hoisted up on her hip. She spins him in a circle before dipping him low. He laughs as she yanks him back up and I remember that same feeling of being weightless. Of being held. My mother singing the words to every song as she carried me around the dance floor. The lights painting her in pretty colors. The smell of her perfume.

The way I clutched her skirt when she tried to put me down.

The last time we danced together was at her aunt's eightieth birthday party. Dad was working late and Miguel was at the movies with his friends. I stayed glued to my phone while Mom floated around the room, hugging and kissing people we only saw a few times a year at weddings and graduation parties and funerals.

At the sound of the electric guitar, she sat down next to me, eyes pleading. "I know you're too cool to dance with your mom." She squeezed my knee. "But it's our *song*, Pepito."

This time when I hear those guitars, my eyes are wet, Mia reigniting the memory by just pressing play.

I turn to her, my throat on fire. "This one."

She takes my hand and leads me to the dance floor and even though I don't feel like dancing, I do. We dance to "A Dios le Pido," Mia spinning me in circles while I cry and laugh and *remember*.

"I'm sorry," I say. "I don't know where this is coming from."

She grabs my face and says, "I do."

And I'm four years old again. Feeling weightless. Being held. Mia wraps her arms around me, and for the first time in so long I'm not begging my lungs to breathe.

Suddenly, the music cuts off and my heart is in my throat, worried they're going to be pissed about me leaving my setup.

"I think we have an audience," Mia breathes.

I look over and the birthday girl's got a giant grin on her face. She wiggles a finger at us and then she changes the song. The violins come in first, mingled with Spanish guitar.

I look in Mia's eyes, at the way the strobe lights strike her skin, and as Reik sings about heaven conspiring in his favor, I remember that bright blue sky the day my mother died, Mia staring up at it, her voice breaking through the storm inside me and making me look up too.

I pull her close and she rests her head against my chest, both of us swaying to "Creo en Ti," like the words were fashioned from between my own ribs. *Mia is light. Mia is safety. Mia is home.*

When the song ends we're still swaying, still holding each other. She looks up, our noses touching again, our mouths only centimeters apart. I feel her rise onto her toes. I lean down, lips parted.

And then I hear the plucking of a fiddle and everyone rushes the dance floor, Mia and I caught up in the current. I shoulder my way back to my setup and then I scan the crowd for Mia. She's standing on the opposite end of the dance floor, cheeks flushed, a hand pressed to her chest like she barely survived being trampled.

"Payaso de Rodeo" plays while people shuffle their feet, the line dance gradually speeding up until it looks like they're all stomping on cockroaches.

And I can't tear my eyes away from her.

Because Mia is light.

Mia is safety.

Mia is home.

16

Mia

I GET TOO CLOSE TO THE EXTERIOR OF AARÓN'S house and the porch light comes on. I freeze, holding my breath. But there are no footsteps, no one coming to the door. It must have been activated by one of those motion sensors.

Okay, you can do this.

It felt more true when I was staring at him from across the dance floor. As if there weren't a dozen sweaty bodies between us. As if we were the only ones in the entire world. But that was three hours ago. What if he's not still lying awake thinking about it like I was? What if coming here was a mistake?

The light behind the curtains is faint, like it's just the glow of his computer screen. Suddenly, the curtains shift. It's so dark I can barely make out his face. I stay perfectly still, not sure if he's seen mine.

The window slides open. "Mia?"

His voice sounds rough and sleepy. It makes my knees weak.

"Mia, are you okay?"

"I'm fine." I inch closer to the windowsill.

"It's late."

"I know."

We stare at each other until it hurts.

"Do you want to come inside?" he asks.

I nod.

Aarón makes room for me to climb inside. It's warm in his room, the kind of warm that collects in a place after you've been holed up there awhile, breathing all alone. Aarón's machines hum like a crackling fire.

We stand in the center of the room, neither one of us sure what to do or say. But that's exactly why I'm here. To say...*do* something terrifying. To finally tell Aarón how I feel.

"Do you want to sit?" Aarón motions to the bed, still made even though it's almost 2:00 AM.

I sit, wrestling with myself.

He can see it. "What's wrong?"

"Nothing's...*wrong*." I exhale, shoulders slumping in defeat. *Just do it already*.

I wait and internally scream, but my own words don't come. Maybe words aren't enough.

I look from Aarón to my phone, and then I scroll through my music library, searching for all the things I don't know how to say.

I find the one. The perfect combination of drumbeats

and synthetic sounds. Then I plug in my earbuds and hand one to Aarón, playing the same game we played at the quince. Only this time it's me who needs help making a move.

Aarón sits next to me, our arms touching. The song starts and the first few notes are a cool breeze over cresting white-tipped waves. The voice is fragile, like glass.

It's a song about being broken. About being mended. The lyrics itch at the back of my tongue. Aarón's jaw tightens. He's chewing on them too.

Listening.

Listening *hard* to what I'm trying to say.

I feel him start to shift and then we both lie on our backs. The lights overhead are black and they look more like thorns than stars.

The song ends. Silence.

In it, I wait for rejection. For him to say he doesn't understand. Or that he does but he doesn't feel the same way.

Suddenly, Aarón reaches for my phone. He taps the screen a few times and then I get my answer.

I can't tell it's a love song at first. But then the singer wails something about the stars, about longing to close the space between them. Aarón's pinky finger brushes my hand.

We take turns, letting the music spill all of our secrets.

Suddenly, Aarón gets to his feet. Then he reaches out a hand.

I reach back and he pulls me against his chest, our

bodies slowly swaying in the dark. The tiny static pulses electrify my skin. He taps out the beat into the small of my back and I shudder.

His other hand reaches for his keyboard and suddenly the lights come to life, twinkling like one of those desert time-lapse videos where the sky is cracked open and glittering. It reminds me of the hummingbirds Nina painted. It reminds me of the scabs on Aarón's knuckles.

It reminds me of my parents. Of the record player spinning. Of my mother dangling a lit cigarette over my father's shoulder as he tried to make her smile. And I almost let go of him, my body retracting from the memory, from the danger we seem destined to find.

He feels me hesitating and he buries his face in my neck, his lips against my ear. "I'm right here, Mia."

I melt, every ounce of apprehension slipping from my skin. Because I am not my mother. We are not my parents.

The song ends and in the quiet, the words finally come. "The other day..." I look up at the lights knotted like mistletoe. "I wanted to..." I press my forehead to his chest. "But I chickened out. And then again at the dance..."

His lips curl into a smile. "What were you afraid of?"

"Making a mistake?" I shake my head. "I don't know...."

"Does this feel like a mistake?"

"No," I say. "It feels like the opposite of a mistake."

He inches closer. "Do you want to try again?"

I lean in, slow.

He takes my face in his hands.

I reach for his lips.

And there is no shock or spark or earth-shattering explosion. His lips pressed to mine, everything is still and calm and safe.

The world doesn't end.

The world *doesn't* end.

Aarón's hands slide into my hair, the earbuds falling out as we roll onto the bed. Tangled up in each other, time stands still. Until a light flicks on in the hallway and the sound of footsteps sends us reeling.

Aarón falls off the bed while I scooch as far into the corner as possible.

A toilet flushes. The hallway light flicks off. Footsteps recede and Aarón finally exhales.

He looks at me for a long time, like he's seeing someone new. "Is this why you came over here?" he asks.

"Yes," I say.

He slides over next to me, our backs pressed to the wall. Then he says, "I'm glad."

I look down at his hands in his lap. The scabs are starting to fall off, leaving behind shiny pink skin. *Healing*. But that doesn't mean his heart has or that it ever will. Maybe that's okay. Maybe that's what he needs me to tell him.

I take his hand in mine, leading us out into the deep end of those memories. "I was so mad after my dad died," I start. "I stole my neighbor's bike and took it up to the top of Trumble Hill. I waited until it was dark and all the skateboarders were gone. Then I closed my eyes and started to pedal. When I picked up speed, I didn't open them." I hug my knees to my chest. "I didn't want to die. I just needed to *see* it. All that hurt. It was so much scarier when it was invisible."

I hold out my arm to show him the scar, the dark spot just beneath the skin. He grazes it, feeling the hardness underneath.

"A car honked and I swerved off the road. The front tire hit a rock and I flew over the handlebars and landed in a cactus patch." I snort. "I cried all the way home. Jazzy and Andrés spent the next hour picking the needles out of my skin." I scratch at the shadow of one of the thorns. "Except for this one. They missed it or maybe it was too deep. Now every time I look at it, I remember the world is made of thorns and that we don't get to choose how many times we get stuck. What matters is having people around to help us dig them out, to dig *us* out when we're too deep in whatever it is we're struggling with."

"Do you still struggle?" he asks, not meeting my eyes.

"I don't think we stop," I say. "But that doesn't mean we have to do it alone." I face him. "You don't have to talk to me about it if you don't want to. You can talk to someone else."

"You mean like a psychiatrist? Don't those cost a lot of money?"

"Sometimes," I admit. "Jazzy, Andrés, and I each got a few free sessions with someone after our dad died. Mrs. Rodriguez at the church connected us with this older woman in an office downtown. But after a little while she started asking us about our mom. No one knew she'd left. We didn't want anyone to find out because then they would have separated us. So we stopped going."

"If you didn't have to worry about keeping that secret, would you have kept talking to her?"

I nod. "She was nice. It was uncomfortable at first. I was twelve, so there were so many things I didn't understand about death and grief. When she would ask me how I was feeling I never knew how to answer. But there was something in her eyes that said I didn't have to know. That I could say the wrong thing and it would be okay."

"I don't know...." Aarón looks down. "I don't want to resurrect her ghost and not know how to bury it again."

"Maybe you're not supposed to bury it."

"But..."—his mouth quavers—"then how do you live?"

We sit together in the silence, underneath those artificial stars, and I don't know how to answer his question. How *do you* go on living when a piece of you is missing? When that hole shrinks and expands when you least expect it?

"The pain is chronic," he breathes. "Like my heart has the flu." He finds my fingers in the dark. "Except when I'm with you."

I kiss him again. Long and hard and hope filled.

Because he's right about the grief making us sick. But there's also this: every millisecond of joy between each ache. Proof that the pain isn't all there is. That in that pain there are cracks wide enough for other things to slip through.

Like hope.

Like joy.

Like love.

17

Aaron

LIGHT BREAKS AND MIA AND I ARE STILL LYING SIDE by side.

I sense it before I even open my eyes. The world is *different.*

My body is different too; no longer free-floating in a starless sky. I am tethered to something and I feel it tugging at me every time Mia inhales. Every time she shifts in her sleep. Invisible binds that make me feel real for the first time in so long.

When I first saw her face outside my bedroom window, I thought I had dozed off. That I was dreaming. But then I reached for her—her arms covered in dew, her hair smelling like the night—and suddenly I was wide-awake.

And then we danced, moving together in the dark. But as I rested my chin on her shoulder, breathing her in, I could still see him. The robot stood in the corner, shaking his head. Admonishing me for even *trying* to pretend. That I'm whole. That it matters.

But Mia didn't have to come. She could have let our almost-kiss hang between us for the rest of our lives. She could have run like we did from our auditions.

The robot glares at me in the dark, his eyes shouting the same.

Run.

But Mia didn't. Not this time.

And all I can think is, *You can't be a coward and then ask someone to love you.*

The hall light flicks on again and I hear my father brushing his teeth. His belt clinks as he slides it through the loops of his jeans. Then the front door slams and the truck rumbles as he leaves for work.

"What time is it?" Mia whispers.

"Must be almost seven."

She sits up, grabbing her head, and then her stomach. It growls.

"Do you want to get something to eat?" I ask.

She laughs. "That obvious?"

■ ■ ■ ■ ■ ■ ■ ■ ■ ■ ■

Mia hooks an arm through my elbow as we walk to Speedy's. The sun washes the storefront in a yolk-colored glow, and I can already smell the chorizo sizzling on the flattop behind the checkout counter.

The bell over the entry door dings, announcing our entrance.

Speedy spots us and in no time the spatula he's holding

becomes a microphone. He belts out something loud and operatic.

Mia's startled and then so is Speedy, his eyes going to our locked arms right away.

He chokes on the next note. "What is this?" he says, grinning from ear to ear.

"It's none of your business," Mia shoots back.

She fills two cups with coffee before carrying them to the counter. "Two breakfast burritos to go, please."

"I always knew there was something going on between you two," Speedy says.

Mia shoots him a death glare. "We'd happily spend our money somewhere else, if that's less of a distraction for you."

"No, no. Don't be silly. I saw nothing. I say nothing." He twists an invisible key through his lips. "Your secret's safe with me."

I pay for the food, and as Speedy puts the money into the cash register he starts singing again. A ballad this time about two lovers reminiscing about being teenagers.

"Bye, Speedy!" Mia calls on our way out.

We've scarfed down our burritos by the time we reach her house.

"Do you think your brothers were wondering where you were last night?" I ask.

"I doubt it. Andrés works late and Jazzy gets to the salon pretty early. They probably thought I was asleep in my bed." She sips on her coffee. "I guess it is a little late to have a rebellious streak. But at the same time it's not like they can say anything. We're all adults. Well, almost."

"Sometimes it doesn't feel that way."

"Yeah, I thought getting into Acadia would make me feel more grown-up."

"Do you think you'll audition again next year?"

She taps her fingers against her coffee cup. "I don't know." She shrugs. "I guess I don't really have anything to lose."

We reach the front porch.

"Yeah," I say, "I guess you're right."

Mia takes a step toward me. "Thanks for walking me home."

"Thanks for coming over last night."

She wraps her arms around me, burying her face in my neck. Over her shoulder I can see the robot. His arms are crossed.

"Text me later?" she asks.

"Yeah."

Then she kisses me and every sensation from six hours ago comes flooding back. I think I might topple over, but she's still holding my hand, steadying me.

When we finally separate, she hesitates, locking eyes with me one more time before she disappears inside.

"Do I even need to say it?" The robot looms over me.

"Say what...?"

"That this is never going to work." His voice softens like he actually feels sorry for me. "You know that, right?"

Last night, this morning, just a few blocks ago I would have said no. That he was wrong. That all I need is Mia. Even with a broken heart, even with *him* in my head, as long as she's with me I can pretend. *I can pretend.*

But the seven-foot robot next to me—with its squealing joints and clunky footsteps and whirring motorized heartbeat—is *not* pretend. It is as real to me as she is. So I can't keep lying to myself about what's possible. Because none of this is—me and Mia, me and Acadia—unless I figure out how to get rid of my ghosts.

Just for a second, I let myself sink into those memories we haven't even made yet. Me walking to Mia's dorm room, meeting her in the library to study, in the student union building for lunch. Us sharing an apartment. A dog. Late nights, both wide-awake and playing with sound. Me helping her get over her stage fright and her helping me get over my fears of everything else.

Mending each other. Growing in the same direction. Chasing the same dreams.

The future pools around me, warm and safe and perfect.

But next to me, so close to my face I can practically feel the vibrations, the robot begins to hum.

And then I snuff out those memories before they've even become a spark. Because hope is not a cure.

■■■■■■■■■■■

This time the post office box isn't filled with cash. There's a brown paper bag, the address written in black Sharpie on the outside.

4218 Manzanito Drive.

"That's the old man's place, isn't it?" the robot asks.

I nod. "Yeah…"

I hadn't heard from Xavier in over a week, but as soon

as another message appeared in my inbox, it felt urgent, like something had changed.

"But did it change for the better," the robot says, "or for the worse?"

I reach inside the bag and then pull out something cold. Metal.

The likeness is so exact I almost drop it on the floor. *The robot.* The robot that has been haunting me for months is toy-sized and covered in scuffs and scratches. The robot that is currently peering over my shoulder is also gripped in both my hands.

The robot that Xavier's father gave to him as a child.

Xavier's father...

His father...

"His father is Mr. Barrero?" I breathe.

The puzzle piece clicks into place and suddenly I know why Xavier trusted me. Because Mr. Barrero trusted me first. But how did he know I was helping him? And what else does he know? Does he know that Mr. Barrero is sick? After so many years of the two of them not speaking, does he even care?

"Maybe that's what this is." The robot gestures to his mirror image. "A goodbye gift."

"That's not how it works," I say. "Mr. Barrero's the one who's sick. He would be the one leaving things behind, making amends."

"Maybe Xavier's sick too." The robot lowers his voice. "Those demons the cop mentioned...maybe they're finally winning."

When I knock on Mr. Barrero's front door it pushes open an inch.

I call out, "Mr. Barrero?"

No one answers. I ease the door open a little more. "Mr. Barrero? It's Aarón."

I step inside before crossing the kitchen, and then I see him.

Mr. Barrero is on the living room floor, arms and legs bent like he's blocking invisible blows, trying to fight off a monster that only he can see.

"Mr. Barrero!" I drop to my knees right next to him. "Are you all right?"

He searches, eyes scanning the space between us until the fear comes out in tight breaths. In tears.

I fumble with my phone. "I'm calling an ambulance." The operator asks for the address and I give it.

Beside me, he shakes, and I can see his bones beneath his shirt, sweat sticking the fabric to him.

He blinks, still searching, trying to see past the tears. Then he looks up. We both do. Waiting for God to intervene. But there is no one else, only us.

Mr. Barrero finally catches his breath, voice quivering and desperate as he says, "Please, don't tell Mia."

18

Mia

AS SOON AS I STEP INSIDE AND HEAR THE SHOWER running, the acoustics amplifying Jazzy's voice as he belts Mariah Carey, I exhale a sigh of relief. He's home and, from the sounds of it, in a semicheerful mood.

Beneath Jazzy's solo shower performance, I hear the clink of dresser handles, Andrés rummaging in his sock drawer. Another sigh of relief.

But then I remember that I'm still in last night's clothes and that my hair is an absolute mess. I've never had rules, so I didn't technically break any by staying over at Aarón's. But that doesn't mean Andrés wouldn't be pissed if he found out I'd spent the night with a boy.

I tiptoe down the hallway and gently twist my bedroom door handle.

"Mia?" Andrés spots me through the crack in his

bedroom door. "Mia…" His eyes widen and I think my appearance has him in shock.

"I'm sorry. I was with a friend. I'm fine. Everything's fine." I push my bedroom door open. "I just want to get out of these clothes and—" I stop.

Because my bed isn't empty. There is a stranger, a woman with her arms wrapped around my pillow, one of her legs dangling off the side of the mattress. She snores, softly, her hair thick and covering her face.

"Who the hell is that?" I cross my arms, horrified that some random woman's body is currently tangled in my sheets, that she's drooling on my favorite pillow, *that she's…she's…*

She rolls, startled by the sound of my voice. Her hair falls away from her face and then I see.

She isn't a stranger.

She's my mother.

I back away, retreating to the hallway.

"Mia…" Andrés grabs my shoulders.

"Mia…?" The woman sits up, rubbing her eyes.

I feel dizzy, like the world has been tilted off its axis. This is not my house. This is not my room. My mother is a ghost. A night breeze. A feral pack of wolves. She does not sleep. She does not stand still. She does not know my name.

"Mia…it's so good to see you." She smiles and it's a punch in the gut.

I clutch my stomach, afraid of puking, of fainting, of cussing her out.

What the hell is she doing here? What does she mean it's "good" to see me? She left. She fucking left us. And now, five years later, she's all smiles like none of it ever happened? Like she didn't destroy our family? Like she didn't kill our father?

"You can rest in my room if you want," Andrés says, trying to move me out of the fire, to help me escape.

Instead, I grit my teeth and say, "Why is she *here?*"

She looks down at the floor and I notice her chipped toenail polish. Bright red. The same color she used to paint on my hands and cheeks and lips. When having a little girl was as easy as dressing up a doll. That's what she used to call me. Her little baby doll.

Andrés sighs. "Maybe we should talk about it after you've gotten some rest."

"No. I want to talk about it now. What is she doing here? Why is she sleeping in my bed?"

This forces her to her feet. She smooths out the blanket before throwing on a shawl. "I'll make us all some breakfast." She steps past us on her way to the kitchen.

And I don't mean to breathe her in but I do. I breathe her in and she smells like vanilla and cigarette smoke. Like flammable memories and rotten dreams.

When she's out of sight, Andrés turns to face me, his eyes welling up. "She's not going to hurt you, Mia. I won't let her."

My body shakes as I hold in the sob. He clutches me tight.

"What about *you?*" I whisper. "Who's going to protect you?"

He clenches his jaw, thinking for a long time before he says, "She's older, Mia. After talking to her last night I can tell she's been through some shit. Maybe...maybe we won't need protection this time."

I remember the mother feeding her daughter outside Pen's Pastelería food truck; the way Andrés's eyes lingered, the way his whole body tensed with longing.

Because she is someone different to him. Three-dimensional; goodness buried under layers of time. He saw it once. He *felt it* once. And he has held on to it like a spool of thread, our mother on the other end, a kite caught in a hailstorm. He thinks she's come back battered and bruised. I can see it in his eyes—he thinks he can mend her.

She leans around the corner, attempting another smile, though her eyes are sad. "I'm a little lost in here. Do you think you could—?"

"Sure." Andrés follows her to the kitchen.

"You reek," Jazzy says. He's in his bathrobe and slippers. "You want to get cleaned up?"

I nod, following him into the bathroom.

He picks at the rat's nest on my head. "I really need to get you in my chair. These split ends are killing me."

I drop my shoes on the floor and then slump onto the edge of the tub.

Jazzy's still going on and on about my hair when I fold in half and begin to sob against my knees. It feels like an earthquake, like the ground beneath me has given way.

"Mia..." He kneels next to me, rubbing my back.

I can't even name the feeling. It's not despair or shame or longing or regret. It's not anger or panic or fear. It's a tornado. A hurricane. A forest fire in my lungs that makes me want to scream.

"I know," Jazzy breathes, rocking with me. "I know…"

We sit like that until I'm empty and my back is aching. Jazzy's cross-legged on the floor with his head resting on my knees. I rub my eyes before brushing my hair back and taking a deep breath.

"I don't want her here," I say.

"I know."

My lip quavers, new tears trying to fight their way to the surface. "I don't want to watch her pretend that she loves us."

"I know."

He holds my hands, lets me get it all out. Every fear, big and small, while he just keeps saying, "*I know, I know, I know.*"

And then, "She doesn't have to stay. She doesn't have to be a part of your life if you don't want her to be." Jazzy tightens his grip on me. "But there are *things* we need to discuss."

I think about all the years it's been just the three of us. All the times Jazzy has done my makeup in that tiny bathroom mirror above the sink. The weekend we helped Andrés retile the shower because it was falling apart.

Every room in this house has been our canvas and on it we've painted a version of home so perfectly imperfect that I can't imagine having it any other way. I don't want to revisit the past because I don't want to paint over those memories.

But Andrés and Jazzy have done everything for me. They have wiped my tears a million times. Don't I owe it to them to listen to her? To try?

"I'll listen," I tell him. "But for you and Andrés. Not for her."

He kisses me on the forehead. "Thank you." Then he reaches behind me and twists on the water. "Now let's do something about that hair."

∎ ∎ ∎ ∎ ∎ ∎ ∎ ∎ ∎ ∎ ∎

My eggs are cold by the time I make it to the kitchen table. I'm not hungry anyway. Things like hunger and exhaustion feel so far away right now. Like my body has flipped a switch and all it can focus on is surviving this moment— face-to-face with my mother after years of silence.

"Your hair's so long," she says, because it's wet and because even when she was still here, it was Jazzy who always had to wrestle me into the tub.

She's still staring at me, eyes flitting across my face like I'm a painting and she's trying to memorize every stroke and stray mark. I wonder what she sees. If she'd forgotten that I have her lips and my father's eyes, or if my face haunts her the same way her face haunts me.

"Is someone going to explain what's going on?" I look from Jazzy to Andrés.

Andrés clears his throat, but our mother interrupts.

"I wanted to know how you were..."

The words light a match inside me. "Are you broke?"

"Mia..." Andrés flashes me a look.

"It's a serious question," I say, turning back to my mother. "Do you need money? Are you homeless? Did the man you left us for throw you out?"

"Mia, that's—"

"It's okay, Andrés." Our mother nods. "I know you're angry, Mia. You have every right to be."

"And you?" I say. "What is it that you think you're entitled to? This house? This family? Because you gave up those things." I clench my fists under the table. "Us? We don't belong to you anymore. You're not my mother!"

Tears stream down her cheeks and pity stings raw at the back of my throat. I can't look at her...so I don't. Instead, I push out of my chair and out the front door, letting the sidewalk sting my bare feet.

I'm three blocks away when my phone buzzes. I know it's probably Andrés or Jazzy and suddenly my anger wanes, replaced by guilt. I told them I would listen to her. That I would try. *For them.*

I lift the phone to my ear. "Hello?"

"Mia?"

It's Aarón. He sounds winded. *Wounded.*

"What's wrong?" I ask.

"It's Mr. Barrero. He's at the hospital."

All of the fear I was wrestling with earlier comes flooding back. But it's different this time. Bone deep. Because Mr. Barrero is more family to me than my own mother. Because I have to tell him. Before it's too late.

I have to tell him.

When I step off the elevator, Aarón is the first thing I see. He's hunched over his knees, kneading his hands like he's trying to start a fire. The chill hits me then, along with the sterile smell of rubbing alcohol and the drone of machines.

A place too cold, too beige, and too quiet for someone like Mr. Barrero. And yet, as I reach the end of the hallway, room 408 coming into view, I know that he is just on the other side of the curtain. Hooked up to one of those humming machines.

Aarón's on his feet. "Are you okay?"

Then I catch my reflection in the glass pane separating the nurse's station from the patients. I look scared.

"I don't know," I say, honest. "Is *he* okay?"

Aarón nods. "He's okay." He moves to sit, motioning to the chair next to him. "The nurses are in there now."

I watch their shoes shuffle beneath the hem of the curtain. "What happened?"

Aarón grabs his backpack and yanks it open. "Xavier sent me on one last errand." Then he pulls out a toy robot, the one printed on Aarón's favorite T-shirt. "Officer Solis told me that Xavier's dad gave it to him when he was a kid."

I reach for it, examining the scuffs and scratches. Proof that it was played with often and well loved.

"And then he sent me to give it back."

I look from the curtain to the robot. "Mr. Barrero? He's Xavier López's father?"

"I think so, but I didn't have a chance to ask. When I showed up at Mr. Barrero's he had already collapsed. I called the ambulance, and after they picked him up I ran all the way here. I haven't been able to be alone with him."

I hand the robot back to Aarón, and it leaves behind a pang that I can't quite place.

I've always known that Mr. Barrero had secrets, but I've been sharing mine with him since I was a kid, the music making me transparent. I trusted him with so much truth, with my fears and questions. But I guess he couldn't do the same.

And yet, that's just skirting the edge of this feeling—betrayal not really at the heart.

Instead, when I think about Mr. Barrero and his son, I feel...*jealous*. Like it's suddenly harder to pretend that Mr. Barrero and I are family now that I know his real one is out in the world somewhere.

But Xavier's not the one sitting outside Mr. Barrero's hospital room. I am. Even though Mr. Barrero stopped being my teacher. Even though the day he stopped is the day he broke my heart. I'm still here...because even if I was only just a student to him, he was never *just* my teacher.

"Would you like to go in and say hello?"

I jump at the sound of the nurse's voice. She smiles, apologetic, before motioning me toward the doorway.

"Are you his granddaughter?" she asks.

I shake my head no, my steps slow as I anticipate how Mr. Barrero might look on the other side.

"Mia...?" His voice is bright and I exhale, relieved.

"How did you know it was me?" I ask.

He smiles, the bedding and his hospital gown gathered around him like he's floating in a vat of whipped cream. "Who else would it be?"

I sit down on the edge of his bed. He smells like rubbing alcohol and aftershave.

He cups my face and I feel a slight tremor. His hand falls back to the bed.

"It's Parkinson's," he says. "I'm sorry I didn't tell you sooner."

And I don't want to cry in front of him, for him to see how scared I am. But when he takes my hand, it feels so impermanent. Like I could blink and he'd be gone.

I think about him lying there all alone until Aarón found him. I think about him being loaded into the ambulance. I think about losing him the way I lost my father, and then I can't stop myself. The tears come until I'm sobbing for the second time today, barely able to catch my breath.

"I'm right here, Mia." Mr. Barrero squeezes my hand. "I'm right here."

His own eyes well up and I remember what I said to him after he told me he wasn't going to be my teacher anymore. I told him that he was just like my parents. I accused him of abandoning me.

But he didn't.

He *wouldn't*.

"I'm sorry," I say. "I'm sorry I was angry. I'm sorry I wasn't there. I'm so sorry."

"Mija..." He pulls me to his chest, lets me drown him in my tears.

I look up. "Do you forgive me?"

He kisses me on the top of my head. "Families forgive. That's what we do."

Aarón rides the bus with me all the way back to Real Street before getting off and heading to a nearby hotel for a graduation party he's DJing.

"Are you sure you're going to be okay?" he asked me.

"No."

He frowned. "You don't have to stay there tonight if you don't want to. If it's too hard to be around her."

"Thanks," I said, not wanting to let go of his hand. "Maybe leave the light on for me? Just in case?"

He kissed me. "Always."

My stop is next, but when the bus finally reaches it, I can't bring myself to get off. Like if I do, if I walk through that door again, they're all going to be sitting in the same place, stunned and staring while I stand there, filling with shame.

I'm still angry. I'm still *hurt*.

But didn't I just do exactly what I can't seem to forgive my own mother for? *I ran*. Away from Jazzy and Andrés. From my family.

I know I'll have to face them eventually, but I haven't cooled down enough to do the same with her. I don't trust myself to say or do the right things right now. And that scares me.

It scares me the same way a spotlight does, the bright light illuminating all my imperfections. I feel like that's what my mother ignites in me too. The *worst* of myself. She brings it to the surface like I'm nothing more than a mirror she finally feels like gazing into after all these years.

I catch sight of my reflection in the window across from me, my mascara smeared from crying against Mr. Barrero's pillow.

Part of me wants to run back there and spend the night on the floor of his hospital room. My mom could vanish tomorrow and it wouldn't be a surprise. It probably wouldn't even hurt. But Mr. Barrero...? I *need* him. I need him to keep bugging me about auditioning and giving me pep talks that I half ignore. I need him to keep pushing me toward my destiny, whatever that is. I need him to keep making me believe I have one.

"¿Querida...?" Mrs. Molina holds out a tissue.

The mascara is down to my chin and the tears lie in dark spots against my jeans.

"Thank you." I try to clean my face with the tissue, but it's already falling apart in my hands.

That's when Mrs. Molina scoots over to the seat next to me. She wraps her arm around me and pulls me against her chest. I bury my face in her blouse and cry so hard that I can't even close my mouth.

I cry for Mr. Barrero and the day he'll no longer be able to lift his trumpet to his lips. I cry for Xavier who grew up without a father. I cry for myself because I almost ended up with the same fate. I cry for Aarón because he hurts and I can't fix it. I cry for Jazzy and Andrés because they still love our mother more than she loves them.

I cry for her too. For all the damage she's caused; how awful that must feel to know that's all you're good for. And last, I cry for my father. Because of the war inside him—his love for us and his heartbreak over my mother. He didn't know how to carry them both. How to exist in a world where both things are true.

Joy and pain.

Love and hate.

Two notes in the same song, each taking the lead in different moments of our lives; other times tangling themselves up into chaos. White noise that makes us forget that life was ever a song to begin with.

I finally lift my head and gaze out the window, trying to hear it. Monte Vista, new and old, every square inch a symphony I've been swaddled in for as long as I can remember.

The bus comes to a stop and on the other side of the window is another mural. This one of a giant wall, a strip of barbed wire at the top. But instead of stretching into infinity, it slowly comes apart, the metal twisting into wings. The wings transitioning from silver to gold. And then an explosion of monarch butterflies.

There must be hundreds of them, some big, some small. They look like flowers. Like leaves. Wings open as they drift toward a big blue sky.

Beauty born from something so ugly. A wall meant to separate so easily overcome by nature. Transformed by a lowly insect that is an expert in just that.

Mrs. Molina rocks me slowly. "He's a fighter, you know?"

I look up at her.

"Mr. Barrero is going to be just fine."

"How did you—?"

She smiles. "Your visitor tag."

I peel the sticker from my shirt. "Oh..."

She pats me on the back. "This is my stop."

We're in front of the library. *Deb*.

"Actually," I say, "it's mine too."

■ ■ ■ ■ ■ ■ ■ ■ ■ ■ ■ ■

"And she just showed up out of nowhere?" Deb pulls two steaming coffee mugs out of the microwave.

She slides one over to me, my hands absorbing the warmth as I tell her all about the drama of the morning.

"Well, while I would love for you to hide out here until all of the return chutes are empty, you are going to have to go home eventually, Mia." She gives me a sad smile. "What will you say to your mother if she's still there?"

I pinch the skin between my eyebrows. "I don't know...."

"You mean you've never thought about it before?" Deb asks.

Maybe I used to. But then the years came and went with no sign of her. Nothing to hang a hope on. Nothing to keep me up at night. Maybe that's what I would tell her. That I see her in my nightmares just as much as in my dreams. That she scares me. That I miss her.

"Nothing I've rehearsed," I admit.

"Why don't we rehearse it now?" Deb says. "Just like when you're getting ready for a big audition."

"I'm not sure I see the similarities."

"Well, both make you want to run and hide, right?"

I laugh. "And both have a way of bringing me to tears."

Her eyes soften. "Both require you to be vulnerable."

My face falls. "And both could lead to rejection."

"She's already rejected you once," Deb says. "And it didn't kill you." She takes my hand. "It *won't* kill you, Mia."

I nod, but I already feel that familiar burning at the back of my throat.

"What do you need to say to her? Not what you think you *should* say. But what you *need* to."

I swallow, take a deep breath. "I need to say... that she hurt me." My hands start to shake.

Deb holds me tighter. "Go on..."

"I need to say... that I'm afraid of her. That sometimes I hate her. That sometimes I wish it was her who'd died instead of my father."

"Tell her what you need...."

Salty tears slip into my mouth. "I need her to leave. If she still doesn't know how to be a mother. If she still doesn't know how to keep a promise, I need her to leave. I need her to leave and never come back."

The coffee is cold and there are no tears left, and I feel like I've shed so much dead weight that I could float all the way home. That I could face her.

I help Deb empty the return chutes before hugging her goodbye.

"Tell her what you need." Deb squeezes me tighter.

"And what if she can't give it to me?"

She brushes my curls out of my face. "Then you'll have to learn how to give it to yourself."

....

All the way home, my pulse is at a steady gallop. I worry about accidentally running into her; that Jazzy and Andrés will still be at work and it'll just be the two of us. I worry that everything I just rehearsed with Deb will spill out of my brain and all I'll be able to do is sob.

But when I push open the front door, I realize all of that worrying was for nothing. She's not here. No one is.

I don't like it when the house is empty. When Jazzy and Andrés are both at work, I'm usually at Mr. Barrero's or the library. Or I sit in the kitchen, the heart of the house, and pump sound through its veins until I don't feel like the only living thing here.

And maybe it's because I want to feel strong, or sure, or in control, but suddenly I *need* my instrument. Because the things I shared with Deb weren't enough. There's more, somewhere deep down inside, where only the music can reach.

I make my way to the hall closet and find my trumpet case where I'd shoved it out of sight. Then I go to my room and open it on the bed. The brass doesn't catch the light quite like it does in Mr. Barrero's garage, and it makes it look like something old and ordinary.

Just a tool.

Except I know how to use it.

I rest my lips over the mouthpiece and for a while I just breathe, testing how faint the sound is when I barely coax it out. I need to hear what's inside me when everything else is at rest; what Jazzy and Mr. Barrero hear, this invisible thing that belongs to no one else.

I inhale, push the air out a little harder until a C-sharp hangs in the air, long and low and waiting. My lungs know what comes next, my fingers follow, and then the lone lightbulb above my bed is the sun. Like those first few weeks when winter and spring are trading places and everything wants to be alive.

When I play I *want* to be alive.

And that's it. What belongs to me and no one else. What Mr. Barrero and Jazzy can hear beneath the notes. What scales my arms with goosebumps and makes me *feel*.

When I play I want to be alive.

When I play I revel in the fact. I *am* alive. *I* am alive.

"It's beautiful." My mother stands in the doorway, misty-eyed and staring at me. "I...always loved music."

I try to speak, to say all of the things I've waited so long to say to her.

But a new rage begins to simmer between my ribs. Because the longer she looks at me, the more she seems to marvel at us both.

I always loved music.

As if she's the reason. As if this gift is my inheritance instead of the fear that keeps me from sharing it with any-one else.

But she's wrong. The sounds don't bloom inside me because she planted the seeds. They bloom because when I was abandoned, desperate for a drink, Mr. Barrero showed me how to summon the rain.

So I don't thank her. No encore. I don't acknowledge her at all. Not until I climb off the bed, make my way to the door, and slam it in her face.

19

Aaron

I COULDN'T BRING MYSELF TO GIVE MR. BARRERO the robot with Mia around. As she held it, her face darkened and I could tell that it grated on her, the idea that Mr. Barrero had a child. As if it made her less of one to him. Even though, the truth is, it probably made his relationship with her mean so much more. How could it not? Watching her grow up. Seeing the scars of her parents' absence up close. As if it was his own son he was trying to heal; his own past he was trying to rewrite.

So instead of bringing it up during our visit, I let Mia and Mr. Barrero talk about his diagnosis; I let them talk about everything.

I listened from the hallway, their shadows on the other side of the curtain turning them into a slow-moving film. The story of a father and daughter who couldn't disentangle their hearts from each other no matter how hard they tried.

Today, Mr. Barrero looks tired, his eyes falling closed as I pull a chair next to the bed.

"I can come back later," I offer.

He waves a hand. "No, no. You stay." He yawns. "I'm sick of this place already. They were in and out of my room every two hours last night."

"They were just trying to keep an eye on you."

He grows quiet and I wonder if he's thinking about how much time he has left in a body that can still play music. I try to imagine how it unravels behind his eyes. Like watching sand in a broken hourglass.

But Mr. Barrero isn't the only one with a time-sensitive to-do list. I've got one too and it includes telling Mr. Barrero about Xavier, and not just that he asked me to give him the toy robot that may have been their only physical connection over the years but that it seems to be part of a bigger plan. One that's either a grand homecoming...or a grand goodbye.

His eyes drift closed again.

"Mr. Barrero?"

He opens them. "What is it, mijo?"

I pull the robot from my bag and for several seconds Mr. Barrero is frozen. He blinks, staring at the scratches and the faded stickers. He looks from the robot to me and then back again, speechless.

"Xavier asked me to give it to you."

His lip trembles. He reaches for the robot with both hands.

"It was really special to him," I say, knowing in my heart that it's true. "You must have been too."

Tears stream down his face, tracing the way time has changed him while his fingers graze the dulled metal angles of the toy robot, feeling how time has changed it too.

"Where is he?" Mr. Barrero finally asks.

My mouth hangs open because it's still the one question I can't answer.

"I don't know. I've been communicating with him online and he seems to care a lot about the upcoming protest. He's been giving people money to help them organize."

Mr. Barrero nods. "He's a good kid." He grows quiet, thinking for a long time before he says, "Will you tell him I'd like to see him?"

My throat clenches. *I'll do anything*, I want to tell him. But that doesn't mean Xavier will come. If he wanted to, wouldn't he have delivered the robot himself? Unless he's afraid. . . .

Maybe if he knew Mr. Barrero was sick he could get over those fears and come see him. Maybe he'd take care of him the way he's been taking care of everyone else.

"Please," Mr. Barrero says softly. "Please, tell him."

I nod. "I will."

He takes my hand, squeezes. "Thank you."

■ ■ ■ ■ ■ ■ ■ ■ ■ ■ ■

Instead of taking the elevator back down to the parking lot, I climb to the seventh floor and emerge at the end of a long narrow hallway. I'm fifteen minutes early for my appointment, taking my time as I scan the room numbers beside each closed door. I finally find the one I'm looking for and knock.

"Aarón Medrano?" A Black woman in green glasses greets me with a huge smile.

"Uh, yes." I shake her hand. "I'm Aarón. Nice to meet you."

"Likewise. My name's Dr. Reid. Come on in."

The office is small. There's a desk on one side and a couch on the other. A wingback chair is angled in the sunlight directly across from it.

She motions for me to sit and then she sits too, pen and notepad in hand.

"Have you ever seen a psychiatrist before, Aarón?"

I shake my head, my skin hot. I walked in here of my own free will and yet suddenly I feel trapped. Like I might suffocate. Or burst into tears.

"Well, therapy is a little different for everyone. Basically, this is just a time for you to talk about what you're feeling and we'll work together to find ways to help you understand and manage those feelings." She looks down at her notepad. "I have here that in the online form you checked off anxiety as one of the reasons for making this appointment. Would you like to tell me more about that?"

I nod, but no words come out. I try to breathe through my nose. I try to count to ten. But it feels like the walls are closing in on me.

"You know, Aarón, lots of people feel uncomfortable during their first visit. It can be really scary to open up to a complete stranger about your feelings. But in this space there is nothing to be ashamed of. You are not burdening me with anything. I only want to help."

I nod again.

One…two…three…four…

"Can you tell me how long you've been experiencing anxiety?"

I exhale. This question is an easy one. "Always."

"So it's attached to some of your earliest memories?" she asks.

I nod again.

"Can you tell me about one of those memories?"

This question is not as easy. I feel myself sweating, so many flammable memories coming to the surface. I close my eyes, trying to tamp down the flames. Focusing on the details instead of the feelings.

"I was two and I was in the hospital getting ready to have my tonsils taken out. The nurses had to rip me out of my mom's arms. When they got me in the surgery room, I kept yanking off the oxygen mask. I thought I was never going to see my mom again."

"Being separated from a parent can be very scary for a child. Do you think that's where a lot of your anxiety comes from?"

I shrug. "I've always been kind of shy. My brother used to tease me and call me a mama's boy. I just needed to be near her."

"And why do you think that is?"

I expect to be overcome by more memories of my mother. Of her working long hours and leaving Miguel and me with one of the neighbors. Of the quiet mornings, me gripping the bars of my crib while I waited for her to come rescue me.

But instead I think of my father, how he flits in and out of my memories, even more impermanent.

While other kids showed up at school with their fathers for Donuts with Dads; while their fathers set up home video cameras at the back of the auditorium to record choir performances and Christmas plays, my father was too afraid to even step inside the building.

His status meant we always had to be careful. Like a game where how well we followed the rules could mean the difference between staying a family or losing everything. My anxious mind understood the stakes, and I trained myself to tiptoe through life, to circumvent obstacles like they were landmines. I was constantly afraid of doing the wrong thing. Of blowing everything up.

But eventually, to survive, I started preparing myself for the inevitable. That one day I might come home and Dad might not be there. There was no changing this fact. There was only swallowing it. A bitter pill that I had to find a way to choke down.

But my mother was different. She was *everything.*

My confidant. My safety net. My shelter in the storm. She was born in this country and no matter how hard the winds blew, how fiercely the rain pelted us, I had her roots to hold on to. I had *her.*

So that's where I put all of my love. In the person who would never be ripped away from me.

Until she was.

Dr. Reid's voice is soft as she says, "What's coming up for you?" She hands me a box of tissues.

I take one, but instead of using it to clean my face, I crumple it in my fist, feeling the levee inside me about to break.

"I'm right here, Aarón." She leans back in her chair. "Take your time."

I clench my fists until I think they might break. Because I am not going to be able to nod my way through this process. I have to tell her the truth or else what's the point?

"My dad's undocumented. Losing him was always a possibility. But not her...not Mom." The tears become a downpour. Like the cloud that has been hanging over me all this time has finally burst.

But it isn't just carrying rain. There's hail too; thunder and lightning. My entire world blown to bits and fluttering down like falling debris.

Dr. Reid's head tilts. "I am so sorry to hear about your mother, Aarón. Can I ask when she—?"

I struggle to catch my breath. "Eight months ago. It was cancer."

"I can tell how much she meant to you. She must have been a very special person."

"She was," I say, my voice raspy and almost gone.

Dr. Reid hands me a heavy pillow that feels like it's full of sand. I hold on to it, letting it pin me to the couch.

"Mothers are paramount in our lives. No one else has that kind of impact on us." She crosses her legs, leans a little closer. "Could you tell me about her?"

I stare at a smudge in the carpet, trying to will my body to form words without completely falling apart. "She was kind," I start, "and spontaneous. She was creative. We had that in common. I played her my songs and she listened like they were the most beautiful thing she'd ever heard. She said that all the time and I would always groan, even though, deep down, I knew she was telling the truth. That whatever parts of me she heard in the music, she thought they were beautiful. Because that's how she made me feel. Like I mattered. Like I was some kind of miracle." I swallow glass. "It's how she made all of us feel—me and my dad and my brother. She made everything better, especially us." My voice breaks. "And I miss her so much. I just wish I could talk to her."

Dr. Reid gives me a sad smile. "What do you think she would say to you right now?"

My heartbeat ticks up as my brain travels to a place I rarely allow it to go. As if pretending my mother is still alive is some kind of poison. Something I want nothing more than to overdose on. But it's too dangerous. Imagining her in these moments...in these hard life moments when I need her advice the most, it feels like a trap. Because no amount of pretending is going to change the fact that she's gone.

"I don't know," I finally say.

"Sometimes when we lose someone we love it can feel like we've lost them forever. But our memories are full of wisdom. All of those things your mother taught you about yourself, about the world, that knowledge still exists inside you. Being able to tap into it means she will always be a guiding force in your life."

I imagine her in bits and pieces. A whisper. A nudge. Was it her who left the audition flyer in the hallway outside stats class? Was it her who pushed me out those auditorium doors to chase after Mia?

I try to sense her in the every day. In random conversations and songs on the radio. I try to sense her in the notes I string together after everyone else has gone to bed. I try to sense her in my bones. In this body that is made from the same stardust she is.

I reach for her...waiting for her to reach back.

Mom. I need you.

But instead, it's the robot that makes an appearance. He leans against Dr. Reid's desk, examining the books on her shelf. He catches me looking and winks.

"But..." I glare at him, daring myself to make him real, to tell Dr. Reid the truth. The *whole* truth. I turn to her. "What if there's *another* driving force?"

She sits up a little straighter. "Do you mean your anxiety?"

I stare down at the smudge in the carpet again. "Sort of..."

The robot appears next to me, imposing and cold. But strangely...he doesn't say a word.

Dr. Reid waits for me to explain.

I close my eyes again, trying to avoid him long enough to get the words out. "After my mom died...I started to feel like...like something was following me. Like my grief was almost human."

"What do you mean *almost human?*"

"Like it...spoke to me."

Her brow furrows. "And what kinds of things would it say?"

I almost look over at the robot, but I quickly cut my eyes away before I can see his disdain. "That I should be afraid. That I'm crazy."

"And do you think it's telling the truth?"

"I don't know...." I hug the pillow a little tighter. "I think that's why I'm here."

"Well, Aarón, I can say with certainty that's absolutely false. Words like *crazy* can be incredibly demeaning, but when we don't have the words we need, maybe because we haven't learned them yet, we sometimes reach for problematic language because that's what's familiar. Sometimes it's out of frustration; a desire to take the blame for our behavior. But you are not to blame for your anxiety, Aarón, or for how it manifests. The truth is that you've just lost the most important person in your life and you're grieving. And that looks different for all of us." She waits for me to meet her eyes. "Aarón, there is nothing wrong with you. Nothing broken. Nothing bad. You are simply human and being human is hard. For all of us."

. . . .

When I get home my mother's voice doesn't startle me. When I hear it floating from my father's bedroom I don't sneak to the door seam, drinking the poison with him. Instead, I think about what Dr. Reid said about grieving and how it looks different for all of us.

This is how my father does it. Alone. Behind his closed bedroom door.

"Jesus Christ…"

I turn and find Miguel carrying in a stack of pizzas.

His eyes are slits, cutting from me to the closed door. His lip quivers and I think he's fighting the same feeling we all are. This endless dread. This gut-wrenching loneliness. But then he pushes past me, banging on the door so hard that it rattles.

"Pizza's here," he says as the recording cuts off.

He rams into me before tossing the pizzas on the kitchen table and storming out the front door.

This is how Miguel grieves. Alone. In a fit of rage.

I think about following him and trying to explain what Dr. Reid said about being human and hurting and how there is no right way to heal. How we are all just trying our best.

But then I remember how much he hates being two halves of a whole. How much he hates *me*. So I don't move.

"Where's Miguel?" Dad steps out into the hall, not looking directly at me.

"He left," I say, following him to the kitchen.

We both sit down, Dad flipping open the box of cheese pizza before reaching for a slice. I'm not hungry, but I don't want him to think I'm being weird, so I reach for a slice of pepperoni and take a big bite.

"You have to work today?" he asks.

The pizza begins to sag, falling limp in my hand. I don't know if I should take another bite or if I should lie and say yes. Or if I should tell him about Dr. Reid.

I don't know anyone who's gone to therapy, besides Mia, and I know my father doesn't either. Therapy is for people with office jobs and corporate health insurance. It's for privileged folks who confuse emotional pain for physical pain, who don't know the remedy is simply a hard day's work. Or it's for people like my Tío Ramón, my dad's youngest brother who lived in the state hospital for a little while. It's for the homeless person who lives under the overpass with a pet rooster.

I know how the people in our neighborhood talk about them. Like mental illness is a punishment from God or the result of being raised too soft. Something to be fixed with prayers, not pills. Something to be shamed and ridiculed for. Something to fear.

But if my father knew I was trying to *fix it*, that I was seeing a real doctor who might help me get better, maybe he wouldn't be so afraid to love me. Or maybe I'm doing exactly what Dr. Reid said I was—using language to talk about myself that only makes me feel worse. Perpetuating that cycle of blame and shame and punishment.

But I shouldn't be ashamed of asking for help.

"Aarón...?" He slides a plate under my pizza before all of the toppings fall off.

"I wasn't at work," I finally say. "I was at the hospital."

"Were you visiting that old man again?" He folds another piece of pizza into his mouth.

I nod. "But then...I had an appointment."

"What kind of appointment?"

I can't look at him. "With a psychiatrist."

He wipes his mouth with a napkin before curling it in his fist. "Why?"

Then I *have* to look. Because I can't believe he just asked me that. After the shit Miguel gives me every night at dinner, the looks, and the sighs, and the *disgust* every time my brain short-circuits and I do something that makes them *remember.* That they're stuck with me now. That they'll never be able to accept me the way she did.

Miguel's familiar rage starts to pound between my ribs. Then I look right at my father and say, "You *know* why."

He shakes his head, pretending to still be confused. *Always fucking pretending.* "You gave money to this doctor?"

I don't know what to say.

"You need to get your money back, Aarón. All that shit's a fucking scam. Do you understand me?"

"No." I keep my eyes down. "I *don't* understand you. And you don't understand me."

"I know you don't need to see a fucking psychiatrist." His face reddens, but I can't tell if he's angry too or if he's embarrassed. If even skirting around the topic of my mental health is making him squirm.

"No, what I *don't* need is a father who can't even talk about his grief, who can't even admit that he's grieving at all. I don't need a brother who lies to everyone, including himself. Who hates me for missing her. Who hates you for missing her too. Even though you'd never say it out loud because you're too much of a coward to—"

He slams his fists down on the table and the whole

thing leaps up, bucking under the weight. Our plates rattle. My stomach drops.

He growls. "To talk to your own father like that, you *must be* out of your goddamned mind."

I push out of my chair before he can see me cry. "To pretend like everything's fine, like you're not just as broken as I am, you must be out of your mind too."

20

Aarón

Mia: I can hear them fighting from the street.

Is this what you've been dealing with?

Aarón: Pretty much.

Mia: No wonder you need my help.

It's only partly true. The other part is that I just really wanted to see her today and I know she wanted to see Mr. Barrero too. He's only been home from the hospital for a few days and of course he already wanted to have band practice.

But when I find Mia, she's not in the garage with the others. She's leaning against the front porch, staring at her phone.

"What did they do?" the robot says. "Kick her out?"

"Is everything all right?" I ask.

Mia reaches for me, her lips finding mine. It's so

unexpected that my knees almost buckle. I press a hand to the side of the house just to hold myself up.

She backs away, smiling. "I just didn't want an audience."

"Oh..." I can feel the blush spreading all the way to the tips of my ears. "Good idea."

Before I can lean in again, Mr. Barrero spots us. He shades his eyes from the sun, a big smile on his face as he approaches.

"I hope it's all right," I say. "I asked Mia to help out today."

He looks from me to Mia, the smile never leaving his face. "So the student has become the teacher...."

Mia rolls her eyes. "I don't know about that."

He squeezes her shoulder. "You know what the secret is to being a good teacher?" He looks between us. "Admitting you don't know a goddamned thing." He laughs. "But trusting that your students will have all the answers."

As Mr. Barrero leads us around to the garage, Mia whispers, "So what exactly do you need me to do? Referee? Put some divas in their place?"

I remember the chaos from our last practice session. All the starting and stopping and stalling. I was so busy trying to get them all the way through a single song that their individual parts just got lost in all the noise.

"I need you to listen."

"So now we've got two babysitters?" Osmin motions to me and Mia.

Mr. Barrero takes Mia's hand. "This girl is a better musician than all of you put together."

While I set up my gear, Mia meets the rest of the band, each of them giving her a ten-second preview while she helps them properly tune their instruments.

"What if it was something more like...?" She hums, making suggestions, giving notes.

They're genius and it doesn't take long for Osmin and the others to warm up to her.

"Are we ready to get all the way through this new song?" I ask.

"Yeah, yeah." Gina waves a hand. "Just count us in."

They're all a little rusty in the beginning and I can see them side-eyeing one another. Osmin glares at Gabriel. Gabriel rolls his eyes at Gina. Naomi yawns and the rest of them shoot daggers at her. Someone's flat, which makes everyone else go flat, and suddenly Osmin's tossing his egg shaker.

"We've been practicing for weeks! What the hell is the problem?"

"It's me..." Mr. Barrero holds his horn against his lap, his hand shaking uncontrollably.

Osmin's anger is extinguished in an instant. "Mierda." He goes to pick up the egg shaker. "It's nothing, Marcelo. Don't worry about it."

Gina nudges Gabriel. "Oye, what's your excuse?"

He jumps back. "What do you mean?"

"You keep screwing up the chorus, pendejo!"

"Me? You're the one whose solo changes every time we do a run-through."

"It's called making art!"

"It's called making it up as you go. Try writing it down next time and then maybe you won't forget!"

"What are y'all talking about?" Mia steps between them. "There were a few mistakes, but it sounded great."

Osmin motions from Mr. Barrero to Mia. "I knew it. *Another* amateur."

"Actually," Mia says, "this time I really do know what I'm talking about." She sighs. "The problem isn't that you're making mistakes. I think the problem is that...you're *afraid* of making them." She tucks her hair behind her ears. "From one perfectionist to another, you're never going to get all the way through this song if you're expecting it to match what's inside your head." She rests her hands on her hips. "Let's try it again but one at a time..."

She motions to Gabriel who quirks his mouth, annoyed, and begins to play. Then she leads in Osmin, letting them work out the tempo before ushering in any other instruments. She circles the garage, listening.

"Hmm, what about this, Gina?" Mia hums an accordion accompaniment, Gina's eyes lighting up when she hears how it layers over the other sounds.

Mia stops in front of Mr. Barrero, humming long notes that his hands fight hard to hold on to. And she doesn't stop humming, hiding the imperfections, leading them all through the chorus and then the bridge. They cross it together, one by one folding themselves into the song, Mia nodding when she likes what she hears.

She paints with the sounds just like Nina and her acrylics, constructing a mural, a story right before my eyes. A story like mango paletas, like birds-of-paradise,

Mexican Coke, and bare feet running through grass. Like streets shut down while people dance under a glowing moon. Like memories. And as they maneuver the notes, winding around one another as gently as the breeze, the light of the past flickers behind their eyes brighter than the sun.

The song ends and I stop recording. No one curses or throws their instrument.

"We play like that on Saturday...people will *feel* every word," Mr. Barrero says, grinning.

Osmin smiles just as wide. "Just like old times."

"No," Mr. Barrero corrects him. "Better."

. . . .

Today there are candles burning on Dr. Reid's desk. The scent of rosewood wrapping around my lungs, commanding them to relax. She gives me the sand-filled pillow before we've even gotten started and I rest my arms on it, letting the weight cue my body that no matter what comes out of my mouth, the world is not ending.

"Eh, I wouldn't be so sure of that," the robot says, sneaking a peak out the window like something terrible is coming.

"Welcome back, Aarón. I'm so glad to see you again. How have things been since we last spoke?"

I should have expected this question. It's the *most* obvious, after all. But I didn't prepare for it and now I scramble for something coherent that isn't just labored breathing and stifled tears.

How have things been? I think of my father. *Awful.* And

Mia. *Perfect*. And Miguel. *Miserable*. But band practice went well and I managed to show up here again.

So things are… "Okay."

She smiles. "What does that mean exactly?"

I clutch the pillow, take a deep breath, and then I tell her about all the people in my orbit. About Mr. Barrero's diagnosis and my feelings for Mia. About Miguel storming out of the house and my father telling me to get my money back for my first appointment.

"I take it he's never been to therapy himself," Dr. Reid says.

"Never."

She sits back in her chair. "You know, my parents reacted the same way when I told them I wanted to be a psychiatrist. They'd never seen one; never told their secrets to anyone besides their pastor. They told me that was the only way to heal."

"That's… harsh."

She laughs a little. "Well, I couldn't blame them, really. They'd never seen a Black psychiatrist before. I hadn't either. Those things seemed off-limits to us. Stuff for rich people with rich people problems."

"Exactly," the robot grumbles. "It's all…" His voice catches. He tries again. "It's all… it's all…" The words keep skipping and I stare at him, confused.

"Aarón?"

"I'm sorry," I say, turning my attention back to Dr. Reid.

"It's all right. But about your father, Aarón, I can't say that I blame him for thinking the way he does. But what I wish I could tell people like that...what I wish I could *show* them is that we deserve to make space for our pain just as much as anybody else. Not only because we lug around more of it but because holding it all inside has never served us well. It never fixes the problem. All it does is make us reservoirs for that pain. And not just our own. But the pain of our families, of our communities. It's a lot to carry. But we can't help shoulder someone else's load until we've lightened our own."

I think of Xavier, of all he's carrying that he won't let people see. I think of my father and Miguel and all of the things they hide from me too. And I wonder if that's why I'm here. Not just to lighten my own load but to help them shoulder theirs. Could I really learn how? Would they even let me?

"So...if I got better...maybe I could help the people around me get better too?" I ask.

The robot hovers over me but for some reason he still can't speak.

"I think when we face our own stuff and learn how to work through it, it makes us better people, and as a result, a better friend, a better son or daughter." Her eyes soften. "But, Aarón, it's not your responsibility to put your family back together. Your father's in a lot of pain right now, and understandably so, but you're still the child in all this. He should be taking care of you."

I look down. "He's never known how to do that."

"Was he better at it when your mother was around?"

I shake my head. "It was just less noticeable." I swallow,

not sure if I want to dive back into those memories again. "He just…he never understood me. Still doesn't. I don't think he wants to."

"Hmm…" She glances down at her notebook. "Aarón, have you ever thought that maybe your father has kept his distance from you for the same reason you've kept your distance from him? Because he's afraid of losing you?"

My throat fills with needle pricks. I always believed that my father couldn't love me because I was broken. What would it mean if he pushed me away all these years because having me close was even more dangerous? Because loving me was too much of a risk.

"But he's closer with Miguel," I say. "He always has been."

"Why do you think that is?"

I shrug. "They just have more in common, I guess. They're both sports-obsessed macho assholes."

"So you and your brother…"

"Miguel."

"Do you and Miguel have anything in common?"

I scoff. "Nothing. We have *nothing* in common."

"And how does that make you feel?"

Those needle pricks start to spread, splitting me open. I swallow hot tears. "Alone."

The robot stiffens, still glaring. But again he doesn't speak.

Dr. Reid doesn't interject either. She doesn't ask me another question. She just waits. While the feelings roll through me. Like a wave shifting the shoreline, peeling back the sand and revealing the hardness underneath.

"When my mom was around it didn't matter," I say. "She kept us together with home improvement projects and movie nights and home-cooked meals. Miguel and I were never best friends, but he didn't hate me. My father and I didn't have a special bond, but we were still connected. But since she died, everything has unraveled. All the bullshit pretending. The happy family facade. Without her, we don't know how to be a family. Without her, we don't even know how to *try*."

"Is that what you want? For you and Miguel and your father to try to be a family again?"

I scrape the tears from my cheeks. "I mean, of course I do. But—"

"I only ask because you seem to have a very specific idea of what a family is. What it should look like. What it should *feel* like. But the truth is, there is no such thing as a *normal* family, Aarón. There's no such thing as perfect. And if it's connection that you're looking for, well that can be found in all sorts of places." She leans forward. "Aarón, your father may never learn to care for you the way your mother did and Miguel may never become your best friend. But that doesn't mean you're 'alone.'" She presses her pen to her notebook. "Is there anyone else in your life, besides your mother, who you feel truly understands you?"

I find the robot's eyes by accident, instinct constantly pulling me in his direction. He's always going on and on about knowing all of my secrets, all my deepest fears. But that doesn't mean he understands me.

He jerks his head, every motion stilted. Like he's trying to nod. Like he's trying to say, *I do. More than you think.*

But he *can't* say it. For some reason, he's stuck. No witty comebacks or rude jokes. He can't say a word.

"Aarón?" Dr. Reid tugs at my attention. "Anyone you can think of?"

I don't hesitate. "Yes."

She waits for me to go on.

"His name is Xavier López."

Her eyes widen, a strange expression on her face, and she begins to scribble.

"He's my favorite musician."

"His music speaks to you...."

I hold the pillow a little tighter. "Not just his music."

"What do you mean?" she asks.

"We've been communicating online."

Her expression tightens, her pen tapping the page open on her lap. "What exactly do the two of you talk about?"

For the first time, she eyes me with a certain wariness, and it triggers something in me like anger. Because no matter what anyone says, I *know* it's him. I know that it's Xavier on the other side of that screen.

So I answer her question. I give her every detail. The lawyer. Virginia Regia's new bakery. The envelopes full of cash. Nina and her murals. The protest. And she writes it all down as if she's constructing her own wall of clues. Trying to figure me out.

"Has he sent you anywhere dangerous? Asked you to do anything you're not comfortable with?" she asks.

I shake my head. "He would never do that."

But it's a lie. I haven't delivered the stones, not just because going back to the cemetery makes me uncomfortable but because I'm scared. I swallow the shame and tell her that too. I tell her about my father's first visit to my mother's gravesite after her funeral and me not being able to get out of the truck. I tell her about my panic attack the night Mia and I came upon the cemetery after running from the police. I tell her about the stones, still in my backpack, a reminder that even when it's Xavier López himself asking me to be brave, I just can't do it.

"These stones have a symbolic meaning for you," Dr. Reid says.

"I guess so."

"What do you think they represent?"

I hear the robot desperately trying to move, metal grinding against metal.

I lean back, closing my eyes until there's space between us, enough space for my own thoughts for once. "I think if I could actually carry them into the cemetery, it would prove that I'm okay. That I can remember her without falling apart."

The robot growls. The only sound he's been able to make. And I can sense his rage bubbling just below the surface.

"And if you had this, proof, as you say, how would that change things?" Dr. Reid asks, her body hidden behind the robot that is still glaring at me like he wants to kill me.

You don't want me talking about this, I think. Not because you care about me or because you and my dad are right. *But because you don't want me to get better.*

"Aarón?"

I blink, focusing on Dr. Reid's voice. On her questions.

On the stones. "I guess it would change what I believe I'm capable of."

The robot is so angry he's practically vibrating.

"And that matters because...?"

I look right at the robot, waiting for him to self-destruct. For the faintest moment, he flickers, like static.

I turn to Dr. Reid and say, "Because if I can change what I believe, I can change who I am."

And *finally*...I know.

I know in my gut what I have to do.

I know how to get rid of him.

············

When I get home, Miguel's in the kitchen, a hammer in one hand and a cell phone in the other. *Dad's cell phone.*

"What are you—?"

He pushes past me on the way to his bedroom before slamming the door in my face. For a few seconds I just stand there, staring at the chipping paint. Then I don't think. I turn the knob and step inside.

"Miguel, don't."

"It's making him sick," he snarls, looking from me to the phone on his bed.

The way he says it, the way he glares at me, I know he blames me somehow. Like I'm the one who brought the illness into this house and Mom's death just made it easier for it to spread.

"He's grieving," I say, grasping for Dr. Reid's words. "We all are."

"No. You and Dad are living in the past. You're driving yourselves crazy while I watch. I'm not going to let Dad drown himself in this." And then the truth falls from his lips. "I'm not going to lose him too." He stiffens, surprised that he actually said it out loud.

"Miguel..."

I don't know what to say, how to keep him in this moment with me, wounds open wide, finally letting me see.

But as quickly as he unraveled, he binds himself up again, no more cracks for my love to slip through.

"I have to." And then he swings the hammer with both hands.

I catch his wrists, forcing him back. He kicks my feet out from under me and we both roll onto the bed. He tries to shove me onto the floor, but I don't let go of him, my arms wrapping around him like we're falling off the edge of a cliff.

He tries to pull my arms away from him, his forehead coming down against mine with a crack. I groan, and he grabs me by the shirt, then the throat. I wriggle out of his hold, scraping the bed for the cell phone. I catch hold of it and he puts me in a headlock.

"Fucking, let go of it, Aarón!"

My vision goes blurry.

"Aarón, let go!"

The room is speckled in black dots. I claw at his forearm and he drags me off the bed.

Then he takes the hammer and rears back before cracking the cell phone screen. He swings again, harder this time, and the face completely shatters. Then he goes for the hard plastic back, the battery breaking off in shards.

He chucks the hammer, shoulders heaving as we both stare at the cell phone in pieces on the bed. Our father's memories. Our mother's voice. In pieces.

Then Miguel turns to me without looking and says, "It's better this way. For all of us."

21

Mia

WE MEET OUTSIDE SPEEDY'S SO NEITHER ONE OF US has to make the trek alone. I locked my bedroom door before crawling out the window. I wasn't sure when I'd be back and the last thing I wanted was to find my mother sleeping in my bed again. Especially not after seeing my father's grave. The place where he ended up all because her love was a grenade.

Standing under a streetlight, Aarón looks ripped to shreds too, and I'm not sure if he's as ready as he thinks he is. My steps slow and I wonder if maybe I'm not either.

"You brought it." Aarón smiles, nodding to my trumpet case.

"You asked."

We close the space between us without a word, staring into each other's eyes while we intertwine our fingers. I try to read him, to measure the danger of what we're about to do. I feel the smooth shiny skin on his knuckles, the scabs gone. What if seeing his mother's grave cuts even deeper? What if there's nothing I can do to close the wound? To put him back together?

"Aarón, are you—?"

He nods, knowing what I mean, that I'm worried.

He reaches into his pocket and pulls out his cell phone. He shows me a photo of something broken, pieces scattered across the desk in his room.

"It's my dad's cell phone." His jaw tenses. "Miguel smashed it to pieces."

"Why would he do that?"

"There was a voice mail on it. The last one my mother ever left him. He listened to it every day, sometimes for hours." Aarón scoffs, staring up at the sky, tears pooling in his eyes. "And Miguel couldn't stand it. He can't stand that she's gone, that we miss her. He can't fucking stand that he wasn't there when it happened. He's just so...*angry*. All the time. Especially when he feels like me or my dad is being weak."

"It scares him." I hold Aarón tighter. "With someone like Miguel it's better to be overwhelmed by rage than grief. Anything feels better than that. So instead of crying, he breaks things."

"Instead of talking about his feelings, he lets them chew him up and then he chews us out. Like we're not really men."

"It's some machismo bullshit."

Aarón lets out a sad laugh. "And now that the last piece of my mom is gone..." He shakes his head. "It was the only thing keeping my dad from locking his heart up for good. Now it's gonna be behind a steel cage just like Miguel's."

I take Aarón's hand and press it against my chest, letting him feel the steady thump. I used to think my heart was something dangerous. Something that could destroy. I savored the sound like a battle song, a warning to encroaching enemies, a way of keeping myself safe.

But the beating beneath my chest, beneath Aarón's palm, isn't a battle song. It's a lullaby. A promise. A heartbreak symphony made up of every moment of raw pain and wild hope—that fist-shaped muscle holding it all.

"I'm here," I tell him. "No steel cage. No lock and key."

He takes my hand and places it on his chest, our heartbeats dancing together.

Aarón looks down at his splayed fingers. "Earlier, when I said I was ready, I was only half sure." He meets my eyes. "But you make me feel like the world isn't trying to devour me. Like life isn't something you run from...but something you chase."

My heartbeat ticks up, my soul already in a sprint. I press my lips to his, forcing away the cool night air, both of us breathing deep. And I don't just feel his certainty. I taste it. I sense it in every fiber of my being that tonight is a night for chasing down memories. For conquering fears. He wraps his arms around me and I suddenly feel like I could conquer them all.

. . . .

But then we reach the cemetery.

The walk was shorter than I expected and the sky

blacker than I ever thought possible. The moon has been swallowed by clouds and the lone streetlight on this side of the church is dead.

For a long time we stand at the gates. The wind rustling the leaves so loud that it feels like it's coming from between my own ears. My thoughts are a tornado and I fight not to get swept up in them.

Because this is where my father is buried.

And I haven't been back since his funeral.

Most people would call that heartless. Maybe even wrong.

Every time those accusations tried to needle their way inside me, I fought them off with accusations of my own. What about what *he* did? Wasn't that wrong? Leaving us behind. Giving up.

No.

I pinch my eyes shut and Aarón notices, squeezing my hand a little tighter.

Those were his mother's words—my abuela who called him a failure. My abuela who took one look at her grubby English-speaking grandchildren and told us we were better off staying here. That we were Andrés's responsibility now.

At the funeral, she didn't shed a tear as they lowered his casket into the ground. Instead, she looked into my eyes and for a moment I thought she was searching for him, that she wanted to say goodbye. But then her own eyes flashed with familiarity, with knowing, and she breathed into my ear, "I hope you didn't inherit his cowardice too."

Her words frightened me, like his death was something I could catch; the look on her face insinuating that I was already exhibiting some of the symptoms. And that's the part I'll never forget—that she *knew* he was sick. It just wasn't the kind of sickness Latino men are allowed to have.

Like Aarón. I see his anxiety and depression as thick as a fog around him. I see how it waxes and wanes. How it seems to settle when his music is near; how it swells when his father is.

Because *real* men keep their hearts in steel cages. *Real* men lock them up and throw away the key. Because *real men* are cowards. They're so afraid of feeling something bad that they can't even tolerate feeling anything good. Because it's just one note on an infinite scale. And once they press play, there's no telling what kind of melody, what kind of siren song will grip their heart and never let go.

But my father gave in to the music, letting it move him even when it hurt. Playing my mother on repeat after she'd left. Spinning the record of their relationship over and over and over. Until she was the only song he knew.

Even now, at the edge of this cemetery, I can still hear their song. The cacophony of it rising up over the trees. And suddenly I don't know if I can do it. If I can be as brave as Aarón and face my father's grave. The place where we left him. The headstone our neighbors had to pay for because we couldn't.

But when something begins to pull Aarón in that direction, our hands still tethered, I have no choice but to follow. That's what I tell myself anyway. That Aarón needs me.

That it's time.

We move through the cemetery without a word, passing headstones with last names I've known my entire life.

At a glance I can see the families that have been here since the beginning, when Monte Vista was just a dirt road and sky. We've just passed the fifth Gonzalez when Aarón comes to an abrupt stop.

I follow his eyes straight down.

"This is it." Aarón kneels, brushing the grass like he's feeling for secrets.

The ground is worn and I feel a pang in my chest, worried that my father's plot will be overgrown with weeds, signs that no one's been there in years.

"Do you think your brother's been visiting her?" I ask.

He shakes his head. "My father..."

"Did you know he comes alone?"

This time he nods, hard, lips tight. Just before he loses his grip, I wrap my arms around him, keeping the pieces together as best I can. Somehow it keeps me together too.

Aarón cries and I let him. Emptying all those things I've been lugging around too. The questions. The regret. It pours from him, rippling through us both. Working its way toward my lips. Begging to be let out.

I feel Aarón reach behind me with his right hand, resting it on his mother's headstone. I imagine her reaching back and suddenly I can *feel* it. The love. The longing. And I'm so grateful that I can feel it, even just for a second, even in this place where I know she is not. Aarón's mother is dead, but unlike mine, she was never gone.

That's what I tell him. "She's still here. *She is.*"

Aarón's hand falls against the small of my back. His head hangs and I can feel how exhausted he is.

No one warns you about that when someone dies. That

you will never stop being tired. Tired from missing them, from dragging around memories you're too afraid to lose. Tired from running from those same memories when they suddenly grow thorns.

"I wish I could have known her," I tell him.

His jaw tightens again, a new heartbreak coming to the surface. He looks into my eyes as he says, "I wish you could have known her too."

We sit in silence until every breath Aarón takes isn't so labored. The night is still, just as silent. No sirens. Not even a breeze. Everything sleeps but us.

"Do you want to see him?" Aarón finally asks.

I'm afraid of what I'll find. Of what I'll feel or won't feel. But instead of saying no, for some reason I can only nod.

I don't remember much about the funeral other than my abuela's scowl. It was summer and the humidity knocked my curls loose from the tight bun Jazzy had fixed to my head. Sweat stained the communion dress I some-how still fit into, the sun burning against my arms and the back of my neck reminding me that I was still alive. That I could still be hurt in a way my father couldn't stand to be anymore.

But tonight, there's barely enough moonlight to see by, let alone feel. All I can feel is Aarón. Still holding my hand. Not letting go.

He stops, spotting the headstone before I do.

I was wrong about the weeds. I was wrong to fear I wouldn't feel a thing. *I was wrong.*

My knees find the grass. No indentions. It's clean and

green and wet, my tears falling fast. Agony forces open my mouth. "I'm sorry, Papá," I whisper. "I'm sorry. I'm sorry."

These are not the words I wanted to say to him. In the days after his death all I wanted to do was scream. In the years that followed all I wanted was to ask him why. But all I can say now is…"I'm so, *so* sorry."

Aarón waits while it all washes over me. He waits and he holds my hand.

Then finally he says, "I wish I could have known him."

I smile and it aches. "I wish you could have too."

Because after tonight, after keeping each other from coming apart, I want him to know that part of me. And every other scared, doubting, dreaming part that I've been trying to keep hidden. I want him to *know* me.

"Did your father ever hear you perform?" Aarón asks.

My stomach knots, seized by the memory. "He tried to. Once." He waits for me to go on. "I was nine and there was a school recital. I walked to center stage and then my parents exploded into this huge fight while everyone watched. It was humiliating."

"Your stage fright," he says, "that's where it comes from."

"My stage fright." I let out a deep breath. "Everything else that scares me."

"I'm sorry, Mia."

I swallow glass. "Me too." My finger barely grazes the headstone, part of me afraid of what I might wake. "I wish he could have heard me play that day…." And then I can't bring myself to say the rest out loud. That I wish he could have heard me play because if he had, he would have heard that the sadness he wore like a heavy coat sometimes weighed me down too. That we were the same in so many ways. That I needed him.

"Why don't you play for him now?" Aarón asks.

There's no crowd. No spotlight. No reason at all to panic. But I feel the spark of it on the tip of my tongue.

"Only if you want to," he adds.

"That's why you asked me to bring it?"

"I don't know. I guess I thought you might need it...."

I try to sift through the anxious thoughts, the doubt like quicksand. Because underneath I feel a different kind of pang. A longing. For my father to hear me, to know that he still exists in me. To know that because of my music, he will *always* exist.

I lift my trumpet, straightening to take a breath. Then I unfurl that first string of notes—the song I recorded in Aarón's bedroom. The one I played for Jazzy. The one I could barely listen to by myself but that I eventually realized wasn't so bad.

But this time when I play it, it feels different. Like this song was never meant to be heard in an auditorium in front of a crowd or even alone behind my closed bedroom door. But that this is where it belongs. Out here, in the dark, in the quiet solitude. Where it can finally tell the truth.

That sometimes being alive is like watching the sun filter through rose-colored glass and sometimes it's like clutching a piece of that broken glass in your palm. There is unbelievable joy and unspeakable pain and the key to being human is learning how to hold them both.

22

Aarón

I WALK MIA HOME IN THE DARK, THE ROBOT JUST A shadow lingering behind us. No more sharp angles or heavy footsteps. I feel him following, but he never says a word. I wonder if he still can or if kneeling next to my mother's grave was the medicine I needed.

What would happen if I gave myself another dose?

Instead of heading home after watching Mia crawl through her bedroom window, I head back the way we came. I reach the cemetery gate and the robot slows, his body hunched over like he's exhausted, every step I take draining him of color.

By the time I reach Iliana López's grave he's just a slow-moving fog. Circling me. And when I finally hear his voice, it's barely a whisper, the sound torn to shreds.

"You're wrong, Aarón. You're doing this all wrong."

"I'm not."

I unzip my backpack and retrieve the stones. They're cold, night wind sticking to them. But they're not as heavy as I remember.

"Aarón, you need me."

I flinch at the word *need*. Because I did *need* him once. When my grief was a tornado, chaotic and unpredictable. I needed to give it a face. *A form*. A trap strong enough to contain it while I tried to make sense of the mess.

Somehow once my grief grew arms and legs it wasn't quite as scary. Until he refused to leave. Because then it wasn't my grief that was trapped. It was *me*.

"I don't need you anymore," I tell him. "It's time for you to go."

The fog bristles, tightening around me. But it's not entirely menacing. It's also warm and, pressed against me, there's something in it that makes me feel safe.

But it's a lie.

Because grief is not a place to grow. Grief is quicksand and the longer I let him hang around, the quicker I'll sink. Until not even Mia, not even my own music can pull me out.

I place the stones atop Iliana López's grave, arranging them in a neat row. Each time I let one go, I imagine the robot sinking instead of me, the weight dragging him down to the bottom of the ocean. The weight pinning him to a starless sky.

I kneel, brushing the stones before pressing a hand to the damp earth. I'm not sure what Xavier would want me to say to his mother. But maybe I don't have to know. Maybe all I need to be sure of is what I would say to my own.

I swallow, throat dry and already aching. "I wish you were here...."

At first it feels strange and I feel stupid. Like during my first appointment with Dr. Reid. But as I stare into the dark, it's clear there's no one here but me. I don't have to hide or pretend or lie.

I can tell the truth.

I can tell *her* the truth.

"It feels like nothing matters." I grit my teeth. "I don't *want* anything to matter. Not if you're not here." My eyes burn and I scrape the tears away. "I just miss you so much. Every second of every day." I feel the weight of each of those seconds, time unraveling between us making it hard to breathe. But then the fog presses in, my grief wanting to swaddle me again, and I know I have to keep going. "But I know that you would want me to *try*," I say. "So that's what I'm doing. I'm *trying*, Mom. Even though it hurts. Even though it's so fucking hard." My heart cracks open. "I need you. Me and Dad and Miguel, we're trying to be okay without you. But I don't know...." I shake my head, tears falling into my mouth. "I don't know. I don't know what to do."

I grip the grass, letting the sensations ground me like Dr. Reid's candles and pillows.

"But I'm trying to hear you, Mom. Because Dr. Reid says you're in there somewhere. That all the things you taught me are still in there. So I'm trying to reach them. To remember your voice and the things you said that always made everything better." I take a deep breath and close my eyes. "Please, Mom. I'm listening. I'm listening. *Please*."

I open my eyes and the night is perfectly still. No moon. No breeze. *But the stones.* They've shifted.

The neat row I placed them in has been split—four piles, four spaces. And I recognize it immediately. Like she's standing right next to me. Like she's holding me in her arms.

I open the Morse code generator on my phone and plug in the dashes and dots. A single word pops up on my screen.

Love.

We buried it the day we buried her, none of us brave enough to dig it back up. Letting it sink into the soil, tangled down in the roots, rather than sift through the muck of our own pain to bring it back to the surface. And now here she is, holding it out for me to take.

Or maybe she's reminding me that it was never lost in the first place. That all I had to do was listen, and not to the voices that feed on heartbreak and tell me lies but to the voice *she* gave me, the one that can shout through any storm.

For the first time in months, I feel that storm beginning to weaken. The rain stops. The clouds break. The thunder rolls away. And with it the fog. *The ghosts.*

I turn in a circle and see only the night and the swaying trees.

The robot is gone. He's *finally* gone.

But as I graze the stones I don't feel alone. Because *she's* here.

In the dark. In the quiet.
Deep down in my soul.
My mother is with me.
She's with me.

. . . .

The entire ride up the elevator, I'm electric. I can't wait to tell Dr. Reid that I did it. I got rid of my grief monster. I stopped fearing my mother's ghost. I *reached* for her and she reached back, sending me a message that I desperately needed to hear.

But when I get to Dr. Reid's office, she's holding a set of keys and locking up her door behind her.

"Dr. Reid?"

I think maybe she's forgotten about our appointment, but when she turns around she doesn't look surprised to see me.

"Hi, Aarón, I thought we'd have our session in another area of the hospital today. Is that all right with you?" She's already walking back toward the elevator.

"Yeah, sure..." I say, confused.

The doors close and we head up to the ninth floor.

"There's someone I'd like you to meet," Dr. Reid says coolly.

My body tenses. *Someone she'd like me to meet?*

There's a ding as the doors open, and I follow her to a wall of windows overlooking the atrium down below. Everything is green and glittering with fresh rain.

"Aarón, I'd like to introduce you to someone."

We approach a man in a thick sweatsuit, staring so

intensely out the window that he's practically up against the glass.

"Aarón, Xavier. Xavier, Aarón."

Xavier turns.

My heart stops.

He laughs. "Whoa, kid, you look like you've just seen a ghost."

I grasp at the air, needing to sit. My body finds a chair and I slump down into it.

"I thought I'd give you two a few minutes to chat," Dr. Reid says. "I'll be back soon." She squeezes my shoulder before leaving us alone.

Xavier has one eye closed, examining me. "Dr. Reid said you ratted me out."

"Huh? No...I—"

He laughs again. "Kid, it's fine." He clasps his hands. "But they did take away my computer privileges for a little while."

"Wait...*they*?"

"I've been staying here. In-patient treatment." He sighs. "I check in every now and then. When things get a little too..."—he motions with his hand—"hectic." I stay quiet and he continues. "Bipolar disorder. Anxiety." He sways. "Depression." Then he smiles. "Guess the day I was born God was just giving the shit away. Lucky me."

"Is that what all this was about?" My throat clenches, remembering all the times the robot claimed Xavier was dead; what Officer Solis said about him having demons.

"You mean, was I in the middle of a bipolar episode when I asked you to..."—he glances around, searching for

Dr. Reid before lowering his voice—"run all those errands?" He chews the inside of his cheek. "It was a scary one this time. I'd been here for months and...I just didn't know. I didn't know if I'd ever leave. If I *should*."

"So you gave all of your money away?" *And I helped.*

He laughs again. "Not even close." Then his face darkens. "I'm not always in control of what people take from me. The music...it reaches enough people and suddenly everyone's a fucking vampire."

"Is that why you took all of your music down?"

"I just got tired of feeding them. All those fucking fangs. Feasting on you like you're just there to be consumed. And when they lose their taste for you, they leave you to rot." He meets my eyes. "All those things I asked you to do, I guess it was my way of choosing who gets a piece of me."

"And the protest?"

"It's important." He stares out the window again, Monte Vista down below and almost small enough to disappear behind my thumbnail. "I was just so tired of feeling helpless. I like to be the one out there shaking shit up, tearing shit down. For the past month treatment has been more important. But I didn't want the people in Monte Vista to think I'd forgotten about them."

I swallow, looking down at the floor. "And the stones...?"

"That was a bad day," he admits. "They come out of nowhere sometimes; have me thinking about my mom a lot. I've been trying to channel it, though. Dr. Reid's advice. You know how much she likes her grounding techniques.

But I needed more than just a weighted blanket to keep me from floating away this time.

"We started talking about my mom more. About the past. All the things I never knew about her that made me feel like I didn't know myself. So I started digging, learning about my own family history. Traced my mom's roots all the way to the Spanish Inquisition." He smiles to himself. "I found out our ancestors were Jewish and suddenly so many things made sense." He looks up. "The stones are their tradition, and there was something about it that just felt *right*. Like it was everything I'd been feeling. Everything I wanted to say that flowers just couldn't."

"Because they don't wither and die like flowers do," I say, finally understanding.

"Exactly," he says. "They persist. They *endure*." The smile slips. "Like grief." But in its place, something else blooms. "Like love."

"Why seven of them?"

"One for every time I mustered up the strength to visit her grave. To make up for all of those dead flowers."

"My mom," I tell him, "...she died of cancer too."

He grimaces. "I hate that for you. Cancer's a fucking monster."

My face warms and I know this is my moment. "Your music...it helped me." I meet his eyes. "It helps."

His own eyes shine, glassy. "Yeah..." He clears his throat. "It helps me too." Then he straightens, rubs a hand over his buzz cut. "Which is why I checked myself out a few days ago. I miss it too much. And apparently, I'm not the only one who needs it." He quirks his mouth. "But don't go sending out some official 'fan club president' announcement or anything."

"Is that why you picked me?" I ask. "To do all those favors for you."

"All those messages you sent me about people in the neighborhood still celebrating me, that's the opposite of being a vampire." He smiles to himself. "And what are the odds that the president of my fan club would be recording my father's first album in almost thirty years? I know he and I haven't spoken...but I still have friends in Monte Vista that keep an eye on him for me; the people he cares about. Turns out, you're one of those people."

"Your friends...did they tell you why he started playing music again?"

His eyes crinkle, confused.

"Mr. Barrero...he's sick."

Xavier turns, staring out the glass again. I think maybe he wants to be alone, that what I've just said is tearing him apart and the last thing he wants is for me to watch.

But then he turns around and says, "I used to hate him. But then I became an old man too." His smile is sad. "I've always known where he lived. I've always known he was just a car ride away. But a young man always chooses pride. So I *had* to get old. I had to grow out of all those old grudges. All of the bullshit." He nods to himself. "Treatment feels different this time too. It's got me thinking about him more. About whatever time we might have left together."

"He wants to see you," I say.

He exhales, rubs a hand over his buzz cut again. "You know, I think I'm ready to see him too."

■ ■ ■ ■ ■ ■ ■ ■ ■ ■

When I get home, my father is waiting. I know he's angry because the veins in his forearms are standing at attention. Then, without a word, he grabs me by the shirt and drags me to my room. He pushes me toward my desk. Toward the pieces of his broken cell phone.

"Dad, no. I was trying to—"

Miguel's drawn out of his room by the noise. His eyes widen when he sees the way my father is fuming, the way he's staring at what Miguel broke.

It wasn't me. It wasn't me.

But instead of making their way to my lips, the words lodge themselves in my throat, choking me into silence.

"You had no right." He wants to scream but it's like his voice, and what he *really* wants to say, is stuck too.

So he doesn't use words. Instead, he swats the lamp on my nightstand to the floor and then flings my laptop across the room. He chucks my keyboard with one hand before sending my speakers tumbling. Then he looks up at the lights and rips them from the ceiling, tacks raining down over our heads.

I can't move. I can't *breathe.*

No. No. No no no no no.

"Dad!" Miguel tries to grab his shoulders, to pull him back. "Dad, please..."

But he doesn't *tell* him. He doesn't tell the *truth*.

Instead, Miguel uses all his strength to hold him still, while he gasps, while he cries. It's the first time I've seen them touch like this. The first time I've seen them lean on each other, unloading every aching thing between their ribs. Our father sobs, still wanting to break things, still wanting to break me. But Miguel doesn't let him. He breaks down too. He holds my father and they just…cry.

"I'm sorry," I finally breathe. "I'm sorry."

They break out of their daze, Dad breaking out of Miguel's hold.

He doesn't look at me as he says, "I want you *gone*."

And still, Miguel just stares, not saying a word.

But then I think about what would happen if he did. Dad might kick him out instead and then who would catch him the next time he falls apart? The next time my father explodes, who will defuse the bomb? They need each other in a way they never needed me.

But Dr. Reid is right. Just because this isn't the family I want…the family I thought I should have, that doesn't mean I'm alone. So I don't argue. I don't beg for them to let me in. For them to love me.

Instead, I just nod and gather my things, chalking it up to another inevitable thing. Feeling that thread between me and my future growing even more taut.

■ ■ ■ ■ ■ ■ ■ ■ ■ ■ ■ ■

When I get to the house on Manzanito Drive the first thing I hear is music. Through the golden glow of the kitchen window, I see Xavier López and Marcelo Barrero listening to old records while sipping on Mr. Barrero's great-aunt Judy's juice. I see them smiling and listening and stealing small glances at each other as they try to make the pieces fit, their shared DNA a sort of puzzle.

I almost don't want to knock for fear of interrupting this moment. But then Mr. Barrero gets up to put his empty cup in the sink and through the window he sees me or, more importantly, the duffel bag thrown over my shoulder.

Inside, the house is warm. As if forgiveness is a crackling fire, the kind you sit and tell stories around, holding your hands up to the flames until the heat spreads all the way to your bones.

"What happened, Aarón?" Mr. Barrero motions for me to put down my bag like I don't even have to ask if I can stay, like it's already a given.

I look from Xavier to Mr. Barrero. "My dad and I got into a fight."

Xavier gets up, gently tugging at my shirt where it's ripped.

"What about?" Mr. Barrero asks.

"It was..." I don't know how to start.

"Here, sit down." Mr. Barrero pulls out a chair.

I sit. And then I tell them everything. About the voice mail and Miguel and the broken pieces I tried to put back together. I tell them about all the things my father broke too. My computer and my instruments...

"It doesn't matter." My eyes sting red. "All I do is choke. I should have known after I blew the Acadia auditions. I should have smashed it all to pieces myself."

"No." Mr. Barrero shakes his head. "We don't smash our dreams to pieces, do you understand me?" He grips my shoulder. "We don't give up."

Xavier watches us intently like we're acting out a memory he wishes he had. He and his father talking about music, about their dreams. His father telling him to keep going. Even when things are hard. When they seem impossible.

You have to keep going, mijo.

Suddenly, there's a knock at the door. This time Xavier goes to answer it. Mr. Barrero and I both look up at the sound of footsteps, and my heart stops for the second time today. It's Miguel, empty-handed, but with a fresh bruise on his right cheek.

━━━━━━━━━━━

We don't speak as Mr. Barrero tosses down some blankets and pillows on his living room floor. When Xavier heads home for the night, I feel guilty for having cut their reconciliation short.

"I'm sorry," I tell Mr. Barrero. "I didn't know where else to go."

He places a hand on the top of my head, squeezes. "*Here*, mijo. You can always come here."

It isn't until Mr. Barrero flips off the lights, leaving us in complete darkness, that I ask Miguel, "Why didn't you just let me take the flack?"

"Because it wasn't true." I can hear the shame in his voice. "You tried to stop me from breaking it. He needed to know that."

I want to ask him, *Since when does the truth matter?* It's not like he ever tells the truth about missing Mom.

"You shouldn't have done it" is all I say.

Then, in the quiet, he says, "Why *did* you?"

"What?"

"Why did you let him think it was you?"

I want to roll onto my side. I want to find his eyes in the dark. To look into them for once without him immediately looking away.

I stay perfectly still. "Because he already thinks I'm damaged goods. It just seemed easier, I guess."

"Easier for me. Not for you."

I don't respond.

"You're not, you know?"

"What?"

I hear him roll over in the dark. I feel him looking at me.

"You're not 'damaged goods,' Aarón."

23

Mia

I EXPECT TO WAKE TO ANOTHER KNOCK-DOWN, drag-out fight between Jazzy and Andrés, Jazzy making one last attempt at convincing Andrés not to make himself a target at today's protest. But then I realize that there's only two hours until sign-wielding activists march on the capitol and that Andrés is probably already there.

I should be too, another set of hands for Deb and the others who have been working tirelessly to get the word out about this event. I think about all the murals Nina painted and all the hours of practice Mr. Barrero and his bandmates have spent in his garage.

No doubt people will be wringing themselves dry today, handing out food and drinks, getting people registered to vote, listening to one another's stories of pain and heartache, praying over one another. Lending their strength so we can all go on to fight another day.

The need to fight is what drags me out of bed and into clean clothes. I throw my curly hair into a messy bun and slap on some sunscreen before heading for the door.

When I spot my mother in the kitchen, I hesitate, wondering for a second if I'm still sleeping. If this is a dream or a nightmare. If she's about to rip my heart out and stomp on it.

"It's early," she says, slight surprise in her voice. "Andrés just headed out."

"I'm meeting him at the protest," I say.

She nods, a little apprehensive.

That's when I spot the suitcase on the coffee table in the living room, clothes neatly packed.

Heat races through my body and I'm so angry, I almost laugh. Instead, all I say is, "I knew it."

She frowns, lip quivering. "Mia..."

"Don't." I raise a hand, so sick of being disappointed. "You *should* go. We don't need you and you obviously don't need us."

"Mia, it's complicated."

"It's not. Dad had demons too, but at least he loved us enough to stay. Andrés was just a kid when he died, but he never abandoned us the way you did. Because when you love someone, you take care of them. You *try*."

"I am *trying*. That's why I came back. But you haven't made this easy."

"*Me?*" I scoff, clenching my fists before my rage turns into a sob. "Yeah, *I'm* the problem. I'm the reason you can't love your children enough to be their fucking mother."

"Don't speak to me like that, Mia."

"What does it matter how I speak to you? You're just going to disappear again. And in a few weeks it'll be like you were never even here. Back to normal with Andrés taking care of everything. Taking care of *us*. But you only think about taking care of yourself. That's all you've ever done. So go. Go do what's best for you and leave us out of it."

I slam the door on her for the second time and wait for some semblance of satisfaction, but I just feel raw. Like all the fight I was planning on taking to the protest has seeped out of me. And I hate that I let her needle her way inside, that beneath my anger and distrust there was *hope*. Even if I couldn't admit it to myself, it was there, waiting for her to be different. To make a different choice this time. To be my mother.

I *wanted* her to be my mother.

How could you be that stupid, Mia?

Suddenly, all the anger I directed at her the minute I saw her suitcase comes springing back in my direction, hitting me so hard in the gut that I almost can't breathe.

So, so stupid.

I close my eyes and count my breaths, fighting back tears so I don't look like a total mess by the time I reach the capitol, and it reminds me of all the other women probably doing the same. Pushing their own pain to the side so they can fight everyone else's battles.

I've seen the women in my neighborhood do it my entire life. Deb creating a community safe haven with her bare hands, Virginia Regia chaining herself to the bakery she built from the ground up. I want to be like them, so sure in my own strength that a little pain doesn't matter. That my mother's rejection won't break me. That *nothing* will.

That's what today is supposed to be about, after all—showing that no matter what the world tries to do to us, when we're together we're unbreakable. So even though it feels like I'm alone, like I'm caught in the middle of a tug of war between Jazzy and Andrés, like my father is a ghost, like my mother is a bad case of déjà vu, I'm not.

I am surrounded by strong people, by hope personified.

That's exactly what I feel as I step off the bus and follow the crowd headed for the capitol. There are kids in homemade T-shirts, hands still stained with paint, some riding high on their father's shoulders or being pushed by their mothers in strollers that have been decorated with flags from the places so many of us used to call home.

Home.

I feel it here too, the community living and dreaming and hoping as one. That this place we call home won't crumble beneath our feet. That we won't be ripped from this land like weeds.

Sunlight glints off the hundreds of signs dotting the grounds like giant Easter eggs, resistance spelled out in every color of the rainbow. It washes over the crowd, speckling people's brows with sweat, pressing bright red thumbprints against our cheeks.

I follow the colors into the crowd where music blares from Bluetooth speakers and old-fashioned boom boxes, sounds summoning us all before the main event.

I see Deb on the capitol steps, helping to mic up the

morning's speakers. Andrés is one of them, he and Celeste in line behind half a dozen others; another half dozen behind them and with more on the way. Voices that aren't supposed to make a sound soon to be amplified for all to hear.

I wonder if any of the speakers are nervous or if there's no time for that when your community's a scapegoat, when so many people you love could be here one day and gone the next.

But people aren't the only things that vanish. When you're under siege, you lose all kinds of things. Language. Culture. Joy. Freedom. They've tried to steal it all from us, bit by bit. Today is about taking it back. With speeches and poems and prayers. With *music*.

I spot Mr. Barrero and his band resting under the shade of a tree and head their way, drawn in by the sounds of them tinkering with their instruments.

"Today's the big day," I say, lowering to sit cross-legged next to Mr. Barrero.

He squeezes my shoulder and I feel the slight tremor I know he must be worried about, whether his mind will be in control of his body today, if the notes will arrange themselves precisely into what he wants to say.

"It feels big," he says, "doesn't it?"

His eyes are closed and I close mine too, feeling the breeze, the motion all around me. Footsteps in the grass, birds chirping, laughter and chatter in so many different languages. The moment orchestrating itself into a song I never want to forget.

I open my eyes and I see the notes in vibrant colors—the

pop of pink bubblegum, bright blue eyeliner and fierce red lips, neon-green chalk paint, and stark white T-shirts, names printed as small as ants down the backs.

They are the centerpiece—Frankie, Mr. Salazar, Estefanía, Mr. V, and all the others we've lost—they're the reason we're here. *And I don't want to forget.*

This is what it means to be Chicane. *Remembering.* Even when it hurts. Because it will, whether the pain stems from being so far away from the past it's barely a flicker on the horizon of your own history or it stems from feeling the flames up close, of staring into a mirror as bright as the sun. This is where we live, where we dance, where we fight. On this tightrope between our ancestors and the stars from whence they came, we build our homes, our families, our futures.

I think about my own future and even though it's still fuzzy, still something fragile that I desperately don't want to screw up, I have one. Because of people like Deb and Nina and Esther and all of the women I've never even met, who held protests like this one, declaring that I am human.

I owe it to them to reach for what I want even if that means being afraid. Because who isn't? Maybe finding joy is how we resist. Which means that following our dreams isn't a selfish act at all. It's as necessary to the revolution as all of this—the marching and organizing and speaking out.

Dreaming isn't just the start of a movement, it's the engine that keeps it going.

I might never get into Acadia, but no matter who the gatekeepers are, I won't let them stop me from *reaching* for this dream. So that maybe the young girls behind me won't have to run as far. So they won't have to scrape their knees or cover themselves in blisters. So they can still be a whole person by the time they get there.

"Mia..."

Mr. Barrero's voice pulls me back to the present. He points at the stage, the crowd pressing forward as one, everyone screaming and jumping, trying to get a closer look.

Xavier López, aka La Maquina, raises a fist. But while everyone's snapping pictures of him on their cell phones, I'm watching the faces behind him; the baseball cap bobbing like the person wearing it is buzzing with nerves.

"Mia, is that—?"

I look closer and then I see him.

Aarón.

24

Aaron

THE PROTEST ORGANIZERS WERE NOT EXPECTING us. We almost get trampled on our way to the stage by die-hard fans trying to get their hands on Xavier, like touching him is holy. The organizers are starstruck too. So when he tells them he's brought the opening act, they don't argue, some of his shine suddenly rubbing off on me.

All because he actually listened to the song I sent.

Because he thought it was good.

A few minutes ago we were sitting in his car, Miguel silent in the backseat, me counting off the streetlights as we rolled closer to downtown.

Until Miguel finally worked up the nerve to ask, "Where are we going?"

Xavier glanced over at me in the passenger seat. "Last night you talked about quitting. You said you blew your audition to get into Acadia."

"You tried to get into Acadia?" Miguel murmured.

"It was stupid," I answered.

Xavier put the car in park. "I was scared too once. Until I realized what the music could do...if I shared it, if I was brave enough to let people in. You reminded me of that when we talked the first time." He met my eyes. "You reminded me that sometimes we *need* to let people in, to let people see us. Because what they see, the *good* they see in us, might make us change the way we see ourselves." He tilted his chin, serious. "That song you sent me is good, Aarón. You should share it."

You should share it.

We don't smash our dreams to pieces.

We don't give up.

"Aarón?"

I turned to Xavier. "Okay."

He smiled. "Okay."

▪ ▪ ▪ ▪ ▪ ▪ ▪ ▪ ▪ ▪

Now Xavier's getting the crowd hyped while I check out the setup. There's a guitar, a keyboard, and a beat-up loop pedal. I wish I had my laptop and all those tracks saved on it; something to build on. But it's even more beat-up than these old instruments. Which means I have to work by memory.

Or...maybe try something new.

Could I really do that? Take Xavier's advice and let people in? Construct something right before their eyes. Letting in every bit of feedback. Watching them rip it to shreds.

Unless they don't.

Unless what they reflect back at me isn't judgment at all but *knowing*. Understanding.

What if they understand?

What if they think I'm good?

I quickly tune each instrument, the heat and the noise from the crowd drenching me in sweat.

"Here." Miguel hands me an orange bandana and I freeze.

It's the one Mom used to tie her hair back when she was elbow deep in soil, planting zucchini and cilantro and strawberries in the garden she started the day after she was diagnosed. My fingers trace the embroidery and I wonder how many times Miguel has done the same, how long he's been holding on to this piece of her.

"I miss her too," he says through clenched teeth. "I know I don't say it...or show it."

"You don't have to," I tell him, because I can see how much it hurts.

He takes the other end of the bandana, both of us holding it for half a second. Like when we each used to take one of her hands on a trip to the mall. Like when we sat by her bedside, both of us saying our own silent prayer, trying to force the healing beneath her skin.

"Maybe she's watching," I say, breathing in the scent of her.

Miguel nods. "She is..."

He lets go, but for the first time in so long, nothing feels severed. Separate, maybe, but not torn. And I realize that even though we didn't get our wish, that Mom wasn't healed the way we wanted her to be, that maybe we can do the healing for her.

As Miguel walks away, I dab at the sweat on my forehead, approaching center stage. Then I rest my hands on the keys. I wish I could pull my baseball cap over my face like a shield. But the sounds are even worse—a murmur passing through the crowd as people wait for me to ignite a bob of their heads, a sway of their hips. As they wait for me to *move* them.

I just have to make myself move first.

"Just play what you know!" Xavier calls out.

The crowd begins to clap, restless, until the noise is a steady drumbeat.

I find Miguel's eyes again. He gives me a nod of solidarity.

Xavier gives me a wink. Another sign from the Universe.

Mr. Barrero's voice swells inside my head. *We don't smash our dreams to pieces. We don't give up.*

I remember the stones. My mother's love that I was so scared I'd have to live the rest of my life without. So scared that I stopped hoping. Stopped dreaming because she wasn't around to see my dreams come true.

But I was wrong. Because dreaming is how we hold on. To memories. To each other. These dreams of mine...they are the light she left behind. Pulling me out of the darkness. Always guiding the way.

I let her guide me now, my fingers holding down a C-sharp until everything vibrates, the sound raining from the speakers. Something nudges me to look up, and in that sea of faces, I see my whole world. The block that made me. The people who raised me.

They're the reason why, when I lost her, the symphony kept on playing. And not just the one spilling from every stoop and storefront in Monte Vista. But the one between my ribs.

I loop the piano section, letting it autoplay as I pick up the guitar. I hit a few sour notes, my hands sweating, but I know this crowd won't turn on me.

I coax out a tight melody and layer it over the piano section. Then I build in the rest, adding bass and drums before returning to the keyboard and swapping out the traditional sound for my signature synth.

I channel Mia's rooftop performance. Her magic and intuition.

I think about Nina's murals. The bold colors. The bravery in every stroke.

I picture Mr. Barrero hugging his horn to his lips, the way it speaks for him. The way it tells only truth.

I see my father ripping the lights from my bedroom ceiling, the stars my mother gave me flickering before going out. I hear him smashing my laptop and my keyboard. I hear him sobbing in Miguel's arms.

Then I remember what Miguel said last night.

You're not 'damaged goods,' Aarón.

You're not 'damaged goods' . . .

I feel it all. Every promise. Every poison. I let the music siphon it out of me. I transform it into something that has my heart racing and my body buzzing.

The crowd moves too, leaning forward like it's quenching something inside them. A thirst none of us knows how to name. All we know is that the music is *it*. The answer to everything.

I work in reverse, peeling the sounds away one instrument at a time until all that's left is synthesizer. I stretch the final notes, making everything shake, and then my hands fall off the keys, and the crowd erupts.

The clamor is so loud, it's more like static, or maybe my brain has been turned to mush. But I'm still in a daze as I make my way offstage, and it isn't until Xavier grabs me by the arms that I feel the sweat I've been pouring. I'm soaked, but I feel...*I feel*...like my body is ablaze and yet nothing burns. I feel alive. Like I'm *supposed* to be alive.

"You killed it!" Xavier says.

But I'm not looking at him. I'm looking at Miguel, who stands far away from the chaos, watching us, watching *me*, with tears in his eyes.

25

Mia

AT THE SOUND OF THE FIRST NOTE, THE NEED TO move pulls me up and onto my feet. I weave my way through the crowd until I can see his face. Cap pulled low, his eyes are hidden. But everything he's feeling is in his hands, summoning note after note that makes the hairs on my arms stand on end.

Suddenly, we all exist on another frequency, another plane of existence where sound is everything, shaking us out of whatever daydream we've been living in. Or maybe *this* is the daydream—the safe harbor between stolen land and a rocky sea. The only place where fear can't touch us.

Because this music is anything *but* afraid.

It is Monte Vista, bustling and brimming with *hope*.

It is the symphony I've always known we are.

When Aarón's hands finally come off the keys, the crowd erupts, swallowing the stage with their joy-filled bodies. I can't see him, but somehow I can still feel him, winding his way through the crowd, closing the space between us.

He breaks through and we reach for each other at the same time. And I don't tell him that it was incredible. I don't tell him that he is too. Instead, I hold him tight, letting him feel the way my heart is racing. He squeezes back, letting me feel the way his heart races too.

And I can still hear it—the ache we share, the pieces of us that are missing, Doubt like an echo between my ears—but they're no longer drowning out everything else, so loud that I can't hear my own voice buried underneath.

It's not buried. It's clear and strong and sure.

I lift the bill of Aarón's cap, our noses touching. "I love you, Aarón Medrano."

His eyes sparkle. "I love you, Mia Villanueva."

I reach for his lips and nothing in me wants to run or hide. Instead, my whole body exhales. Because this is bravery. This is healing. This is *hope*.

The crowd around us stirs, murmurs moving like a wave.

We both turn toward the stage, and there in front of the microphone, her eyes closed as she readies to speak, is Nina.

She looks exhausted, and I wonder if she actually managed to paint the entire neighborhood. Or if it's something she'll never be able to stop doing. Like reliving the memories of her father's death. How many times has it played out behind her eyes?

She blinks, a few tears falling, and I wonder if she's

thinking of it now. "My name is Nina Fernandez. Frankie Fernandez was my father." A low hum passes through the crowd. "And he is *not* dead."

She pauses. Eight whole seconds. Eight bullets. And the crowd is so quiet I can almost hear them too. The *pop-pop-pop*. Flesh meeting pavement. Frankie Fernandez breathing his last breath.

"They want him to be," Nina says. "They want my father to be dead and for his family to be scared. They want his daughter to be quiet. But I won't. Because this is the voice my father gave me. This is the voice he showed me how to use. The voice that holds him here in the present, that keeps him alive. Did you hear that?" She turns to the police who have begun to line up near the street. "My father is alive. My father is *alive* in *me*."

Heartache ripples through me and I feel him so close. Like my father and I are one flesh. Like his still-beating heart is in my chest.

I *feel* him and nothing about it is burdensome or heavy or sad. I feel my father and I feel his love. Joyful, warm, and safe.

Mi hija, he whispers. *My daughter. My daughter. Always and forever.*

"Mia..."

Aarón cups my face with both hands, absorbing what I'm feeling, not letting me feel it all alone.

I wrap my arms around him and bury my face in his neck.

"They're alive," I tell him. "They're alive in us."

He squeezes me tighter and breathes back, "I know."

Then we just hold each other, watching as the tears stream down Nina's face until I feel the ache in my own throat. We listen to Deb talk about Estefanía and I feel the loss of her too. Virginia Regia takes the stage next, telling the story of how she came to this country, and I feel the hot desert sun that chased her all the way here, the relief she felt when she finally reached a church that would take her in.

Celeste performs a poem about monarch butterflies and barbed wire and freedom until I'm tangled up in all of it. Esther speaks next, switching between Spanish and English as she reveals her undocumented status, as she explains that Los Estados Unidos is her home.

One by one, people take the stage, telling stories that I feel in every fiber of my being. The past and the dead resurrected right before our eyes. All of the things we refuse to forget. These memories the only thing the world can't take from us.

"I think Mr. Barrero's band is up next," Aarón says.

I turn to look, Osmin and the others lugging their instruments toward center stage. But Mr. Barrero is off to the side, talking with Deb, and even from where we stand, I can see that he's shaking.

The rest of the band waits while the crowd grows restless, conversations popping up here and there until the noise is overwhelming.

But then I see Mr. Barrero turn. I see him scanning the crowd. Then he finds my eyes and everything is silent. Except for his fear, soundless and striking me in the chest.

But instead of stepping offstage, instead of running,

Mr. Barrero plants himself next to Osmin and Gina and Naomi and Gabriel. He plants himself in front of all those eyes.

Osmin and the others glance back at him and I sense their apprehension. But they don't run either.

Osmin scrapes el güiro, igniting a ratchet sound that has people bobbing their heads. Gabriel comes in next, plucking the strings on his Spanish guitar. The song builds and Mr. Barrero tightens his grip on his trumpet.

I watch his body stiffen, working against the music. But then he closes his eyes, focusing all that fight into the mouthpiece of his trumpet. Then he wails, pushing out every ounce of air. At the last second, he bends the note, the accordion and steel guitar coming in at the same time and crashing into the other instruments—the volume climbing, climbing, before it all crests.

And it's incredible. Wild and *so* alive.

So is Mr. Barrero. Breathing. Fighting. His soul out of his body. His trumpet amplifying everything that soul has ever felt or feared or wanted to be. Soon his body is talking too, moving with the music, and in it I see my own mannerisms. His body a mirror all these years, a form I've slowly been molding myself into. And I realize that Mr. Barrero lives in me as much as my father does. In these lungs that need to play to breathe.

He *lives* in me.

But I'm not the only one carrying a piece of him. I spot Xavier to the left of the stage, lip pinched between his teeth, eyes wet. Watching Mr. Barrero like he's seeing him for the first time. And I realize that he *is*. He's seeing the man who used to revel in crowds just like this one—the man who *chose* music. And in every impossibly beautiful note, he's seeing the reason why. Not because Xavier meant nothing. But because he meant everything. Because even though he made a million mistakes, he was building a legacy for them both.

The song ends and the crowd erupts, igniting one grito after another. The whistles and cheers spreading Mr. Barrero's lips into the widest grin. And then he finds my eyes, sees my smile just as big, and he winks.

I laugh—Aarón and I cheering too. I spot Andrés and Celeste, screaming at the top of their lungs. Around us, the crowd is so raucous, the first pop almost doesn't register. My brain imagines a car backfiring or something else completely innocuous. But then it comes again. And again. Three hard pops in quick succession, and then everyone is running.

I scan the crowd, trying to sense where the gunshots came from. My heart pounds like I'm already in a sprint, but my legs won't move. Mr. Barrero is lost in the commotion. Andrés is nowhere to be found.

"Mia, come on!" Aarón pushes me toward the surrounding trees.

I backpedal, still searching.

Where are you? Where are you?

Please, please, please...

I turn around, and that's when I see the line of police officers cinching in the crowd. They're not the same ones I noticed during Nina's speech. These are masked and holding shields, dressed for a riot that never happened.

Unless *this* is it. The chaos they were hoping for, the chaos *they* created because it gives them the excuse to shoot us on sight.

There's a line of protesters bold enough to confront the officers. They're armed with nothing but their cell phones, shouting questions, giving a play-by-play to people watching the livestream. Batons come down on their backs. Then an explosion of pepper spray.

People cough and scream, gasping for air.

Then I get a better look at one of the men on his knees. His eyes are pinched shut, orange pepper spray staining his face.

No, no, no...

"Andrés!" I scream.

An officer plants a boot in his back, forcing him down to the ground. Then he cuffs him, dragging him off the street. But not before he sees me. Not before he *reaches* for me.

But as they haul him away, there's nothing...

...there's nothing I can do.

26

Mia

"I WANT TO SEE MY BROTHER. NOW!"

The officer behind the counter smirks without looking up from his cell phone.

I slam a fist down on the countertop, ready to tear this place apart with my bare hands. "I watched them drag him away!" I yell. "For no reason. They didn't read him his rights. They pepper-sprayed him and beat him even though he didn't do anything wrong. This is criminal, what you're doing. You're all criminals!" I kick the wall between us, igniting a crack in the plaster.

The cop springs out of his chair and glares at Aarón. "You get her out of here before I throw her ass in a cell too."

Aarón reaches for my arm. "Mia, let's go outside for a minute."

Suddenly, there's a commotion at the entrance, the

front door swinging open, and then there's Deb, followed by Nina's mother, and some of the other organizers I recognize from the library.

"Where's my daughter?" Nina's mother demands.

I rush over to Deb. "They took Nina too?"

Deb pulls me into a hug. "And Esther."

My heart sinks. *Esther?* Esther, who just admitted to a huge crowd of people that she's *undocumented*.

"What are they going to do to her?"

Deb shakes her head, trying not to cry. "I don't know. That's why we have to get her out."

"Mia? Mia!" Jazzy appears, pushing his way through the crowd that has assembled inside the precinct.

"I'm here." I fall into him. "They took Andrés but they won't tell me anything. I tried—"

"I told him not to fucking do this." Jazzy paces. "I told him this would happen."

"But it's not his fault," I say. "He didn't know he'd get arrested—"

"No." Jazzy stops. "But he knew what would happen if he did."

I ease back. "What's that supposed to mean?"

I hear voices chanting—a large crowd gathering in the parking lot. A few police officers get up from their desks to take a look. But Jazzy doesn't take his eyes off me, and the longer I stare into them, the more fear I see coming to the surface.

"Jazzy, what does that *mean*?"

"It means Andrés might not be coming home."

"Why not?"

He lowers his voice, switching to Spanish. "Because to the government, this isn't his home."

The noise around me becomes a drone, and suddenly the world tilts. I'm falling but I don't move. I'm breaking but I don't make a sound.

Andrés.

Andrés has been undocumented this whole time.

This *whole* time he's been at risk.

And I didn't know.

I didn't know that my own brother was in danger. "Why didn't you tell me?"

Jazzy closes his eyes for a moment, wrestling with something, maybe the excuses that kept them from telling me in the first place. "For a long time, *we* didn't know. It wasn't until Andrés turned sixteen and he was trying to get a driver's license." He sighs. "We'd just lost Dad, Mia." He meets my eyes. "We didn't want you to worry about losing him too."

The sob swells in my throat, the sound wanting to be so much bigger than my body will allow. Because beneath the anger and the fear, I sense the safe haven of my brothers' love, of all the ways they have sheltered me and kept me safe. All I want is to be able to do the same for them. To sacrifice and keep terrible secrets. To put myself between them and harm's way.

But I can't trade places with Andrés.

I can't go back in time. I can't drag the border like an old blanket and use it to cover him and my parents. I can't break him out of that cell.

I can only hope. That the God I have never turned to, that I have never trusted, will have mercy on us.

"I called a bail bondsman," Jazzy says. "And Deb's reached out to a lawyer."

"So we might be able to get him out?"

Before Jazzy can answer, I hear glass shatter. Jazzy and Aarón both instinctively block me from the entrance. The crowd is so dense, all I can see are bodies moving in the same direction. I hear yelling. I smell smoke.

"We have to get out of here," Aarón says. "Before they storm the place."

That's exactly what it feels like. A churning storm about to hit land. Angry and desperate and out of control.

"I'll wait for the bail bondsman." Jazzy pushes us toward the entrance. "Then I'll come find you."

I nod, but it takes a few seconds for me to take that first step. As if Jazzy might suddenly disappear too. I squeeze his hand and then keep my eyes on him all the way to the sidewalk. Until people start reaching for me and asking me questions.

I saw them take your brother.

Is he all right?

Where's Esther?

I heard they tossed them into an unmarked van.

I heard they're driving them out of the city.

I heard it's already too late.

I don't know what to say, but most of the people don't wait for me to respond, instead latching on to another horrific conspiracy theory that someone else tosses out. Like their worry is a flame, fear and anger the gasoline. I watch people ignite, throwing bottles and trash at the windows of the precinct. Throwing punches at the glass. Throwing their whole bodies toward the entrance. Trying to tear it down. To get inside.

"Mia...?" Mr. Barrero pulls me out of the bottleneck. "Are you all right?"

I nod but my eyes say no. Then I tell him about Andrés.

"Dios mío." Gina and the others crowd around us.

Something else shatters and I jump. Behind me, I spot the source of the smoke I smelled earlier. There's a pile of trash in the parking lot, the wind tossing flecks of gold across the pavement. Fire catches at the base of a tree and some people try to stomp it out. But then someone else grabs a piece of burning plastic and chucks it at one of the police cruisers.

We all watch it burn, the fire finding its way inside, beating against the tinted windows like the heat isn't real but trapped behind a television screen. Something pretend and faraway.

A baseball bat cracks against the headlights. Then the side-view mirror. People jump on the hood of the car, stomping on it. The sound like war drums leading us into battle.

Aarón's voice pulls my gaze. "Mia, we have to go."

"This way," Mr. Barrero says, trying to forge a path.

The number of cops in riot gear has tripled. They don't even look human. And as we stomp and scream and cry, I realize that's *all* we are. Flesh and bone that means nothing to them. Flesh and bone they want more than anything to break.

If the fire spreads...that's exactly what will happen. They'll kill us. They'll enjoy it.

"We have to do something." I look from the line of encroaching police to the protesters, heart pounding.

There's a bench near the sidewalk, a few kids hopped up on it to get a better look at the chaos.

I look down at the horn still in Mr. Barrero's hand. "Can I borrow that?"

"Mia, what are you—?"

I hop onto the bench, my arms and legs shaking with the weight of what I'm about to do.

This isn't one of Andrés's late-night fights with our father. This isn't a brotherly feud. This is life or death. This is me and my people up against a vicious machine.

But I don't know what else to do. There's nothing else I can do. *Except...*

I lift the horn to my lips and fill my lungs with air. Then I force out the loudest, longest note I can. An announcement over the drumbeat of stomping feet. A different kind of call to arms.

People pause, searching for the sound. When their eyes finally fall on me, I'm not sure what comes next. Beneath the sound of my heart racing, I can't hear the next note. *I can't find it....*

"No, no, no..." Out of the crowd steps Speedy, one hand to his chest as he belts the first line of a song I haven't heard in years, holding out the last note in that same obnoxiously long way he does every time Aarón enters the store.

But this time I relish it. Because he's right. Because it's perfect.

The tinny sounds of a guitar float on the breeze as Gabriel joins me on the bench. Down below, Speedy serenades the crowd.

"¡No, no, no nos moverán!

"¡No, no, no nos moverán!"

Osmin appears, egg shaker in hand.

Gina and Naomi and Mr. Barrero emerge next, raising their voices alongside Speedy's.

Mr. Martín takes off his hat, pressing it to his chest as he lets out un grito that wakes the rest of the crowd. He throws an arm around his nephew Joaquín and they sway to the music.

There's Javi, hands cupped around his mouth as he yells the words.

Soon everyone is singing, the sounds reverberating until we're caught up in a wave that can't be stopped. While the line of police just listen. And it doesn't matter that they don't know what we're saying. That they don't know the promise we've made to one another.

All that matters is that *we* know.

We will not be moved.

We will not be moved.

I feel myself at the center of it all like on the night when my rooftop solo had people honking and hanging out their windows. Like the notes are a thread between our still-beating hearts. And as I glance over at Mr. Barrero, his hands keeping time, I think about all of the hours we spent playing in his garage. All the love he poured into me. For this very moment. So I could pour it back out.

Another story that I hope people will be able to feel with their whole bodies. *My story*. About a girl who believed she wasn't special, who thought doubting was her destiny. A girl with a gift she was so afraid to share until the people who loved her showed her how.

Love.

The song ends, the crowd erupts, and it feels so strange that I start to laugh, relishing the feeling.

And then I see her.

My mother stands among the crowd, wiping tears from her eyes as if I am something to behold.

She watches me and I see the heartache all over her face, the regret I longed to know she carried. I see her pain. I *see* her.

And for the first time, she sees me.

She *sees* me.

And as Gabriel's voice chases away the quiet with another song about liberation, I let her. I let her see the little girl I used to be and the young woman I've become. I let her see that I am still becoming.

"Cambia todo cambia

"Cambia todo cambia..."

She presses her hand to her lips before reaching it out to me, giving me something too. A sign that she sees how her absence has shaped me. An apology for all the wounds and the scars they've left behind.

The crowd sways and she moves with it. Soon, everyone is singing or humming, hands reaching up and turning the song into a prayer.

We pray for all the birds that have left the nest. All the diamonds that have been dulled. All the souls that have been trampled on and ripped from their husks.

I find my mother's eyes, staring directly into them, and I realize that I've been so angry, so wrapped up in my own hurt, that I haven't even asked her where she's been.

The traveler changes his path
even if it leads to pain.

Did the path she chose bring her pain? Was it dangerous? Did it break her?

"Cambia, todo cambia..."

We all sing it in unison. Over and over.

Knowing that this is the only truth that matters.

The only thing we can count on.

This is the curse. This is the gift. That everything changes. *Always.*

Which means that my mother might not be the same person she was when she left us. I'm not the same little girl who watched her parents fight from beneath a burning spotlight.

After all these years, I'm someone different. What if she is too?

■ ■ ■ ■ ■ ■ ■ ■ ■ ■

As twilight descends, people are still singing. "Yo Soy Chicano." "Las Nubes." "De Los Colores."

There are news trucks parked where police cruisers used to be, people with video cameras and sound equipment where armed men once were. Capturing all of it. Our music. Our voices.

Spotlights shine on the entrance to the precinct like an artificial sun. And then, suddenly, into the light, steps Andrés. He squints against the brightness, Jazzy leading him by the arm. Nina is right behind them, her mother holding her tight. Then Deb followed by some of the other organizers. And Esther.

They walk toward the cameras and waiting reporters who are already hurling questions at them.

When Andrés sees me, the horn to my lips, he smiles so wide it knocks the air from my lungs. I jump down from my perch before handing Mr. Barrero his instrument.

"This was your moment, Mia." He kisses me on the forehead.

"Ours," I correct him. "Today was about us."

He smiles. "About family."

He takes the trumpet from me, joining the others, and then I run for Andrés. He scoops me up in his arms like he used to do when I was little. But instead of body slamming me on the couch and tickling me until I scream he holds me tight, keeping my feet off the ground, still keeping the weight of the world off my shoulders.

He laughs into my ear. "Who was that girl up there?"

I lower myself down, grab his face with both my hands, and say, "Who you raised her to be."

He's never heard me say it. That I owe it all to him. That he saved me. That he shaped me into someone I'm learning to be *so* proud of. And I almost didn't get the chance. To tell him how proud I am to be his sister. How proud I am to have *him* as my brother.

He beams with it, the pride welling up in his eyes before streaming down his cheeks.

Another pair of arms wraps themselves around us. Jazzy. He's crying too, head tilted back so his eye makeup won't run.

"Really?" Andrés snorts. "You're worried about looking pretty out here? Who do you think you're gonna meet?"

I spot him before Jazzy does, his body dipping in and out of the spotlights as he makes his way over to us.

"If anyone can make a love connection out here, it's Jazzy." I jerk my head. "Speaking of which..."

Jazzy follows my eyes and then he sees him.

Javi.

Jazzy backs away, adjusting his outfit. "If you'll excuse me."

Andrés stops him for a moment, slipping into his big brother voice. "Don't screw it up this time, Jazzy."

"Yeah," I plead, "because we love Javi *way* more than we love you."

Andrés shrugs in agreement and then the three of us bust out laughing.

It doesn't take long for Andrés to find Celeste and then I'm left scanning the crowd, looking for Aarón.

I finally spot him standing under a tree and when I sneak up behind him, he doesn't jump. Just reaches his hand back to take mine.

"I think you found it..."

I lean my head on his shoulder, both of us still staring out at the crowd rapt in song. "Huh?"

Then he looks down at me and says, "I think you found your why."

27

Aarón

AS THE MORNING SUN CREEPS THROUGH MR. BAR-
rero's kitchen window, all I can do is stare at it, willing it to
stop. I don't want to get out of these blankets. I don't want
to go home.

If I even still have one.

I want you gone.

His words echo in my head and even though Miguel
told him the truth, I still can't help but worry that he
meant them.

What if he doesn't let me inside?

What if I can't go back...ever?

Miguel's still snoring by the time Mr. Barrero gets up
to make coffee. When I hear the water dribbling into the
mug, I extract myself from the blankets. Then Mr. Barrero
hands it to me without a word.

I follow him to the garage and help him roll up the

door, the morning rushing in until everything is washed in a sorbet sunrise.

"Thanks for letting us stay here," I say. "As soon as Miguel wakes up we'll be out of your hair."

"It's no trouble," he says. "But I'm sure your father's worried about you two."

"I don't know if *worried* is the word I'd use."

"You two ever run off before?"

I shake my head.

"Well, maybe he'll surprise you. A few nights without your family, it makes a man think."

I know Mr. Barrero has spent more than a few nights without his family. But when I saw him and Xavier through the kitchen window that night, they'd made it look like mending the past is so easy.

"How did you fix it?" I ask him.

He sits on an old barstool, thinking. "I'm not sure it's the type of thing that *can* be fixed." In his eyes I detect all the sadness I didn't see on the other side of the glass. "You just have to decide, together, to endure the brokenness. To salvage what pieces are left and care for them."

If I'm honest, I don't know if I thought the pieces were worth as much as the whole. That it was worth learning to love my father in all his brokenness. That it was worth forgiving Miguel for all his sharp edges that would never be smooth.

That it was worth accepting myself and all the parts of me that will never fit inside a box.

The three of us, we are all just pieces. Pieces of my mother. Pieces of the past. Pieces of one another.

Pieces we may never be able to put back together. But if we can accept that, if we can learn to see one another's brokenness without running away, maybe we can learn to care for those pieces. To treat them like the fragile things they are.

As fragile as the bruise on Miguel's cheek. As fragile as the crushed bits of my father's cell phone.

He only exploded that day because he was trying to do exactly what Mr. Barrero said we should—taking care of the pieces we have left. Of the people we love. Of the people we miss.

When my father listened to that voice recording, he wasn't just remembering my mother. He was holding her in the palm of his hand. And I have to get her back. So even if it's not my home anymore, even if these past few nights alone haven't forced him to think about changing a thing, I have to go back there.

But not before giving Mr. Barrero a piece of the past that's just as important.

I rummage through my duffel bag before pulling out the CD—old school since Mr. Barrero doesn't have a computer. Six tracks and a paper CD cover Nina helped me make in Photoshop of flowering cacti in the shape of raised fists.

"Beautiful," he says as I hand it to him. "And strong."

"It's what I heard," I tell him.

He clears his throat as he pops the disc into a CD player that's plugged into the wall. We lean our backs against it, listening once all the way through before either of us says a word.

As the last song ends, I turn to Mr. Barrero and see tears streaming down his face. "I hear *us*," he says. Then he squeezes my shoulder. "I hear you too."

I sniff, the tears rolling down the back of my throat. "Thank you. For letting me do this."

He doesn't let go of me. "The first of many, verdad?"

And it's such a delicate thing, a promise we both know we can't keep. But I feel myself nod, making it anyway.

"Absolutely." He hugs me and I squeeze back tighter. "The first of many."

■ ■ ■ ■ ■ ■ ■ ■ ■ ■

When Xavier's sports car pulls into the driveway, my father immediately steps outside. When he sees who's behind the wheel, I'm not sure if he's starstruck or still angry. But he doesn't move until Xavier, Miguel, and I reach the steps.

I expect Miguel to say something first, to reinstate himself as the favorite, but he's not even looking, his eyes stuck to the ground.

Xavier clears his throat and sticks out a hand. "Mr. Medrano, Xavier López."

"I know." My father reaches back. "Come inside."

I knew Xavier wasn't just looking to give us a ride home. I thought maybe he wanted to make sure our father had cooled off, that it was safe. I did not think he'd be sitting at our kitchen table while my father tries to offer him migas and sweet tea.

"Thank you, Mr. Medrano, but I won't be here long."

My hands start to sweat. *What is going on?*

Xavier gives me a wink, a sign to stop freaking out and relax.

"What's this about?" my father finally asks, growing restless too.

"It's about Aarón."

My father's voice hardens. "What's he done?"

I flinch at the sound, still so afraid of being a disappointment. I look over at Miguel, his jaw tense, and for the first time it's like we're finally seeing the world from the same vantage point, like we're finally on the same team, both of us bracing for what comes next.

Xavier pulls out an envelope and slides it over to me. It's blank. No return address. Meant to be hand delivered.

"What's this?" I ask.

"Read it."

I pull out the piece of paper and unfold it in front of me. Miguel pinches one of the corners down. Our father leans forward. Xavier grins.

> *Dear Mr. Medrano,*
> *We are pleased to inform you that you have*
> *been accepted to Acadia School of Music for the*
> *upcoming academic year as a Starfish Scholar.*

"What's a *Starfish Scholar*?" Miguel asks.

I scan the rest of the letter. "It means everything's free." My heart races. "Housing, tuition, a meal plan, everything." *I was right. Xavier was the secret donor.* I find his eyes, my own welling up with tears. "You did this?"

He shakes his head. "You did this." Then he turns to my father. "Your son is an incredible musician, Mr. Medrano. You should be very proud."

My father's neck turns beet red, a sure sign that he is choking something down. But I can't tell if it's pride or if he thinks Acadia is stupid, that I'm stupid for thinking music is anything to hang my hopes on. And I wish he'd just say it. That he'd stop making me wonder if I matter.

Do I? My eyes plead with him. *Does this matter to you? Does anything I've ever done matter to you?*

But he doesn't agree with Xavier. He doesn't congratulate me. He doesn't say anything at all.

Xavier pats at his jacket, chasing away the silence. "One more thing…" Then he pulls out another envelope. "Do you think you can make one last delivery for me?"

I nod, taking the envelope.

"Tell her it's from my father."

28

Mia

I LINGER OUTSIDE THE DANCE STUDIO, LISTENING to the mariachi music and watching the tiny folklórico dancers hoist up their giant skirts. They turn in circles, human rainbows. A sign of hope after yesterday's storms.

A reminder that in Monte Vista, life doesn't just go on, but that every day, in ways big and small, we are carrying our culture on our backs. Dragging it into the future whether it's welcome here or not. These little girls aren't just playing dress-up. They're memorizing an entire history with their bodies.

It makes me wonder about all of the things my body is a conduit for. All the things I carry. My parents' toxic love story. Andrés's sacrifice. Jazzy's unconditional love. Mr. Barrero's atonement. Aarón's hopes. My father's dreams.

But more than any of those things, I feel the weight of all the seconds he didn't get to spend with us. I feel his unlived life like a strong gust of wind against my sails. Propelling me forward. Begging me to make it count.

For both of us.

That feeling pushes me up the ladder, over the edge of the building, and onto the roof. There are no stars tonight, Aarón beneath a lone spotlight, the only thing sparkling.

He smiles when he sees me and for the first time he's not tempering it or trying to hide. He's joyful and it's so unexpected that I can't help but laugh.

"What's going on?" I ask.

Without a word, he hands me an envelope, my name written on the front.

"Open it," he says, still unable to contain the goofy grin on his face.

"Okay," I'm smiling too. Then I pull out the letter... and then I'm shaking. Like I've just been struck by lightning. This one-in-a million thing stealing my breath.

"Mia...?"

I'm still smiling but I'm also crying, tears blurring the words: *Accepted, scholarship.*

"How?" I finally say.

"Someone wrote you a very convincing recommendation letter."

"Mr. Barrero?" I breathe.

Aarón nods. "Not that Xavier needed it. As the scholarship benefactor, Acadia let him have the final say on admissions. But after seeing how you handled that crowd at the protest, he must have realized that everything Mr. Barrero had told him about you was true."

After coming down from that high, I felt different. Transformed, in a way. But also the same. Like I'm still carrying the weight of the world. Except now I'm not carrying it alone.

"Mia..." Aarón comes closer. "I got one too."

I wrap my arms around him, squeezing hard like this moment is just a dream. Like if I can just hold on to it tight enough, if I can just keep it close enough, it might not disappear.

I have been accepted into the Acadia School of Music.

I have been *accepted* into the Acadia School of Music.

And I suddenly realize that it had to happen this way. I had to blow all of those auditions. I had to watch so many things be broken. I had to fill with rage and I had to find somewhere to put it. I had to be scared so I could find the courage. I had to be brave so I could find my *why*.

Just a few weeks ago, I didn't know what it was all for. The music and this yearning to play, to be heard. But now I do. I understand my place in my community and I understand my place in this fight. I might not have all the weapons I need.

But I have this.

This future that is *mine*.

This future that I can forge into everything I need to keep fighting.

That is what my father left me. That is what Andrés and Jazzy have been teaching me to do every single day. We were never cowards. We were never broken.

We were growing up through weeds, fighting for every

inch of soil, grasping at every beat of light. I have been fighting since the day I was born. Through all the fears and doubts, that yearning for *something* was never extinguished.

And as I hold my acceptance letter to Acadia, that yearning begins to change shape, swelling into even more questions, into yet another one-in-a-million dream. Because Acadia is just the beginning. I am *just* beginning.

• • • • • • • • • • •

I forgot to leave my bedroom window unlocked, but it's almost 3:00 AM, and everyone should be out cold. Or at least, that's what I hope as I ease my key into the lock and gently push open the front door.

But I'm wrong.

My mother is propped up on her elbow, watching a silent TV screen. She blinks when she sees me, bleary-eyed, like maybe I'm a dream.

I wonder for a second what I might be like in her dreams, which version of me is tucked away in her sub-conscious. If I'm the daughter she hoped. If we sit and talk. If there is nothing scornful between us. Or maybe her dreams about me are nightmares too. Maybe she's afraid I'm going to hurt her.

I have been. Ever since she got here I've been breathing flames every time I open my mouth, wanting her to feel an ounce of what I do.

But as I look at her, straightening her shirt and smoothing back her hair, self-conscious like I'm some kind of stranger, I realize I don't want to be. I don't want us to be strangers to each other.

I move to sit next to her on the couch. Then I hand her the letter.

She unfolds it carefully, something tugging at her mouth as she reads. Her eyes well up. "Mia, this is amazing."

Something in me stirs. Because I've always *wanted* this. To do something amazing. To make my mother proud.

She looks down. "The last time I heard you play at your third-grade talent show...Well, I didn't really get to hear much at all."

"Because you and Dad started fighting."

Her face darkens, remembering. "But you never stopped practicing."

"I think...it was a way for me to escape. Something that made me happy."

"I could see it," she says. "At the protest, your playing... it took my breath away. You should be proud of yourself, Mia."

She doesn't *say* that she's proud of me. But suddenly, I realize, that I don't need to hear it. Because she's right. I *should* be proud of myself.

"I am," I tell her.

Her suitcase is under the coffee table, but it's zipped shut and I can't tell if it's still packed.

She notices me staring at it. "It was a mistake, Mia."

"Leaving?" I say. "Or coming in the first place?"

"Trying to run from my problems." She grimaces. "I used to think this country was something out of a fairy tale, and after we finally made it, after all those weeks of walking, of hiding, I tried so hard to hold on to that feeling.

To stay hopeful. But every fairy tale needs a villain." She pinches her eyes shut. "I just never imagined it would be us. No money. A crying baby in my arms and one on the way.

"I thought people would help us. That they would *understand*. That they would see that I was a *mother* and they would *understand*. But they didn't and with every passing day the hope just drained out of me. Until there was nothing left. Until my own children were speaking more English than Spanish. Until you started to feel like strangers.

"And I know that's not an excuse. But it ate at me. That here I was, in this place that didn't want me, with my American children who deserved a mother that wasn't so angry, that wasn't full of regret. I didn't know what to do with it all. With this broken heart that was missing my family in Mexico, that was bruised every time I got paid half of what los gringos did, every time someone cussed me out on the bus." She shakes. "I was robbed. Harassed. Told that I was nothing. And then I'd come home and hear you and your brothers speaking in those same voices. Like you belonged to them more than you belonged to me. And I couldn't take it."

She meets my eyes, like she's searching them for the past, to see if I hold any of those same horrible memories. "I'm just not as strong as you, Mia."

The lump in my throat grows thorns. Because all I remember is her strength; the way she left us all battered and bruised. Weakness is what she made the rest of us feel. But now I understand—there was the world inside these four walls and the world outside. And the world outside destroyed her.

"You're not weak," I tell her. "The other night, you could have run again, but you didn't."

"Because you stopped me," she says.

"No," I say, remembering the way I pushed her away. "You stopped yourself. That's not something a weak person would do, is it?"

She leans in, her smile sad. "I'm sorry I left you, Mia. I'm sorry I hurt you."

"I had Andrés and Jazzy."

"You should have had me too."

"And now?" I don't look at her. "Will I...have you?"

"Only if you want."

I look at her. "Maybe I do."

- - - - - - - - - - -

Deb, Celeste, Jazzy, our mother, and the immigration lawyer all crowd around the kitchen table while Andrés looks over a bunch of paperwork that seems to be written in another language. Legalese—just another roadblock between regular people and freedom.

I'm propped up on the kitchen counter, staring down at their heads all pressed together, like they're trying to focus all of their collective brainpower on solving the problem of Andrés being undocumented.

"Our mother recently went through the process," Jazzy says.

"I finally received my green card about a year ago." My mother sighs. "It only took twenty years."

"We talked about sponsorship over the phone," Jazzy adds. "Do you think that's an option for Andrés?"

"I brought all of my old paperwork." My mother slides over a manila folder full of documents.

"Wait…" I look from Jazzy to my mother. "Is that why you came back? To sponsor Andrés so he could get his citizenship?"

"Jazzy got in touch." She reaches for Andrés's hand, squeezes. "He said your brother needed help." Her eyes burn red. "It's the least I could do. I'm the one who got him into this mess…."

"No." Andrés's voice is firm. "You did what you thought was best. For your family."

With those three words, she crumbles, as if he's just given her the greatest gift. As if we didn't truly belong to her until now. And I wonder when it happened. When she first realized that she missed us; that we mattered. But as I stare into her eyes, it occurs to me that maybe we always did. Maybe it was *her* who didn't think she mattered.

Jazzy turns to the lawyer. "Do you think it could work?"

The lawyer frowns. "That would require Andrés to leave the country. He can't apply from the States. And if he goes back to Mexico, it might take another twenty years before he gets approved."

"I'm not going back to Mexico," Andrés says. "I don't even remember it."

"So he'll apply for Dreamer status," Deb cuts in.

The lawyer nods. "Right now, DACA is the only way. But it's constantly under attack, new rulings sometimes leaving recipients in limbo. So there are risks involved, and you'll have to be diligent about reapplying and keeping track of your paperwork."

"I can help with that," Celeste says.

"Good. Then I'll get the process started." The lawyer stands, shaking hands before heading for the door. He pauses. "You've got a lot of support here, Andrés. That matters right now because this won't be easy."

"I know," Andrés says.

The door closes and Jazzy exhales. "Maybe we should have told him we've been through worse."

He's right. We've been through so many other things that haven't been easy. That have been hard and seemingly hopeless. *We can do it again. Can't we?*

Deb and Celeste head outside, both off to work. Our mother follows them out, and I hear her thanking them for all they've done.

I take a seat at the kitchen table—just me, Jazzy, and Andrés. My family. My home.

I turn to Andrés. "Are you scared?"

He taps his fingers on the table. "A little. But...maybe being scared is good."

"What's good about it?" Jazzy asks.

"It means I'm alive," Andrés says. He looks at each of us. "It means I have something worth losing."

That's the root of it. We *fear* because we love. We fear because we *are loved*. These fragile things are what make life worth living, but they're also what makes it so dangerous. Because nothing is safe. But maybe the fact that life is fleeting should make us love it even more.

I look at my brothers and I see the boys they once were. I see the men they've become. I see all the years that are ahead of us, tiny moments made of glass.

"But you won't," Jazzy promises. "You won't lose us."

At first I think that's a promise he can't make. But then I remember Nina's speech and all the ways her father still lives inside her. I think about all the ways I still sense my father in me. In my music. In the way I see the world.

Jazzy was right when he said that Andrés raised us. Which means that no matter how far away we are from one another, no matter how many miles or years have wedged themselves between us, Andrés will always be around. In that loud-quiet moment before I take the stage. In the silence between the notes. In the stomach-turning exhilaration after a show.

I will carry my brothers with me the way I've learned to carry everything else.

29

Aarón

I UNROLL MY RATTY COMFORTER ONTO THE TWIN mattress, place my new laptop and keyboard on the adjacent desk, shove my guitar case under the bed, and tack the painting Nina made for me onto the cork board by the window.

Next to it is one of Mr. Barrero's fedoras. He had about a million of them and as we were packing up his things and getting ready to move him in with Xavier—where he'd have access to a full-time nurse, cable television, and a private pool (which he was very excited about)—I asked if I could have one.

Instead of grabbing one from the back of his closet, he removed the one he was wearing, knocked off my baseball cap, and placed it on my head.

"There," he said, "now you look like a real musician."

Three months later and it still smells like his aftershave,

the small air conditioner in the window mixing it with the scent of musty dorm room. Not like home.

I didn't think I was going to miss it, but as Dad and Miguel and I were packing up my room—every box on my father's truck like the eraser end of a pencil, wiping away the memories and the little boy who lived them—I found myself moving slower. Touching things one at a time. Savoring memories I never thought would matter.

But they did. The moments of joy twisting me up just as much as the moments of pain. All of it mattered because all of it made me.

My mother. My father. Miguel. The way our family used to be and the broken mess it became. I miss it all. Not because all of it was good but because moving out, moving on, is another end as much as it's a beginning.

And endings hurt.

As much as cutting off a limb. That's what this feels like. Like I'm lighter but also bleeding. Like I'm relieved but also bruised.

Like I'm following my dreams but also leaving something behind.

My father pushes through the door, back first, as he carries the last box inside. He sets it down on the desk before pulling a rag from his pocket and dabbing his forehead.

"I'm getting old," he says.

And he is, lines that haven't yet been etched in my memory cutting across his forehead.

He looks around the room, taking it in for the hundredth time today, like he still can't believe it's real. That I did this. That I'm leaving. Miguel was always going to find a way. I was the one who was lost, who wasn't ready to go out into a world without her.

Now my father is the one who looks lost. Like Miguel and I are as irreplaceable as our mother's voice mail. Like he's losing the only pieces of her he has left.

I dig through my backpack and pull out the USB stick. Then I plug it into my laptop and wake up the screen.

My father watches, maybe wondering if he's finally going to hear what Xavier did; this thing that made me special enough to get into Acadia.

But when I press play, it's not one of my songs coming through the speakers.

"I'm feeling so much better today. I think I'm going to take the boys to the park, maybe get some ice cream."

My father inches toward the sound, breathless.

"The sun's finally out after all that rain. Here, the boys want to say hello. Say hi, Miguel."

Miguel's yelling from the backseat. "Dad, we saw the biggest spider ever and it almost—"

Mom laughs. "I swear I haven't even given them any sugar yet. Aarón, say hi to your father."

My mouth is too close to the phone. "Hey, Dad, we'll save you some ice cream. Mint chocolate chip with gummy worms. Your favorite."

The words strike me—this version of myself that knew my father's favorite ice cream. That wanted him around.

As he closes the space between us, a hand on my shoulder, still listening, I realize that maybe I still do.

"We can't wait to see you when you get home." Mom lowers her voice. "I wish you were here with us."

Tears land against my shirt and I'm not even sure who they belong to.

I pull out the USB stick and hand it to my father. He closes it in his fist like I've just handed him back his North Star.

It burns between us, a reminder that the relationship between father and son is sometimes one forged through fire. That sometimes it hurts.

We hurt together, in the middle of my musty dorm room, faces stained with tears. And when the hurt becomes too much, my father reaches for me. He wraps me up and we let it all pour out.

He stretches out an arm, reaching for something, and then I feel Miguel pressed against my back. I feel his grief trying to fight its way out.

It's safe here, I want to tell him. *Your sadness is safe with me.*

But I don't have to tell him. He can feel it.

He can feel it in the rawness of this moment. In every fragile, shaking breath.

We cry together, remembering all the ugliness and all the beauty. Her sickness and her fight. The way she *fought* for us. To stay and keep being the glue. To stay and keep our hearts from breaking.

She *tried* . . . and now it's our turn.

It's our turn to take these pieces of her we have left, to summon the same strength, and figure out how to be a family. Not whole. Not perfect. But *here*.

Here for one another.

"I'm sorry," my father breathes into my ear. "I'm sorry, Aarón. I'm so sorry."

"Me too," I tell him.

"I love you. I love you, boys." He holds us. "My boys. My boys."

I hold him back. "I love you too." And I feel Miguel squeeze me tighter.

⬛⬛⬛⬛⬛⬛⬛⬛⬛⬛⬛

"Aarón?" Mia eases the door open, a basket hoisted on her hip. "I brought goodies."

She's covered in just as much sweat and dust as I am from moving in all day, but she's also beaming.

"Try this." She sets the basket down on the bed before stuffing something sweet and flaky in my mouth.

"It's delicious."

"Deb dropped off cocadas and besos from Pen's Pastelería." She pops a beso in her mouth too.

"What else is in the basket?" I ask.

"Just a few things." Mia pulls out a wooden frame and flips it over to face me. It's a photo of us at graduation, caps off, hair frizzy in the Texas humidity. She places it on my desk next to my laptop.

I laugh. "And...?"

She turns away, reaching into the basket again. "And... this." She hands me a cardboard box of multicolored Christmas lights. "I thought we could hang them up. Like the ones in your room."

I sink down onto the mattress.

Mia sits down next to me. "I packed some things of my dad's. His pocketknife and an empty bottle of cologne that still sort of smells like him. I know he's not here. Not really. But it makes me feel like, if I close my eyes, he could be."

I tear open the box and start unraveling the giant strand of lights.

"I know they're just pretend," Mia says. "I know having my father's things around is just my way of pretending that he's a part of this moment somehow. Like all of the other kids whose parents are helping them move in." She finds the plastic plug and presses the prongs into the pads of her fingers. "But maybe it's okay to pretend sometimes."

My throat clenches, raw from crying so much today already. But this time it feels different. Because Mia *knows*.

She knows that as much as I want to celebrate this day, I can't help but mourn the fact that my mom isn't here to celebrate it with me.

Unless we put up the stars and pretend. That she's in her paint-stained overalls and cranking up the stereo on her favorite eighties pop songs. That she's holding the step stool steady while Mia tacks stars to the ceiling, looking back at me with a wink. A sign of approval. *I like this girl, Aarón. Don't screw it up.*

I reach for Mia's hand, curling it in mine. Then I kiss her, tasting the powdered sugar from the besos we just ate.

"Let's pretend," I say.

She grins.

We climb on top of the bed, on top of furniture, on top of each other. With just a small section of ceiling left to go, Mia's sitting on my shoulders, both of us laughing as she arranges and rearranges, trying to create the perfect constellation.

I'm pouring sweat again. "I don't think I can hold you much longer."

"Just a second."

My shoulders burn. "No, Mia, I'm...I'm falling!"

We land in a heap on the bed, Mia laughing and gasping for air, my body sinking into the mattress like Jell-O.

"Let's see." Mia plugs in the lights.

Then together, we look up. At the stars and the space between them. Shining even though they're already ghosts.

I used to feel like one. Like something on the verge of disappearing.

But Mia makes me feel something else.

And I realize that falling in love is like writing the perfect song. Like the world is suddenly a symphony, the chaos of life transforming into chord structures, into a melody that only the two of us can hear.

Love is the soundtrack, the heart-pumping rhythm inhabiting my whole body. Making my heart swell so big that I can't imagine it ever being broken.

My favorite song is Mia Villanueva and when life gets quiet, when life gets loud, I close my eyes and sometimes I can hear the way our melodies intertwine. I can feel the rise and fall of the notes in my chest. I feel her unfurling my clenched fists and wrapping her arms around me.

I *feel* the universe open wide and it sings to me the truth. That my flesh and bone are powerful instruments and my mind...my mind, in all its disarray, is the conductor.

I am not damaged goods.

I am a whole universe. Expanding instead of shrinking. Wishing on stars instead of waiting for them to fall.

Instead, it's *me* who's falling.

Falling, for the first time, without worrying where I'll land, if it'll hurt.

I know it will sometimes, but there will also be this. Me and Mia curled around each other. Me and my music in the middle of the night. Me and my dreams slowly coming true.

ACKNOWLEDGMENTS

I'm trying my hardest to remember all the incredible people who shouted about and supported my debut novel, which launched very anticlimactically during the pandemic and which I was so terrified would simply disappear into the ether.

But it didn't. Because of the generous people who wouldn't let it, like Laura Taylor Namey, Eric Smith, Yvonne Palos Vitt, Syrena Arevalo, Kathie Weinberg, Natalie Aguirre, Marytza K. Rubio, Yvonne Tapia, Mariana Calderon, Cathy Berner, Jessica Sinsheimer, Julie Kingsley, Jen St. Jude, Sawyer Lovett, Liz Lawson, Becky Calzada, Tirzah Price, Astrid Pizarro, Vanessa L. Torres, Laura Rueckert, Gloria Amescua, Terry Catasús Jennings—the list goes on.

Thank you for tagging me with photos of the book out in the wild, for writing the loveliest blurbs and reviews, for inviting me to your book clubs and festivals or to work with your incredible organizations, and for spreading the news far and wide about my debut. I needed that encouragement when I was trudging through the drafting of *Heartbreak*

Symphony, a book that turned out to be the most difficult thing I've ever written.

A very special shout-out to the Latinx bookish community for doing the absolute MOST for my debut, as well as a HUGE thank-you to my local indie bookstore, Book-People, and especially Eugenia Vela, for making my launch experience so special.

I also want to thank the LBYR team, including Savannah Kennelly, Bill Grace, Victoria Stapleton, Christie Michel, Marisa Russell, as well as the countless others behind the scenes, who worked tirelessly to keep my debut afloat in a digital landscape that sometimes felt impossible to navigate. Thank you for doing whatever you could to get my book into the hands of the young people who needed it most. Thank you for putting forth the same heart and effort to make sure *Heartbreak Symphony* does the same.

I'd like to thank my editor, Sam Gentry, and my agent, Andrea Morrison, for continuing to be such incredible advocates for my work. You both have invested so much time and energy in me and I feel so fulfilled by all we're building together for Latinx readers. Sam, thank you for your creativity, compassion, and understanding (and all those deadline extensions). Andrea, thank you for seeing the potential in everything I do (and for reading the millions of things I send your way). To both of you, thank you for handling me with such grace.

I also owe so much thanks to my fellow Musas for helping me reach the end of this project and for tending to my battle wounds on the other side. Thank you to Mia García for reading the final version in a rush in order to reassure me it wasn't terrible. Thank you to Jonny Garza Villa, Crystal Maldonado, and Olivia Abtahi for Slack chats and DMs that always make me laugh. I'm also sending love to Angela Velez and Amparo Ortiz for your friendship and support. And thank you to the entire collective for all of the ways you've lifted up me and my work.

Teachers, you hold a permanent place in my acknowledgments section. The world asks so much of you and yet you still find ways to give even more. Including to authors like me whose first introduction to a teen is so often facilitated by you. Thank you for introducing my work to your students. Thank you for giving us both that gift of being seen and understood.

I especially want to show my immense gratitude for educators Keri Burns, Jenny Hoober, Katrina Owens, Stephany Gaines, Pearl Perez, Becky Calzada, and Lauren Vicente. Thank you for everything you did to get my books to teachers, in classroom libraries, and most importantly, in the hands of kids. Special thanks to Keri for being the BEST hype woman ever and to Pearl for believing so strongly in my abilities to create and lead. I appreciate you all so much!

To my family—you lived the pain of this story with me. Thank you for making sure we survived it together.

To JD—when I started writing this book in 2017 it belonged to only me and putting down these words was only possible because of the life and love we'd built together, a safe place to process my grief after losing my dad. Now this story belongs to us both. I hate it. I'm sorry. I love you.

To my readers—thank you for celebrating my work, and as a result, my culture and community. Thank you for lifting us up, for fueling this dream, for showing me your hearts. Thank you for taking care of mine.

LAEKAN ZEA KEMP

is the author of *Somewhere Between Bitter and Sweet*. She has three objectives when it comes to storytelling: to make people laugh, cry, and crave Mexican food. Her work celebrates Chicane grit, resilience, creativity, and joy while exploring themes of identity and mental health. She lives in Austin, Texas. Laekan invites you to visit her at laekanzeakemp.com or follow her on Twitter @LaekanZeaKemp.